LOVE,
LIES AND
SCANDAL

Earl Sewell

LOVE, LIES AND SCANDAL

sepia™

LOVE, LIES AND SCANDAL

ISBN-13: 978-0-373-83140-1
ISBN-10:   0-373-83140-4

Copyright © 2008 by Earl Sewell

www.kimanipress.com

Printed in U.S.A.

Love makes your soul crawl out from its hiding place.
                                        —Zora Neale Hurston

Acknowledgments

When I begin a book, most of the time it's because a concept, idea or a slice of a conversation has decided to marry itself to my thoughts. I'm not given the courtesy of selecting which thought or dialogue gets to stay and which ones have to leave. The information moves in like family members who feel that the world owes them something just for being born. I suppose it's a unique talent to be able to take a thought and create characters, a story line and eventually a novel from it. I've been writing my books this way for so long that to me it's as natural as breathing air. However I know that for many people just trying to figure out where to start a novel can be a challenge. One day, as I rode the train into downtown Chicago, I overheard a man having a rather loud conversation on his cellular phone. He was sharing with someone the discovery of an affair his brother-in-law was having on his sister. The man was in support of his brother-in-law getting a little action on the side as long as the affair was kept on the down low. I listened as inconspicuously as I could but I wasn't able to gather much more than what I'd initially overheard, because the man exited the train before I did. Ironically, a few days later a public official had to step down because of an inappropriate relationship. It is from these two separate occurrences that *Love, Lies and Scandal* was born.

When I began writing, the only thing I truly had was a catchy title. I did not know who my characters were, where they were from or what adversity they'd have to overcome. While on a book tour in California in 2007, I stayed at my favorite hotel, the Concord Hilton (hey Yanta, what's up), which has the Iron Horse Running Trail nearby. I decided to go out for a short run. The moment I began my run, the characters for the book came forward and introduced themselves and told me their story. Before I realized it I'd run twelve miles. My characters talk too much.

I have so many people to thank for my continuing success in this profession. To my family, Annette and Candice, thank you for putting up with my craziness and keeping me on track.

I have to give a big thank-you to my editor Glenda Howard, who not only loved the story idea but also pushed for sexier book covers. I truly hope you guys like the new packaging. There are so many book clubs from around the country that have been supporting and encouraging me for years. So another big thank-you goes out to the following book clubs: African Violet, Born Readers, Come As You Are, Different Shades of Black, Rawsistaz, Sisters on the Reading Edge, Sweet Soul Sisters, In the Company of My Sisters, Circle of Sisters and all of the other book clubs out there that have been supporting my work.

To all of you bookstore owners and managers— Lisa Williams in Detroit, Donna Liptrot in Kalamazoo, Michigan, and Cindy Smith, Calumet, Illinois. Thank you for recommending my work to your customers.

To Pam Nelson and the Levy Home Entertainment family. Thank you so much for all that you do. Pam, you're a godsend and I truly appreciate all that you do. To my Soul Expressions Bus Tour authors, ReShonda Tate Billingsley, Lori Woolridge-Bryant, Naleighna Kai, Rochelle Alers, Brenda Jackson, Nina Foxx, Beverly Jenkins, Selena Montgomery, Teri Woods, Francis Ray, Donna Hill, Nikki Turner, Tracie Howard, Daaimah Poole, Stephanie Perry Moore and Crystal Hubbard. We had a blast during our bus tour and I look forward to seeing you all soon.

To Barbara Keaton and L.A. Banks. You guys are a blast to be around. I'll never forget how Barbara got me, L.A. Banks and a few friends from downtown Chicago to Oak Park (which is thirty minutes away) in ten minutes flat so that L.A. wouldn't be late for her book-signing. Barbara should have been a NASCAR driver.

In case I forgot anyone, which I often do, I apologize, and please know that it wasn't intentional.

Please feel free to drop me a line at earl@earlsewell.com. Please put the title of my book in the subject line so that I know your message to me is not spam. Make sure you check out www.earlsewell.com and www.myspace.com/earlsewell.

Finally, be sure to visit Earl Sewell's Travel Network at www.earlsewellstravelnetwork.com. Sign up for my free deals and steals travel newsletter and finalize all of your travel plans. Whether you're going on a cruise, taking a vacation to the Caribbean or going to visit friends and family, let Earl Sewell's Travel Network take you there.

All my best,

Earl Sewell

CHAPTER 1

WILL

Will admittedly looked debonair in his tailored Versace suit. He was handsome, charming and sexy all rolled into a nice package. He stood in front of the bathroom mirror making sure that his cuff links were securely fastened.

Anyone with any sense of style could tell that he was most certainly a man who was serious about his appearance. He paid handsomely for his wardrobe. The black suit had cost $1,695. The Versace striped shirt hit him for $300. He smiled at himself because he knew that women would be adding him up the moment they saw him. It wouldn't even matter that DaNikka was accompanying him. *A well-dressed and handsome man has the power to drive a woman crazy, there is no doubt about it,* he told his reflection.

He adjusted the strap on his Movado timepiece before picking up his bottle of Unforgivable cologne. He tilted his neck to the right and depressed the pump once before switching to the other side and repeating the process. As he rubbed away the wet spot on his neck with his fingertips, he saw an imperfection that annoyed him—his wedding ring. He smirked. *I won't need this tonight. Especially since I plan on being a very bad boy.* He removed the inconvenient reminder and placed it in his black Gucci travel bag on the countertop.

"Just like Justin Timberlake said, I'm bringing sexy back." Will laughed to himself as he studied his flawless chocolate skin and well-groomed mustache. "You're a suave brother who has it all. Money, power, a wife at home and freak on the side. Now, let's go make your forty-third birthday a memorable one," he said aloud, popping his collar and winking at himself before exiting the bathroom.

He was in Philadelphia, staying at the luxurious Ritz Carlton Hotel. He'd paid good money for a penthouse suite that could be accessed only via a private elevator. His nineteen-hundred-square-foot suite had two bedrooms with super-king-size beds, two and half baths, a living room, dining room, a den, full kitchen and an incomparable panoramic city view. Will poured himself a glass of wine before he moved toward the window, drew back the drapes and took in the beauty of the city. He exhaled as he stuffed one hand in his pocket and shifted his weight from one foot to the other.

"DaNikka, how much longer are you going to be?" He spoke loud enough for her to hear him. She was still in her private bathroom getting ready for their evening together.

"Not much longer," she answered him.

"You'd better not be," Will threatened as he took a sip of wine. "I want tonight to be perfect." Will loathed having to wait for her but since a lot of what he was showing his young and naive mistress was new to her, he was patient. After all, this trip marked the very first time that she'd ever been outside of Pittsburg, California.

He glanced down at his almost empty wineglass and laughed a little as he thought about the craziness of his secret life. Living a double life was an exciting adventure to him. He enjoyed entertaining the more primal side of his nature. He enjoyed the freedom it afforded him. The women, the secret rendezvous, the private clubs and secret societies he was a part of were all designed for men like him. Men of wealth, power and social status who needed to be discreet.

"I'm almost ready." DaNikka updated Will on her progress. "I'll be out in a moment."

"Okay," Will answered as he felt the cellular phone vibrating in its holster. He looked to see who was calling him.

"Donna," he whispered to himself. "I've told you a million times that it's over and that you need to stop calling me. Women trip me out with wanting to end a relationship as friends. If I'm done with you, I don't want to be your damn friend. Just leave me the hell alone."

"Who are you talking to?" DaNikka finally exited the bathroom.

"No one. I'm just talking to myself," Will said as he put away his phone.

"So how do I look?" DaNikka struck a pose for him.

"Just the way I want you to," Will said, smiling at her lustfully. She had on a gray Diane von Furstenberg dress with a hemline that stopped well above her knees. The dress wrapped around her body, leaving a fair amount of her ample breasts exposed.

"What about my hair? Do you like the way it looks?" DaNikka asked as she twirled around and modeled the short, cute Halle Berry–style haircut.

Will sat down on a nearby straight-back chair and draped one leg over the other as he studied all of DaNikka's assets. She was blessed with the body of a goddess. She was tall like him, had curvaceous mahogany legs that he loved holding during the throes of passion. She had full hips, a full and voluptuous apple-shaped ass that he loved to spank and bite on. She had a set of luscious breasts, with round chocolate nipples that were the perfect size for teasing with his lips and tongue. Her succulent lips, alluring bedroom eyes and energetic youth rounded out her package. She was his showpiece, his personal playmate and the thing that made his ego purr. Physically, DaNikka was perfect in every way. However, when she opened her mouth, it was painfully obvious that her body was her only asset. It didn't matter; Will didn't need her to think or be smart. He already had an intelligent wife.

"Do you like my shoes?" asked DaNikka pointing out her Prada high-heeled shoes. Will brushed his tongue across his lips.

"Yeah, I like those a lot." Will smiled devilishly.

"You sure?" DaNikka asked again.

"I'm positive. I'm more interested in what you have on underneath that dress. Do you have on the lingerie I purchased for you?"

"Yes, I got them on." DaNikka positioned herself directly in front of him. Her love mound was at the right height for his lips to kiss. Will leaned forward and spread his legs open.

"Stand right here." He pointed between his legs. DaNikka did as he asked. "Now, turn around," Will directed her. Will lifted up her gray dress and exposed her perfectly fabulous chocolate ass, which was accented by the presence of the gray silk thong.

"Damn." Will massaged her big, spankable ass. He then began to place kisses all over it. DaNikka cooed and responded to him by leaning forward and resting her hands on her knees. She made her ass jiggle playfully for him because she knew how much he liked to see that.

"I am definitely an ass man. There is no doubt about it," Will uttered as he spanked her derriere once more before covering it back up.

At that moment Will's cellular phone rang again. He pulled it out of its holster.

"Is that her? Is that your wife again? Because I know that's who you were talking to when I came out of the bathroom."

"Calm down and get your emotions in check," Will said before answering his phone. "Hello," he greeted the caller. "Good, we'll be down in a moment," he said and then ended the call. "That was the limo driver."

"Oh," DaNikka said softly. "I just got a little twisted because I thought she was calling you."

"You need to put those childish emotions of yours away.

If you're going to be with me, you have to be a big girl, understood?" Will stood up and took her face in his hands. He wanted to taste her lips. He drew her to him and kissed her tenderly.

"You know that I'm your man, don't you?" Will whispered in her ear.

"Yes," DaNikka responded softly.

"And you will do what I ask," Will stated.

"I'll do anything for you. I've told you that before. I'm so lucky to have a man like you in my life, and I'll do anything to be with you and to make you happy."

"That's my girl. Come on, let's go. We have to be at Zanzibar Blue in fifteen minutes. I want to make sure that I don't miss Diana Krall's opening number."

A short while later, DaNikka and Will were sitting next to each other, enjoying a light dinner and listening to Diana sing the classic jazz tune "Fever."

"I've never heard this song before," DaNikka said as the melody finished.

"It's a hot little number, isn't it?" Will said, turning his attention away from the stage and back toward DaNikka.

"Yeah, I like it. I'm not that big on jazz music, but I like that song."

"See, that's what I'm talking about. I'm going to show you things that you've never seen before. I'm going to take you places you've never been. As long as you remain loyal to me, good things will happen."

"Well I appreciate you wanting to show me things and take me places, because it beats seating around the house all day wondering what's going to happen next. I can handle being sophisticated as long as you show me how." She gave him a bright smile.

"Tell me something that you like about me, DaNikka," Will

demanded, taking her hand and placing it on his thigh. He focused on her breasts and felt his erection begin.

"I like the fact that you're a powerful man. I like the fact that you buy me things, and I like the fact that you're teaching me things that I never knew about. I like how you make me feel sexy. I don't feel self-conscious with you. I feel desired."

"Touch me," Will commanded. "Stroke it for me."

"You want me to do it right here?" DaNikka whispered. "Right now?"

"Yes," Will answered. DaNikka unzipped his pants, removed his erect manhood from its confines and began stroking it.

"You are so hard," DaNikka said as she leaned toward him and kissed him. Will's erection tightened up even more once their lips met. "You want to do me bad, don't you?" DaNikka whispered in Will's ear.

"Just as bad as you want to do me," he answered, sliding his hand beneath her skirt and wiggling it up toward her womanhood, which was hot and wet.

"Oooh," DaNikka cooed aloud as Will's fingers touched her. "Can you tell that I'm moist?" Will was attempting to get around the fabric barrier of her thong, but DaNikka stopped him when she noticed their waiter returning.

"Would you like to see the dessert menu?" the waiter politely asked.

"I'm cool," said Will. "What about you, babe? You want anything?"

"No," DaNikka answered, laughing nervously because Will's fingers were still trying to crawl upward. It was clear by the expression on the waiter's face that he knew exactly what was going on. With a smirk, Will made eye contact with the waiter.

"I got this," he said just as his fingers slipped inside DaNikka.

"Oh, damn!" DaNikka buried her face in Will's shoulder.

"I see. Would you like me to take a picture of you this

evening?" the waiter asked. Will knew that he was being sarcastic, but DaNikka took him seriously.

"Yes. Take a photo of us with my camera phone, please," DaNikka said.

"What?" Will was surprised by DaNikka's suggestion.

"Remove your hand, please," DaNikka whispered in his ear. "You can't get me all hot and bothered while I'm wearing this dress." She reached into her purse, set her phone and pointed out which button should be pressed in order to snap the photo. Will and DaNikka posed for their picture. The waiter returned DaNikka's phone and placed the bill for dinner on the table before them.

"I'll be back," the waiter said and left.

"Baby, I had to stop you. Your fingers were driving me crazy," DaNikka explained.

"Shhh, I'm just getting my dessert." Will licked her essence from his fingers. "That's what I'm talking about. Hot all of the damn time."

"Only for you, daddy," DaNikka purred.

"Are you ready for the rest of your surprise?" Will asked.

"Yes," DaNikka answered.

Will calmed his manhood down and placed it back inside his trousers. He called to make sure his limo driver was outside waiting before placing enough cash on the table to pay for dinner.

"Come on, it's time to go," Will said.

Will had the driver take them to Secrets, which was an exclusive nightspot that specifically catered to wealthy men and women who had an unshakable appetite for sexual exploration. The exclusive club was owned and operated by a woman named Jade who had clients from all around the world. The limousine pulled into a parking lot surrounded by brick buildings in the warehouse district. The driver parked the car and then unlatched the trunk. He got out and held open the door for Will and DaNikka.

"Wait for us," Will instructed as he stepped out.

"Yes, sir," the driver answered before going to the rear of the car and removing a black messenger bag. "Sir, I've picked up the items on your list." The driver handed Will the bag.

"Thank you." Will took the bag and moved toward the entrance.

"I'm nervous," DaNikka confessed as she looped her arm through Will's.

"Relax and go with the flow. You'll be fine," Will reassured her. DaNikka held on to Will a little tighter as they entered the building and moved down the dimly lit corridor, illuminated by candlelight. At the end of the corridor, a man dressed in black stood beside a big steel door.

"Do you have a reservation?" he asked.

"You should have a reservation for two under the name of Daddy Long Stroke." The man looked at his list and located the name.

"Take these masks, put them on and enjoy your evening," he said as he opened the steel door. Will and DaNikka put on their festive masks and entered the club, encountering a flood of the uninhibited and the bold. There were topless waitresses walking ready to serve clients. Other employees of the club were carrying trays of colorful drinks. The staff appeared very attentive to ensure that their every need and desire was met. Some patrons were fully clothed, others partially and others completely nude. But no one seemed to notice. It was as if being in a place like this was as normal as breathing air. Will took DaNikka by the hand and guided her through the crowd to an area where there was seating for two on a sofa.

"So, what do you think?" Will asked as they sat down.

"This is straight-up wild, that's all I have to say right now." DaNikka scanned the room, taking in every detail. To her right, there was a dance floor with a stripper's pole. A full-figured and voluptuous woman had an audience of men surrounding her as she worked the pole wearing nothing but red high-heeled shoes. Directly in front of DaNikka were several pool tables. Wall-mounted television screens were showing X-rated films. To her left, several other sofas held folks sitting and talking while others allowed their passions to rule their behavior. One activity in particular caught DaNikka's eye.

"Damn, those guys are all over that woman. She looks like she's about to lose her mind." DaNikka tilted her head in the direction of a woman who was being pleasured by two men. The woman was reclining comfortably on the sofa. One man was between her thighs, circling his tongue around her clit as well as using his fingers to play with her honey pot. The other man was sucking on her breasts. It was clear by the sounds of the woman's moans that she was experiencing exquisite pleasure.

"Does watching them turn you on?" Will asked.

"I'm just surprised that they aren't nervous about doing it out in the open where everyone can see." At that moment, the woman began trembling uncontrollably and screamed out as she rode the wave of an intense orgasm. She tried to push her lovers away from her but they wouldn't move. The fun wasn't over yet.

"Being self-conscious is the last thing on their minds. This place is all about fantasy and pleasure. And tonight it's about you fulfilling one of my many fantasies." Will captured the attention of a waitress and ordered drinks.

"Look at what I have for us." Will unzipped the bag he'd taken from the limousine driver. He removed a vibrator with a rotating head, cock rings, edible panties and handcuffs.

"You're going to have to show me how to use some of that stuff," DaNikka said nervously.

"Don't worry," Will said. "I plan to." At that moment their topless waitress returned with their drinks.

"Is it okay if he spanks my ass?" the waitress asked DaNikka. "I like having my ass spanked."

"It's okay with me. It's his birthday and I want to make it perfect for him," DaNikka said as Will spanked the woman's ass several times. She then handed them their drinks.

"As soon as you're done with your drink, I want you to get undressed," Will informed DaNikka as he caught the attention of a male employee.

"Good evening, sir. How may I serve you?" asked the man.

"We're going to be getting undressed in a moment or two. Take care of our clothes for us, will you?"

"My pleasure, sir," said the employee.

"Oh, and turn around and let her spank your ass," Will ordered the man. DaNikka laughed as the man offered his derriere to her. She spanked him lightly and sped him on his way.

"Okay, I may need two or three drinks before I can comfortably get undressed in this place," DaNikka said, smiling at Will.

When DaNikka was ready, they both got completely undressed and left their clothing in the care of the male employee.

"Come on. Follow me," Will said seductively, as he grabbed DaNikka and the bag of toys.

"Where are we going?" DaNikka asked, apprehension clear in her voice.

"The oral sex room," Will said plainly.

"What do they do in there? I mean, I know they have oral sex, but is there something more?"

"You'll just have to wait and see now, won't you?" Will chuckled.

"Come on, tell me! How freaky do they get?" DaNikka asked.

Will laughed a little louder this time. "Extremely freaky," he said.

"Well, you know me. I'll try anything once," DaNikka said with shaky confidence.

"That's my girl," he said with a wink. "You turn me on when you talk like that."

They walked into the room, which was filled with participants. On one side of the room, several men reclined on a sofa with women between their legs. On the other side of the room, several women were positioned on their backs with men kneeling, their faces buried between the women's thighs licking their wet pussies as though it was their last meal. Will had his back pressed to a wall in a dark corner of the room. DaNikka quietly worked her bare-naked ass against his manhood as they both watched men and women have one pleasurable orgasm after the next.

"Watching this and being here with you has me turned on," Will said in DaNikka's ear. He nibbled on her earlobe and caressed her naked body. DaNikka raised her arms up high and caressed the back of his head as she pressed her ass against him harder. Will's fingers toyed with her pussy and stirred her passions.

"I want to fuck you so bad," DaNikka said. "Every time your fingers touch my pussy, I get weak."

"Are you going to fuck me in front of an audience like I want you to?" Will made his desires known.

"Yes, I will. I want to make you happy any way that I can," she answered as Will slipped two fingers inside her. DaNikka's knees buckled and she moaned.

"You're driving me crazy, Will," DaNikka cooed.

"Are you ready for me?" Will was eager to get the action started.

"Stop teasing me, baby, and give it to me, please," DaNikka begged. Her words were music to Will's ears. Will took her by the hand and led her to another room where there were several beds lined up against a wall. Topless employees were placing fresh linens on the empty ones.

"How often do they change the sheets?" DaNikka asked.

"Every time a couple uses a bed, the linen is changed right away so clients are always on fresh bedsheets. They'll even rip open a new package of fresh linen upon request," Will said.

DaNikka noticed three couples were on one bed making love while several people watched.

"Come on." Will was eager to feel DaNikka's warm folds. They stood by one of the free beds. Will signaled for an employee to come over.

"I want fresh sheets directly out of the package," Will said to the employee who immediately complied with his request.

Will positioned himself on his back and DaNikka mounted him.

"Oooh," she cooed as she began to ride him rhythmically. "Damn, this feels so good," she whispered.

"Come on. Stop holding out on me. Do the move that I like. Ride the tip of me. Ride the head."

"Okay," DaNikka said, lifting herself up and allowing only the head of his penis to remain inside her. She circled her hips, which caused his manhood to pulse with excitement. Will placed his hands on her ass and guided her movements to his liking.

"Yes, that's it, baby," Will encouraged. "That's it, just like that," he instructed her.

"Damn girl, are you sure you can handle all of that?" asked a female who was positioned doggy-style on the bed next to them.

DaNikka answered the woman by taking all of Will inside of her and flexing her ass and pussy muscles with authority.

"Oh, damn," Will cried out as DaNikka began to ride him hard.

"Damn, man, your lady has some nice moves," said an overweight man who was also watching.

"Her pussy is like dynamite. It blows me the hell away," Will said.

"Oh, it's like dynamite, huh?" DaNikka began screwing him harder and with more passion. She leaned forward and placed her hands on his chest.

"Come on, don't just lie there," DaNikka challenged Will, and he began thrusting his hips. "Come on. Give it to me. Stop playing around. Hit my spot, baby." Will worked his hips harder, but he couldn't keep pace with DaNikka. Tonight she was too much for him to handle. Her energy, her youth and her enthusiasm caused Will to come before he was ready to.

"Oooh, you were saving it up for me, weren't you?" DaNikka asked as she rested her sweating body against his.

Will was breathing hard. Once he caught his breath, he spoke. "Yes. I was saving it for you. I have more, just give me a minute to recover." After a few minutes, Will said, "Come on. Let's go get in the whirlpool and play with the toys I got."

Later that evening, during the drive home, Will thought about his wife, Angela. He didn't feel one ounce of guilt because he'd told her about his fantasies and desires, but she wasn't willing to satisfy his needs. So his solution was to find someone who would. And in his mind, there was absolutely nothing wrong with it as long as he kept his mistresses a secret.

CHAPTER 2

ANGELA

Angela rolled over to the right side of her bed and picked up her cellular phone from the nightstand. She checked it to see if she'd missed a call from Will during the night. When she saw that he hadn't attempted to contact her, she set the phone back down and tossed the comforter aside before sitting upright. She stretched, yawned and slipped her feet into her house shoes, which were at the side of the bed. She then walked toward her balcony. She drew back the drapes before opening the French doors to take in the fabulous mountainous California skyline and the view of the Bay. She took a moment to enjoy the warmth of the morning sun kissing her skin and sat down in a chair that was situated on her balcony to relax and think.

She thought about her life and how blessed she felt to have such a successful career and marriage. She loved the life that she and Will had built together. She loved living in their two-million-dollar, three-story, Mediterranean-style custom home. She adored the fact that her home was part of a gated enclave, which allowed for even more privacy. Since she and Will had such different tastes—Will had a more modern flare while Angela was more traditional—they had hired a designer to furnish the home and balance out their styles.

Angela shifted her thinking to the reality-show proposal she'd forwarded to Bobbi Franklin, one of her sorority sisters and the owner of a local cable network. Bobbi was in the process of revamping the network's programming and was looking for original show ideas. Angela was hoping her show idea called *Love, Lies and Scandal* would interest Bobbi, though a few weeks had gone by and she hadn't heard.

Angela's moment of solitude and her thoughts were interrupted by the sound of her neighbor's dog howling.

"I swear, I'm going to shoot my neighbor and that mutt of his one of these days," Angela said aloud. On more than one occasion, she had complained to her neighbor about how disruptive it was to hear his brown-and-white St. Bernard dog howling loudly first thing in the morning. She made a mental note to speak to Will once again about contacting the local authorities to have them enforce the noise ordinance. To the relief of Angela's ears, the howling didn't last for very long.

Angela got up from her seat to mosey back inside and head downstairs to the kitchen. She flipped on the light, turned on the countertop radio and went into the bathroom on the other side of the kitchen. Once she'd freshened up, she went about the business of brewing her morning coffee, then poured herself a cup. Angela was about to sit down at her kitchen table to enjoy it while she watched TV, but was interrupted by the ringing of the house phone.

"What's the deal, pickle? Is everything kosher?" It was Regina, Angela's lively girlfriend from Chicago. "How is life out in California with all of the beautiful people of the world?" Regina and Angela both laughed.

"Where have you been? You don't answer your cell phone or your house phone and you don't return voice or text messages until you feel like it. Why have been treating me like a bill collector?"

"Pimpin' isn't easy, girl," Regina boasted, as if that career was the most glamorous one in the world.

"Pimpin'? What the hell are you talking about?" Angela asked, perplexed.

"I'm big pimpin' nowadays. I have a couple of men on the

street right now. Matter of fact, I'm about to roll up on one of my men who is standing on the corner. He'd better have money when I stop." Angela laughed loudly.

"Stop lying, Regina. You're not cut out for pimpin'."

"You don't know what I'm cut out for." Regina continued her charade. "All I need is a few good-looking brothers who just got out of jail and can go all night long. I know plenty of women who could use a good stiff one and would probably pay well to get it."

"Regina?" Angela tried to pull her back to reality.

"What?" Regina laughed some more. "I'm just saying. If I were a pimp, I'd be one wealthy sister."

"And you'd be in jail. Let's not leave that part out."

"You know a fine-ass mickey fickey like myself would not make it behind bars." Regina had a habit of saying *mickey fickey* instead of *motherfucker*. She only used the actual words when she was extremely upset.

Angela loved her girlfriend for her uniqueness as well as her quirks. Regina could always make her laugh even when she was in the worst of moods. Regina's spirit was infectious and contagious and she always tried to see the positive side of the most awful situations.

"No, you wouldn't. Besides, I don't want the police to come and lock you up," Angela said, taking a sip of her coffee as she sat back down at her table.

"Speaking of the police, honey, let me tell you about what happened at my cousin Jesse's barbecue last weekend. You're not going to believe the mess that jumped off."

"Mess? Was there some kind of trouble?" Angela asked.

"Girl, a fight broke out." Regina said it as if she couldn't hold on to the juicy information any longer.

"Stop lying. No one started fighting." Angela laughed.

"I am not lying," Regina said firmly.

"Who was fighting?" Angela was now curious and wanted to know all of the details.

"You know his wife and her entire family are some retarded mickey fickeys, right?"

"Yeah, you've told me a thousand times that Jesse's wife, JoAnn, isn't the brightest woman to ever walk the earth."

"Well, neither is her fifty-two-year-old alcoholic sister, Jackie. In fact, I might as well tell it like it is. All of the women in JoAnn's family are alcoholics, even their grandmother. They're all ugly, as well. All of them look like they've done hard time down in Statesville. I'm still puzzled by why Jesse even dated JoAnn. She must be taking it all kinds of ways because Lord knows, she can't pull a man based on her looks."

"Regina, stop talking about the woman like that," Angela scolded her friend.

"I'm serious, Angela. JoAnn is wearing these dreadlocks that make her look like that creature from the movie *Predator.*"

Angela started laughing. "Regina, stop," she pleaded with her friend as she tried to control her laughter.

"Hey, it is what it is, honey. Like I said, JoAnn must be casting spells on Jesse or she's flipping her shit upside down."

"Come on, get to the good part and tell me what happened." Angela pushed Regina to give her the details.

"See, what had happened was..." Regina toyed with the popular slang saying.

"Stop stalling, Regina!"

"Okay. Jesse was having a barbecue, just a few friends and family members, nothing really big. JoAnn's sister Jackie was there. Jackie's thirty-year-old, baby-breeding daughter, Felicia, was there, as well. JoAnn's mother, uncle and grandmother were also there. And let me tell you, all of them mickey fickeys can swallow down alcohol like water running down a drain pipe. Anyway, Jesse also invited a few of his running buddies and me over. Jesse and I were sitting out back on the deck shooting the breeze about his sporting goods stores and how he was planning to run the Las Vegas Marathon in a few weeks.

JoAnn, Jackie, Felicia and the mother, uncle and grandmother were sitting around the kitchen table drinking and playing cards. Everything was cool until JoAnn got a little too drunk and started accusing Felicia of wanting to sleep with Jesse."

"What?" Angela almost spilled her coffee.

"You heard it right. JoAnn started accusing her niece of wanting to sleep with Jesse."

"Oh Lord. Well, was it true?" Angela asked.

"Girl, I wouldn't put it past Felicia to at least tempt Jesse. She conducts herself like some dog in perpetual heat. Anyway, JoAnn started talking about Felicia's tight clothes, bad weave and promiscuous ways. 'Don't think that I haven't peeped you trying to catch Jesse in a weak moment. I saw how you sat down in front of him and flopped your legs open. He doesn't want that funky stuff between your legs that every Tom, Dick and Harry has been jumping up and down in,' is what JoAnn said to Felicia."

"Oooh, damn."

"Wait, it gets better. Felicia looks at her mother and says, 'Did you hear what she just said to me?' And her mother, Jackie, says, 'Yeah, now go handle your business.'"

"'Go handle your business'?" asked Angela. "What was that supposed to mean?"

"I was wondering the same thing until Felicia leaped up out of her seat and swung on JoAnn like she was Laila Ali."

"What?" Angela's voice was loud with excitement.

"Felicia coldcocked JoAnn. Hit her in the face so hard that JoAnn fell over backward in her chair and hit the floor."

"Oh, hell no. That's just unacceptable. You don't go over to someone's house and literally get into a fight." Angela had a difficult time wrapping her mind around the concept of brawling at a family gathering.

"Well, honey, these jezebels went at it. It was almost comical. Thirty-year-old Felicia knocked forty-six-year-old JoAnn flat on her back. Felicia took a few swings at JoAnn while she was down but JoAnn quickly got to her feet, grabbed a fistful of Felicia's hair and started tossing her around with her weight. They knocked over chairs, slammed into the refrigerator and eventually crashed into a wall. They both began throwing wild punches at each other while continually calling each other a bitch."

"That sounds like some deep-rooted animosity," Angela commented as she took another sip of her coffee.

"Wait a minute, it gets wilder. JoAnn's mother got in on the action. She got up, snatched the kitchen broom and started hitting Felicia on her back with it. She kept saying, 'Turn her loose, Felicia,' but Felicia wouldn't. That woman was caught up in the moment and she was getting JoAnn for old and new."

"Was JoAnn able to defend herself at all?"

"JoAnn was able to get in a few hits of her own. But by the time she did, Felicia had done some damage."

"So what did Jesse do?"

"I think he was in shock. Once he realized that JoAnn and Felicia were really throwing down, he went over and broke them up. Needless to say by that point the damage had been done. Jesse's guests began leaving and one guest called the police out of fear that the situation was going to turn into an all-out riot. Within five minutes, three squad cars pulled up in front of Jesse's house."

"Oh, that had to be a real embarrassment. I'm sure the neighbors got an eyeful," Angela said sarcastically. "So what did you do?"

"I did what any person in that situation would do. It was time for me to grab my purse and leave. Especially after the police arrived. You know, a pimp like me has all kinds of warrants." Regina laughed at her own joke.

"Girl, you'd better stop saying things like that before you really do catch a case."

"Oh, believe me, if the fight had come my way at any time, I was going to represent," Regina boasted.

"Regina, you know you can't fight." Angela shrugged off Regina's comment.

"I can fight better than you. Do you remember that night you were trying to get an interview with that crazy dentist?" Regina paused. "What was her name?"

"Hayward. Dr. Charlene Hayward. That chick was crazy enough to be placed in a padded room."

"That's her. You had me come with you to sit in the car to watch your back in case Charlene snapped and became violent," Regina reminded Angela.

"I remember. Dr. Hayward had been dating some married guy and when he refused to leave his wife she somehow got him to come to her dental office to 'talk' about it."

"Yeah, then she used nitrous oxide to knock his ass unconscious and pulled out all of his teeth, right?" Regina was trying to recall all of the shocking details.

"Yeah, that's what she did. Any sister who got mad enough to yank a man's teeth out of his head was clearly, at least in my mind, at the end of her rope. I didn't know what she was capable of. I was just an ambitious reporter trying to secure an exclusive interview."

"Well, ambitious or not, you knew who you needed to have in your corner if girlfriend decided to turn into Mike Tyson."

"Okay, I'll give you that one. So have you heard from Jesse since all of the drama unfolded?"

"Not a word. He'll call me when he's ready. I'm sure he has his hands full dealing with his rough-ass in-laws." Regina laughed again. "So where's Will? Did he have a good time on his birthday?"

"He's out of town on business. So what's on your agenda today?"

"I'm treating myself to a massage today, then I'm going to go run a few errands. What about you?"

"I'm going to work on one of my stories a little more this

morning and—" Angela paused because her cell phone beeped. She quickly looked at the caller ID and saw Will's name. "Regina, I've got Will on the other line. I'll call you back."

"Okay, love you," Regina said.

"Love you, too. Bye." Angela disconnected from Regina and took the call from Will.

CHAPTER 3

JoAnn

Although it was only 6:30 a.m., JoAnn's thirst for alcohol was strong.

"I could use a dirty martini or two. Naw, fuck the martini, I could use some hundred-proof rum," she said softly to herself. She'd been lying awake in her Las Vegas hotel bed for only a few moments, contemplating whether to reach for the phone and order up her drink. She closed her eyes again then repositioned herself in the super-king-size bed as she tried to locate Jesse's warm body. When she couldn't make contact with him, she focused her attention on the sound of the room. She heard muffled voices passing by her door in the hallway and the sound of water running continuously.

"Damn, he's already up," JoAnn whined as she wondered why he'd decided to get out of bed without cuddling first. She hated the fact that he moved around like the damn Energizer Bunny on caffeine. The sound of the water ceased and a moment later Jesse exited the bathroom.

"Hey, I'm glad you're finally awake. The bathroom is all yours." He began to dry off and dress. "I need you to get up right away because we've got a ton of work to do. We've got to get down to the convention center early and set up the booth. I also need to see what other vendors are charging for particular items so that I can see if I need to offer some additional discounts to potential customers. I don't want to be undersold. I've spent a lot of money on the booth space as well as shipping a boatload of merchandise to sell. Did you remember to bring the credit card machine?" Jesse was now fully dressed and ready to attack the day and JoAnn felt like going back to sleep.

JoAnn knew that if she'd suggested that they order up breakfast and a few cocktails, Jesse would disapprove. She knew he'd say things like, "You just recovered from your alcohol and gambling addictions, why are you even thinking about drinking?" JoAnn knew that Jesse would blow up at her if he knew she'd lost control over her urges and had been secretly drinking and gambling behind his back.

"Stop yelling out orders at me," JoAnn snapped at him. "I'm not some damn machine."

"Baby, we've got to get moving. We can't afford to move at a slow pace. Time is money, so let's make this happen." Jesse popped his fingers at her. "Our competitors are probably already at the convention center waiting to meet customers." He stepped over to his suitcase.

"Why can't we just relax in this bed for a little while, huh? Why don't we just say 'fuck it' for today and skip the sports-and-fitness expo and just enjoy each other?"

"JoAnn, stop playing and get up. This is the third day of the expo. We want to make some money." Jesse went into the closet and removed a pair of running shoes.

"I'm serious, Jesse." JoAnn positioned herself on her knees. "We could just lie in this bed, make love and order room service for a day. Doesn't that sound like fun? I could do some really freaky stuff to you." JoAnn thought the promise of a wild sexual experience would be more than enough to slow Jesse down.

"We don't have time for all of that right now, JoAnn. I came out here to make some extra cash for the sporting goods store, do some networking and run the Las Vegas Marathon. I've already agreed to stay on a few extra days afterward to enjoy the city."

"You're not going to enjoy walking around with me after you've finished the marathon and you know it. You'll be too damn sore and you'll be complaining the entire time." JoAnn wanted to change all Jesse's plans so that they could spend time with each other walking the strip, gambling and seeing the shows.

Jesse gave her an icy stare. "JoAnn, I don't have time to debate this with you. You knew exactly what the deal was when we came here. Why would you purposely try to change things now?"

"Because, I don't—" JoAnn stopped herself midsentence. "Never mind, Jesse. I'll get up. This trip is all about you, as usual."

"Good. I'm going to run down to the lobby and grab a luggage cart so that we can haul our equipment over to the convention center." Jesse sat on the edge of the bed and began tying up his shoelaces.

"I'm just some old workhorse to you," JoAnn grumbled as she got out of bed.

"And I'm just some inconsiderate jerk who's been paying all of the bills, putting food on the table and working hard to keep the business in the black instead of the red. Last time I checked, a hardworking black man was still in style," Jesse quipped.

"Whatever, Jesse. You can toot your horn for as long as your ears can stand to hear you speaking." JoAnn finally entered the bathroom. "You're just an inconsiderate overachiever who doesn't know how to take time and enjoy life."

"What did you just say to me?" JoAnn could tell by the tone of his voice that Jesse was more than ready to have an argument with her this morning.

"I said that you don't know how to enjoy life. You don't know how to be spontaneous and just go with the flow," JoAnn said, not backing away from the swelling conflict.

"Honey, I'm more exciting than you'll ever be. *You're* the one who can't keep up with *me* in the sack."

"News flash, Jesse. No girl wants to have marathon sex every time she gets intimate. You don't even know how to relax when you're having sex. Everything is about competition with you. I swear, sometimes when we're together, I feel like you're running one of your damn races. You just keep going until I dry out."

"Hey, if my lovin' is too much for you to handle, just let me know." Jesse now stood in the doorway of the bathroom. JoAnn looked him in the eyes and she could tell his temper was rising. At that moment, she decided to back down and let him win this round.

"You're missing the point, Jesse. Never mind, I'll be ready to go in a few moments," JoAnn said as she placed a line of toothpaste on her toothbrush.

"Good. Leave our argument in this room. Do not bring it to the convention center." JoAnn didn't say another word. She slightly pushed him out of her way as she exited the bathroom. She picked up the telephone on the nightstand and dialed room service.

"Did you hear me?" Jesse asked.

"I heard you," JoAnn answered him just as room service picked up the line. Jesse began walking toward the door as JoAnn placed her order for two apple martinis to help her get through the day.

JoAnn both admired and loathed Jesse's natural charm, magnetism and charisma when it came to working the public. He had a gift. He could talk to anyone at any time and make them feel immediately comfortable. No matter what walk of life they hailed from, whether it was wealthy, middle class or the underserved, Jesse knew how to relate to people. JoAnn didn't have that natural aura. Whenever people—especially women—met her, they seemed to judge her and size her up. Before she could even speak, she could sniff out their attitude toward her.

She wasn't a fitness fanatic or a hyped-up marathoner like Jesse and the people who surrounded him. She was just a middle-aged black woman with an ample ass, thick thighs and a belly that would balloon up from time to time when she ate something that didn't agree with her. By no means did she consider herself to be a sloppy-looking woman, but she certainly wasn't trying to look as if she were in her twenties.

"The running shorts are thirty-five dollars and the matching top is twenty-five, but if you buy them together, I'll let you have them for an even fifty dollars." JoAnn listened and watched as Jesse worked his charm on two women who were noticeably flirting with him. He was all business though. If a woman wanted to have Jesse, she'd have to pretty much toss him on the ground and rape him before he'd pick up on the fact that she wanted to screw his brains out.

"I am so sick of these Barbie bitches," JoAnn muttered as she approached Jesse from behind.

"Okay, handsome, I'll buy them from you," said one of the women, allowing her eyes to dance all over Jesse. It was obvious she was having herself a quick little fantasy about the two of them as he bagged her purchases and gave her a receipt.

"Now you have a safe run tomorrow and shoot for your best," Jesse said as the woman took her purchases.

"Maybe I'll see you out there," she said as she and her girlfriend stepped away, looking at him longer than necessary.

"Maybe I'll see you out there," JoAnn mocked the woman as she stood next to Jesse. "Who were they? Some of your running groupies?"

"No, that was Lisa and Monique. They're runners from the Bay area."

"They were both smiling at you awful hard. I thought you knew them or something."

"No, they were just being friendly, that's all," Jesse said.

"Do you have your wedding ring on?" JoAnn asked.

"Of course I do." Jesse gave her one of his evil glares. "What's wrong with you?" He had no clue as to why she was irritated.

"You just make sure that you let these running groupies know that you're taken already. I don't feel like having to beat a bitch down today."

"JoAnn," Jesse said through gritted teeth. JoAnn knew that she'd unintentionally struck a nerve. "Put that damn attitude of yours in check."

"I'm just letting you know, okay? I'll beat a bitch down in here."

"The last time you got into a fight, you didn't do so well, remember?" Jesse began moving away from her to help a man who was looking at a pair of sunglasses. His comment hurt her and stirred up a multitude of bad feelings. There was no need for him to bring up the fight she'd had a few months back with her niece.

"I need another drink," she whispered to herself. She looked back at Jesse who was finalizing another sale. She reached for the flask in her purse and drank the vodka and orange juice she'd mixed up and poured into it.

"I feel so much better now," JoAnn said as she exited the hotel bathroom wrapped in the complimentary bathrobe. She'd decided to take a shower while Jesse counted the day's cash and receipts. "My legs are aching from standing up all day. Will you rub them for me?"

"Yeah, in a minute," Jesse answered as he continued to count money.

"Do you mind if I turn on the television?" JoAnn asked as she positioned herself on the bed.

"Yes, I do. Just give me one more minute," Jesse said as he continued mumbling to himself and writing down numbers. JoAnn huffed as she waited patiently for him to finish.

"Okay, it appears as if we didn't do bad at all. It cost forty-five hundred dollars to ship merchandise out here, pay for our airfare and hotel expenses, as well as cover the cost of the booth space. I have eight thousand, five hundred dollars in cash and another six thousand dollars in credit card receipts. So that adds up to fourteen thousand, five hundred, minus expenses, which leaves the business earning a profit of ten thousand dollars. We've made a handsome amount of money over the past three days." Jesse smiled.

"You know what we should do, babe?" JoAnn had what she thought was a grand idea.

"What?" Jesse asked as he placed the money in a secure bag and then moved toward the safe in the room.

"We should take some of the money and have a little fun. We should go gambling just for the hell of it."

Jesse laughed as if he agreed and then stopped abruptly. "No," he said with conviction.

"Why not? Let's live a little, let's be spontaneous and enjoy ourselves. We can afford it," she said with glee.

"No, that's called being irresponsible. Besides, you know that I don't gamble. I work too damn hard for my money to throw it away."

"We're in Las Vegas, Jesse. That's what people do here. They have fun," JoAnn argued.

"Babe, I have a marathon to run which means that I'm not going be up all night fumbling around at a casino. Besides I was reluctant about you even coming on this trip because I know casinos aren't a very good place for you."

"It's not like that anymore and you know it. I know how to control myself. We can splurge a little during our extended stay. Let's just budget out a certain amount."

"No. My idea of fun is sticking to what we agreed to. We're going to enjoy a Las Vegas show or two, have romantic dinners and go dancing. Gambling is just not in my nature."

"Not even a little? You won't even play the penny slot machine?" JoAnn asked, slightly horrified by his unyielding position.

"That's right. Now, tomorrow, while I'm running the race, I want you to wire the money to the business account back home."

"Fine," JoAnn said as she picked up the remote and turned on the television. Jesse locked the safe and then went to take a shower. "Can we at least order some room service?" JoAnn asked sarcastically.

"Yeah." Jesse shouted out his answer.

"Cheap bastard, I can't stand your ass sometimes," JoAnn mumbled as she picked up the room-service menu. "I'm going to order the most expensive item they have," she said as she scratched the palm of her right hand. "I must have some un-expected money coming my way. That's what it means when-ever the palm of your hand begins to itch for no reason at all." JoAnn smiled at the thought of having a large sum of money at her disposal to do whatever she pleased with. With that thought, both palms began to itch. "Shit, luck must be on my side."

There were thousands of people preparing to run the 26.2-mile run and no matter how many times JoAnn had witnessed the number of people who were crazy enough to participate in the race, she was always amazed by their dedication to it.

JoAnn had just finished helping Jesse stretch up and was walking with him to the starting point of the three-hour-and-forty-five-minute-pace group.

"So, do you actually think you'll finish the race in three hours and forty-five minutes?" JoAnn asked.

"If I finish it in four hours and fifteen minutes, I'll be happy. But if I can hang with the pace leader the entire way, it would most certainly be a personal best for me."

"Well, good luck and don't hurt yourself," JoAnn said, giving him a light kiss on the lips.

"At what mile marker should I be looking for you?" Jesse asked.

"Look for me around mile ten. That will give me time to wire the money," JoAnn explained.

"Good." At that moment, a loud air horn went off indicating that the race had begun.

"Okay, baby. I'll catch you later," JoAnn said as she stepped away from the crowd. She watched as Jesse disappeared in the sea of runners.

As she made her way back to the hotel, the palm of her hand began to itch again.

"Damn," she said as she scratched. "It's a sign. I can feel it. Luck is with me, I know it is." When she returned to the hotel room, she unlocked the safe with the key Jesse had given her. She pulled out the cash and held it firmly in her grasp. JoAnn began to feel the need to gamble. She was quite familiar with the symptoms. Years ago, gambling had been a problem for her, but she had learned to quell that compulsion. Now those old familiar pangs lured her back. Itching palms, feeling lucky and having cash in her hand excited her. She knew she should resist.

"Damn, girl. Do the right thing," she muttered to herself.

CHAPTER 4

JESSE

At the mile ten water station, Jesse was feeling strong and was still on track to finish the race in three hours and forty-five minutes. He looked on both sides of the street and scanned the cheering crowd in search of JoAnn, but she was nowhere to be found. He didn't think much of her absence, assuming that it had been too difficult for her to get back to that location at the exact time he'd be there. He knew for certain she'd be at the end of the race waiting for him. He adjusted his white running cap to keep the blazing sun out of his eyes and began to think about how blessed he was to be healthy. This was his twelfth consecutive marathon and he had no intentions of stopping anytime soon. His body type wasn't that of a marathoner. He was two hundred and ten pounds of solid muscle as opposed to a lean and wiry elite runner. He had no desire to compete with the elite runners for the half-million-dollar purse because there was no way in hell he'd be able to run 26.2 miles in under two hours. As Jesse approached the fifteen-mile water station, he decided that it was time to turn on his iPod for a bit of extra energy and motivation. The song "Just Fine" by Mary J. Blige blared through his headphones as he pressed on, still feeling strong. By the time Jesse reached the twenty-mile water station, he was feeling completely different. The blazing Nevada sun had taken its toll on him. Sweat was cascading off his body as if he were a walking waterfall. He feared that he was well on his way toward dehydration.

Between miles fifteen and twenty, he'd seen a significant

number of runners collapse from exhaustion. Jesse's legs felt as if someone had poured quick-drying cement in them. He'd fallen slightly behind the pace group by fifty meters and, in spite of his pain, willed himself to pick up his feet and catch up. Once he did, he settled into his stride once again. At the twenty-two-mile water station, Jesse had to stop running. Heat exhaustion was trying to steal away his glory and was doing a damn good job of it. He asked one of the aides to pour water on his head. The cold water felt good and it cooled his skin down. Jesse continued to walk to the next mile marker. At mile twenty-five, he found himself shuffling along on fumes.

"Come on, you can't stop now," a woman said as she approached him. "You've got to keep moving." She smiled and sprinted past him. He glanced up briefly and noticed that Lisa and Monique, his customers from yesterday, were jogging next to him.

"That's right," Jesse muttered, "I can't stop now."

For the remainder of the race, the three of them ran together in silence. When they crossed the finish line, they hugged each other and thanked one other for the encouragement to continue.

Jesse finished the race in four hours and thirty minutes, which was slower than he'd have liked, but he wasn't about to complain about it. After he picked up his completion medal and draped it around his neck, he searched the crowd for JoAnn. When he couldn't locate her, he decided to have a seat beneath a tree to get out of the hot sun. He remained there for an hour resting and talking to other runners about how tough the race had been and how gratifying it was to complete it. Jesse was hoping JoAnn would come along so that they could head back to the hotel and she could give him a massage that would relax him into a deep sleep. But JoAnn never surfaced.

He finally decided he'd go back to the hotel alone. He

walked over to the gear tent, collected his belongings and caught a cab. Walking through the lobby of the MGM Grand Hotel, Jesse had only two things in mind—a hot shower and a soft bed. When he entered his hotel room, JoAnn was nowhere in sight. He removed his clothes, went into the bathroom and took a shower. Fifteen minutes later, Jesse exited the bathroom feeling moderately refreshed. Just as he was about to lie down, he heard JoAnn come into the room. She gasped the moment she realized she wasn't in the room alone.

"Damn, you scared the hell out of me," JoAnn said, as she placed her hand over her heart and closed the door. Jesse only glared and waited for an explanation.

"Is your race over already?" JoAnn asked.

"You didn't come at all, did you?" he asked.

"Baby, I'm sorry. I was walking around sightseeing. You know how big these casinos are. I didn't realize how quickly the time went by."

"You should've looked at your watch, JoAnn." Jesse's aggravation was obvious.

"You're right. You are so right and I am wrong. I'm sorry for not being there for you. Let me help you get in bed." JoAnn approached the bed and pulled back the covers for him. "How do you feel?"

"I'm a little stiff and achy but I'll be okay," Jesse answered.

"You know what, let me rub you down. Hang on and I'll get the baby oil," JoAnn said as she went to the bathroom to retrieve the lubricant.

"Aren't you going to ask me how I did?"

"Knowing you, baby, you probably finished in record time," JoAnn said as she exited the bathroom.

"Well, not exactly, but it was still a decent time," Jesse stated.

"Sit up and take off your robe so that I can give you a good massage." JoAnn smiled and poured oil into her palm. Once

Jesse was completely naked, JoAnn kneaded his muscular caramel-colored legs and his feet.

"Oooh, you don't know how good that feels." Jesse sighed.

"Shhh, just relax," JoAnn said as she massaged his thighs and his manhood, which had become erect from all of her caressing.

"How can you get hard after running all of those miles?" JoAnn asked.

"I got it like that," Jesse boasted.

"I see," JoAnn murmured as she wrapped her hand around him to see how strong his erection was. "Solid as a rock," she stated.

"I told you, I got it like that."

"It seems to me like you have a little energy left to do something," JoAnn said without enthusiasm.

"Suck on it. Put it in your mouth."

JoAnn glared at him. "Are you serious?" she asked.

"Do I feel like I'm serious? You're the one holding my dick in your hand." JoAnn turned her head away from him.

"Come on, baby, do me," Jesse begged. "I'll just lay here and let you work me over."

"And then you'll go to sleep?" JoAnn asked.

"Honey, the minute I pop a nut, I will be out like some busted headlight."

"Fine," JoAnn agreed. She got on her knees and placed his dick in her mouth. She used both of her hands and sucked on him as only she could. She made sure his shaft was slick with her saliva as she stroked him with one hand and caressed his thighs with the other.

She circled her tongue around the mushroom head and took him deeper into her mouth, pushing down until the tip of his dick was at the back of her throat. She then suctioned her lips down on his glistening shaft and slowly pulled up while simultaneously sucking.

"Oh, shit." Jesse sighed. She repeated her signature move several times until he had an orgasm. Within seconds of his release, Jesse was fast asleep. She went into the bathroom and cleaned herself up. She brushed her teeth and gargled with mouthwash, then washed her face. She looked at herself for a moment in the mirror and, before she could stop them, tears began falling.

"Damn, JoAnn, why did you do that?" she whispered directly at her reflection. "You've gambled away half of the cash. Girl, you're a better gambler. You've got to bring your A game in order to win. Get yourself together, get the rest of that money and go triple it. You can do it. Just take your time and pay attention to what you're doing. And stop crying. Jesse doesn't know yet and what he doesn't know will not hurt him. Just go win the money back and everything will be fine." JoAnn smeared away another teardrop and began to scratch her palm.

"It's a sign," she said to her reflection. "Mama always said that if the palms of your hands itch, it means that you've got unexpected money coming to you." JoAnn teased her hair with her comb and then stepped out of the bathroom. When she looked down at Jesse, he was snoring loud enough to cause a person to go deaf.

"You're not going to wake up anytime soon." She went to the safe, opened it up and took the remaining cash and headed for the blackjack table.

CHAPTER 5

WILL

Will was disturbed out of his sleep by the stewardess asking that he bring his seat back into the upright position in preparation for landing. As she moved forward, he glanced at her pear-shaped ass as it ballooned against the fabric of her skirt. The stewardess was now several rows ahead of him, leaning forward, relaying the same message to another passenger.

She doesn't have on any underwear, Will surmised. He could tell by the way the fabric of her skirt folded into the crease of her ass. The visual beauty of her behind and the knowledge of her secret turned him on. He fantasized about standing in the aisle with his pants around his ankles, pulling her hair and penetrating her from behind. In his mind, he could hear her primal moans, her heavy breathing and the sound of her ass slapping against his thighs. *Damn, I wish I could have her right now,* he thought as he scanned his surroundings.

The airplane was practically empty, thirty passengers at best. He reached over DaNikka, who was still asleep, and opened up the window shade. He noticed the sun was beginning to peek from beneath the horizon but hadn't fully risen yet. Off in the distance, he saw the red steel arches of the Golden Gate Bridge knifing through a few clouds. He closed the window shade and focused his attention on DaNikka. She had a copy of Kim Catrell's book *Sexual Intelligence* resting on her lap. He'd picked up the book for her before their trip to Philadelphia. The book explored sexual intelligence, the mystery of sexual fantasies and the power of arousal. He'd gotten it for DaNikka so that she'd understand not only herself but him, as well.

"Good lovers are taught, not born," he had said to her when he gave her the book. He was hell-bent on making damn sure she was a highly skilled and a well-trained lover. She'd been reading the book at the beginning of their flight back home. Will studied her body language as she read and saw that she'd become aroused. It was the way she crossed one leg over the other and bounced it, signaling that an erotic impulse was stirring around the folds of her paradise.

"Are you getting hot? Are you getting wet?" He had to know.

DaNikka stopped reading and met his gaze. "Yes. I seem to stay wet whenever I'm around you." Will smiled, then glanced down at the swell of her breasts. Her thirty-four double-Ds were a constant source of pleasure. Will tossed one of the small blue blankets that had been given out at the start of the flight over her legs.

"Let me feel how wet you are. Spread your legs for me."

DaNikka looked around. "Are you serious?"

"Yes. No one is near us. I just want to feel it. I want to put my fingers on it and play with you a little."

"You are going to make me scream," she muttered as she unbuckled her belt, unzipped her jeans, slumped forward and spread her legs slightly.

"I'll try not to make you moan too much," Will assured her, skillfully gliding his fingers through the triangle of hair on her mound. She cleared her throat as she checked to make sure no one was coming down the aisle before spreading her thighs a little wider. DaNikka guided his hand around the rim of her lips as Will's middle finger dipped inside her. DaNikka moaned and then clutched his hand. She cradled the back of his head, pulled his ear to her lips and allowed him to hear her sensual moans. The wave of passion swelled up within her and she quickly crossed her legs to contain it before she informed the entire plane that Will's finger was deep inside her.

Will could feel the walls of her paradise pulsing against his finger.

"My very touch sets you off, doesn't it?"

"Yes," DaNikka whispered. Will was about to place a second finger inside of her when DaNikka stopped him.

"The stewardess is coming," she whispered, hastily removing his fingers, clapping her thighs shut and fastening her loose clothing.

"Are you two okay?" The stewardess stopped at their seat. Will placed his glistening finger between his lips and circled his tongue around it.

"Everything is delicious," he'd finally answered with a devilish smile.

Will now squeezed and coaxed his erect manhood—which he had fondly named Homicide—in an effort to satisfy Homicide's unyielding and perpetual thirst for sex. *She's so young and she's all yours to teach and train to be loyal only to you and your most titillating fantasies.* He considered DaNikka to be the perfect mistress for a man in his circumstances. She hailed from Pittsburg, California, an economically depressed community filled with scores of poorly educated black people. DaNikka's mind wasn't strong like Angela's, and was therefore ripe for molding. DaNikka was the youngest in her family and by far the most beautiful. And what man wouldn't want a woman around who idolized, adored and worshipped him no matter how he treated her?

"DaNikka." Will tapped her leg to wake her up. "We're making our final descent into Oakland," he whispered to her and then kissed her on the cheek.

"Tell me you love me," DaNikka mumbled as she looped her arm around his and nuzzled her face against his shoulder. "I want to hear you say it."

"You know I do." His words held absolutely no truth.

"We should just run away and leave California behind. We could buy a new house and start a new life together. I could have a son for you and a girl for me. The four of us would be so happy together. I just know we would. Don't you think it would be nice for us to be together all of the time?" she rambled.

"Get your mind right, DaNikka." Will unlatched her from his arm. "Remember your place. Remember our agreement."

"I'm sorry, I was just thinking—" she quickly apologized.

"Don't think. Just do what I ask you to and you'll benefit from it. Who is the man who buys you nice clothes?"

"You."

"Who is the man who makes sure you have money in your pocket?"

"You."

"And who is the man who has been helping out your mother?"

"You."

"Now why do you want to mess up this perfect arrangement?"

"I don't want to mess it up, baby. I just—" DaNikka stopped talking out of fear she'd say something wrong.

He stared coldly at her so there would be no mistake. "Make sure you don't start thinking like that again or I'll cut you completely off."

"I'm sorry, okay?" She tried to give Will a kiss, but he refused her affections. DaNikka sat completely upright and remained silent as the plane landed at the Oakland airport. Will turned his cell phone back on and checked his messages.

"I've ordered a car for you," Will said as the aircraft taxied toward the gate. "The driver is at the luggage carousel waiting for you."

"You're not riding back with me?" DaNikka pouted.

"No. Angela is picking me up." DaNikka remained silent. Will knew that made her unhappy, but she'd get over it. They exited the aircraft and began walking through the airport.

Will directed her to step over to the side away from the flow of traffic. "Here, this is for you." He handed her an envelope filled with one thousand dollars in cash. It was the largest amount of money he'd ever given her. "Do something nice for yourself."

The money changed DaNikka's attitude. "You know that you're my boo, right?" DaNikka smiled slightly as she tucked the money inside her purse.

"I'll call you when I can, most likely after my committee meetings."

"Okay." DaNikka closed up her purse and tried to kiss him once again.

"We're back home and in public, DaNikka. This is the part where Mr. Rourke and Tattou appear out of nowhere wearing white suits and say your fantasy has come to its end."

"Who?" DaNikka was confused.

"I forgot you're too young to remember that television show. Just make sure you don't get too caught up in our fantasy getaways."

"I'm sorry. I just want to say thank you," she explained. "My mom and I can really use the money."

"Well, you have what you need, so go pick up your luggage. Your driver is waiting for you."

Will watched DaNikka as she sucked up her emotions and was swallowed into the massive herd of people moving forward toward their destination. Will then walked over to Starbucks and ordered himself a cup of coffee. As he took his first sip, his cell phone rang.

"Hello," he answered.

"Hey, baby. Where are you?" It was Angela.

"I just got off of the airplane."

"Okay, I'm down at the baggage carousel waiting for you."

"I'll be there in a few minutes."

"Did you miss me?" Angela asked.

"Of course I did. I thought about you every day."

"I thought about you, too. I missed you."

"Well, you won't have to wait much longer. I'm on my way," Will said as he completed their call. He went to the bathroom to freshen up.

"The last thing I want is for Angela to get a hint of DaNikka's scent on me," Will whispered to himself. After he'd washed his hands thoroughly, he decided to visit a few airport stores to give DaNikka enough time to get her luggage and exit. As he came down the escalator near the luggage carousel, he noticed that there appeared to be some type of delay. Their luggage hadn't been removed from the aircraft yet. He also noticed that Da-Nikka was standing behind Angela, glaring at her with contempt.

"There you are. Hey, baby." Angela walked over to Will and stepped into his embrace. As he hugged Angela, DaNikka trapped his gaze, her eyes swelling with hell's fire. At that moment, the luggage carousel began moving.

"It looks like the luggage is finally here. Why don't you go pull the car around?"

"Do you need any help?" Angela asked.

"No. I'll be outside in a moment." Angela left and Will waited for his luggage. When his luggage arrived, he grabbed it and stood before DaNikka. He looked into her tear-filled eyes and quickly kissed her on the cheek.

"Keep it tight and wet for me," he whispered and then continued onward.

CHAPTER 6

ANGELA

When Angela saw Will finally emerge from inside the building, she popped the trunk on her gold Infiniti. Will placed his luggage in the trunk and got in the car. He kissed Angela on the lips and then buckled his seat belt.

"How was your trip?" Angela asked as they drove toward the highway.

"It was good. We did plenty of team-building exercises and I attended a seminar about conflict resolution."

"How many people were there?" Angela asked as she reached for her bottled water sitting snugly inside the cup holder.

"I don't know the exact number, but I think about sixty," Will answered as he yawned. "Man, I'm tired."

"Well, it was a long flight. You're probably a little jet-lagged. You should soak in the whirlpool when we get home."

"Yeah, that sounds like a plan. Could you put some of your sea salts and aromatherapy in it for me?"

Angela smiled. "I'd love to but I have to head down to the station once I drop you off at home. I'm also going to be late getting in tonight because of the Black Journalists' meeting."

"Oh, yeah. I forgot about your meeting. You're speaking to high-school students tonight, right?" Will asked as he reclined his seat and yawned once again.

"Stop that. You know yawning is contagious."

"Can't help it, babe. Long business trips completely drain me." Will laughed.

"Well, did you get any type of sleep while you were out there?"

"Not really."

"Why not?" Angela asked.

"Sometimes it's hard to get comfortable in a strange bed. The bed was a little lumpy and the pillows were not as soft as I would have liked them to be," Will complained.

"I know how that can be," Angela agreed. "Your brother called early this morning. That fool called the house at 5:00 a.m."

"What the hell did he want?" Will asked.

"He wanted to know when you'd be home. He said that he needed to talk to you right away."

"I'll catch up with Smokey when I feel like it. I'm just not in the mood for any of his bullshit today."

"You two really should consider selling that house in Pittsburg," Angela said as she began driving through their gated community.

"Smokey doesn't want to leave there. I've talked to him about it several times and he refuses even to consider selling the property. His reasons for staying are silly, but we both own the house. I can't sell it unless he agrees."

Angela parked the car in the driveway. "Maybe he'll change his mind. It would be safer for him if he moved. Well, get your things. I'll see you later on tonight," Angela said.

"Okay, baby. I'm going to go in and take a nice long bath." Will groaned as he exited the car. He pulled his luggage out of the trunk and entered their home through the garage. Angela backed out of the driveway and continued on to work.

When Angela arrived at the television studio, she made her way toward her office. The place was buzzing with telephones ringing and multiple conversations. Her coworkers were busy getting the facts on various news stories and writing down copy for the midday news.

Angela peeked inside the control booth and said hello to Royce, a camerawoman. She continued down a narrow corridor and made her way past the office of her boss, Steve Stone.

"Angela, can I speak with you for a moment?"

Angela turned and saw that Steve had gotten up from his desk in order to catch her. Steve was a short, mousy-looking guy with a receding hairline who was fond of wearing suits that were too big for his small frame. Angela turned and walked back into Steve's office.

"Have a seat." His outstretched hand indicated a chair in front of his desk. "I saw the piece you did last night on fraud and home-based businesses."

"Did you really?" Angela asked. "What did you think?"

"It was very good. I was impressed. I wanted you to know that the station has received an unbelievable amount of phone calls asking that you do an investigation on several more companies."

"Really?" Angela smiled inwardly. She knew that Steve was more than just pleased with her investigative work.

"Yes. It appears is if this problem is more widespread than we thought in the Bay area."

"Well, I could've told you that." Angela chuckled.

"Have you ever gotten one of those e-mails from some foreign country asking for your bank account information in exchange for a ridiculous sum of money?"

"I get them all the time."

"There's a very large-scale effort to defraud people here in the Bay area. This time the crooks are not asking for bank-account information. They want cash. I'm going to forward you several e-mails that I've gotten. I want you to play along and send the monopoly money to whatever address they give. When they pick up the package, I want you to be there to expose them. Are you game?"

"You know that I am. This sounds like an assignment I'm going to enjoy."

"I thought you would." Steve and Angela both laughed. After a little more small talk, Angela headed back to her desk to work on her story for the five o'clock news broadcast.

After the broadcast of the evening news, Angela unhooked her microphone and walked toward her office. She sat down and began going through her mail. As she was reading a letter, her cell phone rang.

"Hello, this is Angela," she greeted the caller.

"Why are some men so damn retarded?" It was Regina. Angela chuckled.

"What are you talking about?" Angela stopped reading her mail, reclined in her seat and gave her full attention to Regina.

"I'm talking about a hell date that I went on."

"Hell date? Oh Lord. This is going to be good. Where are you?" Angela asked. "I hear a lot of noise in the background."

"I'm walking down the street to my car. I'm just leaving my belly-dancing class."

Angela chuckled. "When did you decide to take up belly dancing?"

"When I saw that they offered the class at my gym. Tonight was my first night and the sister who teaches it knows how to work her hips. She had the class try a few basic moves and I swear, I think one of my kidneys got dislocated."

"You can't dislocate a kidney." Angela laughed out loud.

"Well, I'm telling you that it feels as if I've shifted my damn kidney. But anyway, that's not why I called."

"Well, come on, spill the beans and stop playing."

"Okay. I met this brother named Craig at First Friday's last month."

"How come you didn't tell me you'd met someone? Why have you been holding out on me?"

"Because I wasn't ready to talk about my traumatic experience yet."

"Traumatic?"

"Yes, traumatic. Now are you going to let me finish?" Regina asked.

"Go on, I'm listening."

"Craig is drop-dead fine. Tall, well-groomed, pretty smile, athletic build and a product of an historically black college. But little did I know his name was Mr. Diva."

"Mr. Diva? What's that supposed to mean?"

"Will you let me finish?"

"Sorry, you know it's just my nature to ask questions."

"So, like I said, we met at First Friday's. I learned that he was a vice president of sales at Soul 98, a hot new radio station here in Chicago. We really hit it off. He had a great sense of humor, he made me laugh and he paid attention to me. The brother was making all the right moves. We exchanged phone numbers and spoke on the phone a few times. I learned that he has a loft on the near-west side of the city where they've gutted and remodeled a lot of the old warehouses. We decided to set up our first date. He took me to the Wine-Tasting Room near Harpo Studios."

"What's that place like? I've never been there before."

"It's very nice. I'll take you the next time you're in town. It's a place where you can sample different wines, listen to poetry and jazz…"

"Sounds romantic," Angela said.

"It's very romantic. So we go there, order chocolate fondue, have a great conversation and taste several different wines. Needless to say, after a few glasses, my ass started getting hot, and Craig was well on his way to getting his world rocked. We listened to jazz, shared a few kisses and drank more wine. Then he asks if I like the singer named Silky. To which I replied, yes, I love his music."

"Oh, I like his music, too. Especially that sexy song 'Instant Message Passion,'" Angela chimed in.

"That's one of my favorite songs, as well. Not to mention Silky is drop-dead sexy. Because I'd do him in a New York minute. So Craig says that Silky is an old college buddy of his. 'He's in town for a fund-raiser. Would you like to hang out with Silky for a little while?' he said. I was like, boom, let's go kick it with Silky, not a problem with me. So we leave the Wine-Tasting Room and head back toward the Ritz Carlton Hotel before the fund-raiser. When we get to the Ritz Carlton, we head on up to Silky's suite. We get off of the elevator and my legs suddenly feel weak. I think it was a combination of the wine and the excitement of meeting Silky. Craig knocks on Silky's door and Silky opens it up. And, girl, let me tell you. That man looks even better in person. I mean he made me want to scream like some nerdy high-school girl."

"You weren't acting all retarded, were you, Regina?"

"Girl, no. You know that I played it calm, cool and collected."

"So what did Silky say to you?" Angela was anxious to know.

"Angela, he looked at me and I swear he was undressing me with his eyes. He said, 'Hello, baby, my name's Silky. What's yours?' I told him my name as I trailed behind Craig inside the suite. Once inside the hotel suite, I took in the beauty of the room, which had floor-to-ceiling windows and a spectacular view of the city. As I was admiring the view, I noticed that Silky slapped Craig on his ass. I didn't think anything of it because it was the kind of ass-slapping I'd seen football and basketball players do all of the time. I asked Silky where the bathroom was so that I could go freshen up. 'It's the last door down that corridor over there,' he says.

"So I head to the washroom to make sure that my makeup is still in order and that I still look as fabulous as ever. When I came out of the bathroom and walked back into the room where I'd left them—girl, I could have been shot with a bag of shit and left hanging to stank when I saw what they were doing."

"What were they doing?" Angela was on the edge of her seat with anticipation.

"Girl, they were tonguing each other down!"

"Get out of here! They were kissing?"

"Kissing, squeezing and sucking each other's bottom lip."

"You're bullshitting!"

"You know, when I first saw them doing that, I said, now hold on, girl. Maybe you've had too much to drink and the shit you're seeing just isn't real. So I turned around, went back into the bathroom and placed some cold water around my eyes. I came back out and they were still going at it."

"So, what did you do?" Angela asked.

"I stood there stunned and traumatized."

"Oh, hell no! I would've been, like, what the fuck is going on with you two?"

"Well, I did interrupt them."

"What happened after you interrupted them?"

"I said, are you guys gay? And they both looked at me and said, hell no!"

"Bullshit. If you're kissing on another man and slapping his ass, you're gay," Angela said. "What happened next?"

"I did what any sister in her right mind would do. I left. I went downstairs, had the doorman hail me a cab so that I could go home. I must've brushed my teeth and tongue for a full hour once I got in the house. Then I got pissed off. I mean, how dare that motherfucker bring me to his bitch's house! I mean, honestly, what kind of shit was that?"

"I don't know, but damn! Silky is on the down low. This would make a great topic for my show, *Love, Lies and Scandal,* if Bobbi ever calls back. Celebrities with secret love lives."

"What are you rambling on about?" Regina asked.

"I submitted a proposal to someone for a reality show called, *Love, Lies and Scandal*. Do you think you could put me in touch with Silky's lover? Perhaps if I can convince him to let me do an interview it would—"

"Now, you've pissed me off, Angela," Regina snapped angrily.

"I'm sorry, okay. I didn't mean to sound so insensitive. I'm sorry that you went through that."

"I am, too. Anyway, I'll talk to you later." Regina sounded hurt.

"Don't be mad at me. I just got caught up in the sensationalism of your story."

"I'm tired of talking about this. I'll talk to you later," Regina said and hung up the phone.

"Shit," Angela hissed. She knew that she'd inadvertently trampled on Regina's feelings. She made a mental note to herself to send flowers to her friend's office in the morning as a peace offering. She knew that Regina's wound was still raw, but with time she'd be okay.

Angela looked at her watch and realized that if she didn't get a move on she'd be late for her meeting. She gathered up her belongings and headed toward the conference room where she'd be giving her speech to high-school students interested in careers in journalism.

CHAPTER 7

JOANN

Over two days, JoAnn had traveled between three hotel casinos: the Bellagio Hotel, Caesar's Palace and the MGM Grand Hotel. At each hotel and at every gambling table, JoAnn suffered heavy losses because she couldn't bring herself to stop.

JoAnn lost three thousand dollars playing blackjack at the Bellagio. She suffered another three-thousand-dollar loss at Caesar's Palace playing poker. She lost an additional fifteen hundred dollars playing roulette and four hundred and fifty dollars at the slot machines at the MGM Grand Hotel.

JoAnn was now sitting in front of a slot machine, hoping her luck would change and she'd win big. She decided to play three slot machines at the same time. She wasn't about to allow someone on either side of her sit down, pull the handle once and win.

In a short amount of time, JoAnn gambled away the last of the money she'd taken from the safe. She closed her eyes and dropped her chin into her chest. Hastily, she brushed the tips of her fingers across her eyelids several times to smear away the tears that threatened to fall.

JoAnn held her head up and took in a few deep breaths. "My hand was itching," she said to herself. "And whenever the palms of my hands itch or tingle, I know that it means I'm about to hit it big. It's a sign. That has always been my intuitive signal which lets me know that money would be coming my way." JoAnn felt a massive migraine building. She gathered up her belongings and stepped away from the slot machine. She slowly wandered to the end of the slot-machine aisle, dreading having to go up to her hotel room. She stopped when she heard a loud ringing coming from one of the slot machines behind her. She spun around and noticed that a woman had sat down at one of the machines she had been playing and had just hit it big.

"No, no, no!" JoAnn hustled back toward the woman who was screaming for one of her girlfriends to rush over to her.

"That's my money," JoAnn shouted out above the noise. "That's my machine and that's my money!" she screamed at the woman. "Did you hear what I said? That's my money."

"Yeah, right." The woman huffed as she began placing coins into her bucket.

"I want my money. I was playing this machine and I put my money in it."

"I'm not giving you a damn thing," the woman snapped as her girlfriends arrived.

"I want my damn money! You were probably sitting somewhere watching me just waiting for me to get up." JoAnn made a quick move and tried to snatch the bucket away from the woman who fought her off.

"Come on! You want some of me?" The woman removed a can of pepper spray from her purse and aimed it at JoAnn. The two women glared at each other for a moment before JoAnn finally conceded.

"Fuck it! Just fuck it, and fuck you, bitch!" JoAnn turned and walked away as quickly as she could. She made her way to a sitting area and sat down. She cried before pulling herself back together. She asked one of the waitresses who was passing for the time.

"It's one o' clock," the woman said.

"In the afternoon?" JoAnn asked because she couldn't believe that she'd been gone all night.

"Yes," the waitress answered and continued on her way.

"Damn, Jesse is probably searching for me." JoAnn reached inside her purse and pulled out her cell phone. Sure enough, there were several missed calls from him.

"Okay, girl. Pull yourself together. It's not that bad. Jesse will understand. He'll be mad but he'll understand." JoAnn tried to convince herself of her own words. There was no logical reason for what she'd done and she knew it.

"I have to get Jesse to understand that I just made a mistake and I'll make all of this up to him. He'll accept that. I'll just tell him how sorry I am and that it will never happen again." JoAnn sat in her seat for another hour talking to herself and thinking so hard that her stomach turned sour. She finally got herself together, took a deep breath and headed up to their room to apologize.

JoAnn placed her door key inside the slot. When she crossed the threshold, she could hear Jesse on the phone. Once inside the room, she froze. Jesse sounded as if he was on the phone with the bank.

"Are you sure there was no deposit or wire transfer placed into the account?"

She peeked around the corner. Jesse's back was toward her and he hadn't heard her come in. JoAnn took a few steps forward and noticed that he had opened up the room safe.

Damn, she thought. He already knows the money is gone.

"Are you sure that there isn't some mistake? The money should have hit the account yesterday."

JoAnn felt nauseous. Jesse finally turned and acknowledged her.

"Never mind. Thank you for your help. My wife's here. I'll ask her for the confirmation receipt and call you back," Jesse said and hung up the phone. "Where have you been?"

"Don't yell at me," JoAnn whined as she sat down at the foot of the bed. "I'm getting a headache."

"Where have you been?" Jesse asked with a calmer tone. "I need your help. I've called the bank and they have no record of money being deposited. Give me the wire transfer receipt so that I can help them track where the money is."

"Jesse, baby." JoAnn looked at him as teardrops raced down her cheeks.

"JoAnn, where is the receipt?" he asked again with a little more authority.

"It's hard to explain." Her voice trembled.

"Where is the money, JoAnn?" Jesse folded his arms across his chest and waited for an answer.

"I was just trying to win a little extra money for us, that's all. I had good intentions." JoAnn's words came out in spurts.

"JoAnn! What the fuck are you talking about?" Jesse shouted and waved his arms like a madman.

"Just calm down, baby. I'm going to make it up to you. I promise."

"JoAnn, where in the fuck is the eight thousand, five hundred dollars that I asked you to deposit?" Jesse began clenching his fists.

"I blew it, okay? I'm sorry." JoAnn began to slap her head with the palms of her hands as if she were trying to beat some sense into her brain. "I didn't know how to stop. I got caught up. I—I—I made a bad judgment call and I'm sorry but I gambled away the money," JoAnn said as tears streamed down her cheeks.

"You mean to tell me that you gambled away eight grand in two days!"

"I'm telling you that I wasn't myself. I didn't know how to stop. My palms kept itching. I knew I was going to win, it was just a matter of time. When my palms itch, it always means that I have money coming my way. This is the first time that it hasn't worked."

"I don't believe this shit!" Jesse began pacing like a caged tiger.

"I've been to the support groups with you for gambling. I've been to the Alcoholics Anonymous meetings with you. I've been through so much bullshit with you, JoAnn. I've gone from trusting and loving you to being suspicious and leery of you and back to trusting you again. I thought we'd moved past your addictions. Don't you realize that your issues have the power to destroy our marriage? Don't you realize you can financially ruin us?"

"I just messed up a little money, Jesse. It's not the end of the world." JoAnn hoped to downplay the severity of what she'd done. She caught his gaze and noticed his eyes were laced with anger and damnation.

"There is no doubt in my mind that you fully understand the impact of your behavior. I'm tired, JoAnn. No, wait. Forget I said that. I'm not tired. I'm pissed off about this. Do you have any idea what it took for me to excuse your faults and flaws and learn how to trust you again? Do you have any idea of how many times I had to tell myself that I wasn't an idiot for loving you the way that I do? I can't believe you've done this to us again."

"I'm sorry," JoAnn said softly. Jesse stopped pacing and she could see that he was calculating something.

"You planned this. That's why you didn't show up to support me at the race. You were out gambling then and lost track of time." Jesse glanced at JoAnn who was horrified that he was able to figure her out so easily.

"Then, when I came home from the race, you pulled an orgasm out of me quick so that you could run off and gamble some more while I was sleeping." Jesse once again looked at his wife, and, based on the expression she had on her face, he knew that she'd deceived him.

"I never thought I'd have to go through some shit like this with you again—the last time was bad enough," Jesse growled at her as though some evil spirit possessed him.

"You'd better not hit me, Jesse," JoAnn warned.

"I'd better not *what!*" Jesse's evil rage was in control of him now. "I'd better not do *what?*" he barked at her again.

"I know that I fucked this up. Believe me, I feel bad about—" Jesse lunged at JoAnn and locked his hands on her throat and began choking her. As she fought to free herself from his grip, they tumbled to the floor. Jesse was too strong for her and easily positioned her on her back and straddled her. JoAnn had her hands locked around his wrists and was trying to pry them away from her throat.

"Eight thousand dollars! You blew eight thousand of my goddamn money! I should kill your ass!" Jesse slammed her head against the floor several times. JoAnn slapped and punched him on the side of his face, but her blows didn't do any damage.

"You don't fuck up money like that!" he shouted as JoAnn began gasping for air. She could feel herself beginning to black out. "Do you hear me?" Jesse lifted her head up and slammed it against the floor again. "Why!"

"You're killing me." JoAnn managed to find enough breath to squeeze out those few words. Her eyes began to float upward into her skull. At that moment, Jesse immediately released his pit-bull clasp. JoAnn sucked in air, coughed and managed to crawl from beneath him. Jesse rose to his feet as JoAnn crept into the bathroom, slammed the door shut and locked herself inside.

CHAPTER 8

JESSE

Jesse rushed out of the hotel room to calm himself down. He needed to get away from JoAnn because his mind was telling him to strangle her to death and then drive out into the desert to dig a hole for her corpse. He'd been with JoAnn for well over a decade and she'd done a lot of ignorant and stupid things during the course of their relationship, but this latest idiotic act of hers outdid them all. He'd never put his hands on her before. He didn't understand how JoAnn could be so reckless and then want him to easily forgive her.

"She must be out of her damn mind," Jesse said out loud as he walked down the Leg Vegas strip. "How in the fuck did she blow all of the damn money and think that I was going to be okay with that shit!" He continued to rant loudly as he wandered the streets. He caught the curious glances of a few people who moved out of his way when they realized that he was on edge.

"I should've never hooked up with her ghetto ass. Everyone in her damn family is ignorant. None of them amounted to anything. They're all just a bunch of alcoholics, leeches, welfare queens, wannabe pimps and idiots." Jesse began walking away from the strip and toward the University of Las Vegas. Once he made it to the campus, he wandered over to the football field and took a seat on the bleachers.

He exhaled a few times and began to think about happier times with JoAnn. He thought about how they'd met at the Essence Music Festival. She'd accidentally bumped into him with her tray of food and spilled it all over him. She was so apologetic about ruining his clothes but he didn't care. He continually told her that it was okay but she wouldn't stop apologizing. Once she stopped brushing food off his clothes, he met her gaze and saw a kind and generous woman he wanted to get to know. Without thinking twice, he asked her name, where she was from and if she'd like to attend the Frankie Beverly concert with him later that evening. She said no at first, but then quickly changed her mind and told him she'd go with him if her sister came with them. After the concert, Jesse took her out for a late dinner. His attraction to her was strong, and as they got to know each other, a level of comfort developed that made him feel as if he'd known her for years.

After the music festival, they exchanged phone numbers and promised to keep in touch. Jesse didn't think he'd see JoAnn for at least a few weeks, but it turned out they were both on the same flight from New Orleans to Chicago. They rearranged their seats so they could sit next to each other and talk more during the flight home.

During the course of their courtship, Jesse and JoAnn enjoyed attending celebrations and enjoying nightlife with friends. For Jesse, it was a nice diversion from the chaotic and stressful world he lived in. JoAnn had the ability to make him laugh and feel as if he could accomplish anything with a woman like her at his side. After a year of dating, he asked JoAnn to marry him.

"I'm going to have to end my marriage. I can't go on like this. I can't continue to live in the house with a woman who insists on drinking and gambling. We are two completely different people. I knew it when I married her. Marrying her was a stupid move on my part." Jesse exhaled in an effort to release some of his frustration. He couldn't come up with a clear and decisive answer as to what he should do about his strained relationship with JoAnn. There were a multitude of things he needed to consider before going down the road of divorce. He would have to contend with the emotional trauma for their daughter, Trina. JoAnn would also have the right to ask for her fair share of his business profits and the value of their home.

"Damn, damn, damn!" Jesse shouted as he weighed all the facts. He no longer liked JoAnn, and he damn sure didn't trust her anymore.

"A marriage without trust is going to fail," he said aloud. "Our marriage is a relationship that should have been buried a long time ago," he murmured to himself. "I can't believe that I wanted to kill her. It's not cool that I lost it like that," Jesse said as he ran his fingers over his hair. He sat on a bench until sunset, mulling over his thoughts and the pros and cons of different scenarios centered around ending his relationship. He finally grew tired of placing so much mental energy into his problematic marriage. He decided that he'd walk back up to the strip and treat himself to a nice dinner and show to take his mind off JoAnn.

The following morning, Jesse went to the convention center and packed up all his remaining merchandise so that it could be shipped back to his store. When he was done late in the afternoon, he returned to the hotel room. JoAnn was sitting on a chair having a phone conversation. When she saw him, she ended her phone call and remained silent. Jesse could tell that she'd been crying because the whites of her eyes were still red. He didn't say anything to her because his heart didn't have any sympathy whatsoever. He opened the closet door and pulled out his suitcase and began packing. He was ending their stay early.

"Are we leaving early?" She broke the silence between them.

"I don't care what you do," Jesse answered bitterly. "I'm taking a five o'clock flight home."

"I don't blame you for the way you reacted," JoAnn said. "It's understandable, but I don't want you ever to do that to me again."

Jesse still refused to acknowledge her.

"You're not going to talk to me at all?" JoAnn asked. "We can work this out, you know. It's not as bad as it seems." She smeared away more of her tears. "Do you still love me?" JoAnn stood up and approached him. "Will you ever forgive me? I've forgiven you for choking me." Jesse's heart and feelings for her were completely iced over.

"Do yourself a favor—don't say a fucking word to me," he said as he moved toward the bathroom. Once inside, he shut the door, locked it and turned on the shower so that he could freshen up before heading to the airport.

When they arrived at the airport, Jesse paid the cabdriver, grabbed his luggage and immediately went to the ticket agent to change his seat assignment. He ended up with a seat at the rear of the aircraft near the toilet, but he didn't care. He didn't want to sit next to JoAnn during their flight home. Once he got his boarding pass, he didn't bother to wait for JoAnn to receive hers. He continued on his way as if she were a complete stranger to him. He took a seat at the gate area and glared out the window at planes arriving and departing.

"Do you want something to eat or drink?" JoAnn arrived and sat next to him.

Jesse couldn't believe that after all that had gone down, she still had the nerve to be in his face like a fly buzzing around a picnic table. He caught her gaze and showed her that his contempt for her was still very much alive.

"Don't look at me like that, please," JoAnn begged.

"Leave me alone, JoAnn. What part of that don't you understand?"

"We have to talk about this, Jesse. I'm so sorry for what I did. I got caught up. I wasn't myself, okay? I don't know what to say. I don't know why I—"

"Shut up, JoAnn." Jesse didn't want to hear another word

fall from her mouth. She swallowed heavily and moved away from him. Jesse went back to the business of watching planes arrive and depart. After he got bored with that, he decided to walk over to a magazine stand and select something to read. As he did, he spotted JoAnn sitting at the penny slot machine searching her purse for any loose coins to gamble with. He shook his head disapprovingly. He picked up the latest issue of *Runners World* and went back to his seat.

"Here." JoAnn interrupted his reading. He glanced up at her from the page. "Your daughter wants to talk to you," she said as she tried to hand him her cell phone. He didn't take it. JoAnn pressed the mute button.

"You can be mad at me all you want for as long as you want. But don't take out your anger on Trina." She attempted to hand over the phone once again. Jesse took the phone, released the mute button and spoke.

"Hey, butter cookie," he said to his preteen daughter, Trina.

"Hey, Daddy. I can't wait for you to get home. I've missed you."

"I've missed you, too, honey," Jesse answered.

"Daddy, guess what?" Trina asked.

"I don't know, what am I guessing about?"

"I'm on the volleyball team at school."

"You made it. Well, congratulations. We'll have to celebrate when I get home."

"Thank you. I didn't think I was going to make it at first, but they posted the results of the tryouts today after school and I saw that I'd made it. I'm so excited."

"When is your first game?" Jesse asked.

"In a few weeks."

"That's wonderful. I can't wait to come watch you play." Talking to Trina made Jesse feel a little better. Before he realized it, JoAnn had sat in the empty seat next to him and removed his magazine from his lap to thumb through while he spoke with Trina. He stayed on the phone with his daughter until it was time to board the plane. Once he ended the phone conversation, he gave JoAnn back her cell phone, took his magazine back and walked onto the plane without saying a word to her.

CHAPTER 9

WILL

After Angela dropped Will off at home from his trip to Philadelphia, he began unpacking his luggage. He checked all of the pouches in the suitcase to be sure that no evidence that would expose his affair with DaNikka was inadvertently overlooked. Afterward, he made his way to his office and began working on a draft of his speech regarding an amendment to a resolution on public housing. As he was proofreading his work, his cell phone vibrated on his hip. He ignored it; he'd check it after he finished. A few moments later, his house phone rang and Will once again ignored it. He made some revisions to his speech, printed it out and read over it once again. No sooner had he finished reviewing that his cell phone rang again.

"Who in the world is calling me like this?" Will unholstered his phone, glanced at the caller ID and saw that it was Smoky, his brother.

"Where in the hell are you at, man?" Smoky growled.

"I'm at home," Will snarled back. He wasn't in the mood for Smoky or his attitude. At times Smoky was both offensive and abrasive.

"I need your help, Will. I'm in a bad way," Smoky explained.

"Smoky, I'm not about give you any money and you know that," Will said as he sat the phone on his desk and pressed the speaker button.

"You don't have to give it to me. Just give it to the city so I can get the hell out of jail."

"Jail! Smoky, what the hell are you doing in jail?"

"I need you to come bail me out."

"What did you get arrested for?" Will asked, irritated that his plans were about to be interrupted.

"They're trying to jam me up on some bullshit-ass charges. I told them that they didn't know who the fuck I was. But they brought me in anyway."

"On what charges, Smoky?" Will asked once again.

"What the fuck does it matter, man? Just come get my ass out of here before I hurt somebody. You know that this place is not equipped to handle me."

Will sighed. "Smoky, you are far too old to be getting arrested. What station do they have you at?" Will opened his desk drawer and pulled out a pen and a notepad and wrote down the information. "I'll be there within the hour," he said and hung up the phone.

When Will arrived at the station in Martinez, California, he learned that Smoky had been arrested for buying marijuana from an undercover narcotics agent. Will posted the one-thousand-dollar bond and waited for an officer to escort Smoky from his jail cell.

Forty minutes later, Smoky was rolling himself toward Will in his wheelchair. Will stood up as his brother approached. Before Will could react, Smoky had curled his fingers into a fist and punched Will in the gut.

"What the fuck is wrong with you?" Will coughed and was about to strike back.

"It's unlawful to hit a man in a wheelchair," Smoky said quickly.

"What the hell did you hit me for?" Will asked.

"For not answering your damn phone," Smoky said as he rolled away.

"Smoky, I swear, if you weren't my brother I'd beat your ass and I wouldn't feel guilty about you being in a wheelchair," Will said as he trailed behind him.

"Yeah, whatever. Suck it up, congressman, and come on before someone recognizes you and starts asking too many damn questions," Smoky said as a woman held the door open so he could wheel himself out. "You know there's nothing like being with a handicapped man, baby," he said to the woman. She didn't respond, only smiled as Smoky continued on his way.

"Why were you messing with that woman?" Will asked.

"Because she was hot," Smoky answered. "Oh, by the way, I need you to run me by the barbershop so that I can get a haircut."

"Who said that I wanted to drive you around all day? Maybe I've got other things to do," Will argued.

"Your plans changed once you came and got me, so stop your bellyaching and take me to where I need to go." Smoky wheeled himself next to Will's passenger door. "You know that ever since I had my accident I've depended on you. Why do I have to continually go through this shit with you, man?"

"Because you keep messing up the schedule I set up. I have everything scheduled for you. Your trips to the grocery store, visits to the doctor, all of that stuff."

"You know that I don't like schedules."

Will and Smoky were as different as night and day, but they hadn't always been so dissimilar. They were raised in a middle-class suburban home with both of their parents. Their father was an electrician and their mother was a top-selling real estate agent for a local agency. Their parents had them late in life; Smoky had come along when their mother, Vera, was thirty-seven years old and their father, Joe, was forty-four. Four years later, to their parents' surprise, Will was conceived.

Both Will and Smoky were very smart, did well in school and were always very competitive with each other. After high school, Smoky went on to graduate from the University of California at Berkley with a degree in business. Will graduated from Morehouse College with a degree in political science.

After losing both of their parents within two years, Will and Smoky became very close because they only had each other. Smoky worked as a real estate agent for the same company that his mother had worked for and eventually purchased the company. After college, Will landed a job working for his local congressmen.

While vacationing in Lake Tahoe, California, six years ago, Smoky and a few of his friends got intoxicated and decided to go racing through the wilderness on their rented snowmobiles. Smoky lost control of his snow craft and had a horrible accident which left him without the use of his legs. After the accident, Smoky became deeply depressed. He began drinking heavily and experimenting with drugs. Eventually he lost his business, his home and his nest egg. Will stepped in and made sure that Smoky saw a therapist and signed him up for rehab, but none of his efforts helped. Smoky had decided that his lifeless legs gave him the right to abuse himself until he got too tired to continue.

"How is that little girl that you have on the side treating you?" Smoky asked as Will lifted him out of his wheelchair and sat him inside the car.

"She's doing fine."

"Boy, that's a nice piece of ass you have there. Does she still do whatever you tell her to do?"

"She doesn't give me any grief, if that's what you mean," Will said. He got in the car and began their journey back toward the barbershop.

"See, that's the kind of woman I need. One who knows how to obey." Smoky laughed at his comment. "You'd better be careful though. Those young girls are kind of crazy. They'll turn on you in a New York minute."

"I'm not worried about DaNikka doing anything. I have her exactly where I want her. She lives in public housing and I'm her last hope."

"And what about Angela? You got her where you want her?" Smoky asked.

"I know how to manage my women, Smoky. Angela knows that we're perfect for each other. She isn't going anywhere."

"I taught you well." Smoky held his hand out so that Will could slap him five.

"Yeah, right." Will chuckled.

"What? Do I need to remind you that at one point I was holding down four women at the same time? Do I need to remind you that I had all four of them together in the room and kept all of them in check?"

"No, you don't need to remind me, Smoky." Will smiled. He wanted to remind Smoky that all four of the women eventually left him but he didn't feel like bruising his brother's ego. At this point, those memories were pretty much the only thing Smoky had left.

"Man, I need a hundred dollars from you," Smoky said.

"For what?" Will asked.

"I need to pay for some pussy. It's been a minute." Will was about to argue, but he didn't know how to respond to his brother's comment.

"Smoky, you really shouldn't be messing with streetwalkers, man. You could get sick."

"I'm already sick." Smoky didn't like Will's judgmental tone.

"Yeah, but—"

"But what? I'm still a man! I still have needs. My shit still gets hard. Now I'm asking you for a favor. I want to get me a haircut, an order of chicken wings, smoke some good weed and have sex with a prostitute. Is that too much to ask for?"

Will shook his head. "It's your life, man. I can't stop you from doing what you want to do."

"That's right. Because I'm going to do whatever I want whether you like it or not," Smoky said just as Will pulled up in front of the barbershop.

* * *

Inside a Lincoln Town Car, Will was being driven to the airport. He was headed to D.C. for the next congressional session. The driver stopped at a corner and Will noticed a man with one leg swinging himself across the street on crutches. The man had a sign taped to his back that read, End the War in Iraq. The sight of the disabled man made Will think not only about the war but about his brother, Smokey, as well. He wanted so much more for his brother. He wanted his brother to move out of their parents' old house. The neighborhood had changed and now it was infested with drugs. He wanted his brother to get on the right track, but Will could want for eternity. Smoky had lost the will to do better and that pained Will's heart.

In Washington, Will spoke before the House of Representatives regarding Resolution H.R. 3940. He'd been appointed to a congressional subcommittee to deal with the demolition and rebuilding of public housing.

After Will's impassioned speech, there was a loud chorus of supporters for his amendment when the chairman intoned, "All of those opposed to the amendment please signify by saying nay." Only one voice was heard. "The amendment passes," said the chairman.

Will exhaled as he sat back down in his seat, pleased with the victory.

Will finally returned to his hotel room just before midnight. He sat on the edge of the bed, removed his shoes and loosened his necktie.

"Damn, I'm tired," he muttered to himself as he stood up and made his way to the bathroom to take a shower. Once he was done, he put on his pajamas and rested comfortably on his bed. He picked up the television remote and clicked the power button. He surfed through the channels in search of a program that was entertaining, but he wasn't able to find anything, so he settled on a twenty-four-hour news channel. There was a special report on about professors dating their students and how university officials across the country were trying to create policies that would ban such behavior.

"What the hell," Will said to the television. "If the two people agree to get involved with each other, the university has nothing to do with that. People are going too far with this. I'd be mad as hell if my employer dictated to me who I could and couldn't sleep with." Will became so disgusted that he turned off the television.

He positioned himself comfortably on the bed and closed his eyes for a moment. He saw images of his beloved wife submerging her naked body in their swimming pool. His body began to yearn for her as he allowed himself to fully recall an erotic encounter he and Angela had a few months ago. He remembered that it was one of the most explosive sexual episodes they'd ever shared. When he saw her naked form enter the water, he didn't hesitate for a second before removing his clothes and joining her. He plunged beneath the water and swam to her. When he resurfaced, he was standing directly in front of her, looking at the flames of desire burning in her eyes. She didn't say a word to him. There was no need to. She crushed her lips against his and slipped her tongue past his wet lips. Their kiss was passionate and spirited. Her tongue danced inside his mouth as he lifted her up so she could lock her legs around his waist.

"What's gotten into you?" he asked as his hands traced the fullness of her ass.

"In a minute, you'll have gotten into me," Angela said as she nibbled on his bottom lip. Her words sparked his passion. His manhood pulsed with anticipation, and he was filled with a hunger that demanded to be satisfied.

"Oh, so you're a bad girl tonight. You want it rough?" Will said, ready to feel her warm folds.

"On the steps of the pool. That's where I want you to fuck me," Angela said. They maneuvered over to the steps. Angela spread her legs and leaned forward to rest her hands on one of the higher steps, placing her ass and the entrance to her paradise just above the surface of the water. Will entered her and began thrusting deep inside her. Angela released sensual moans that encouraged him.

"Yes!" she cried out as he spanked her caramel ass.

"Come on. Give it to me," Will demanded and Angela complied. She spread her legs a little wider so that Will could push harder.

"Oh, baby," Angela cried out as her orgasm made her body quiver. That was the reward Will was searching for—the moment he got it, he exploded inside her.

Will felt a sudden burst of energy and needed the comfort of a woman. His nature was demanding and at times, untamable. He thought about booting up his laptop computer and watching some adult videos, but he didn't. He didn't want to talk to Angela because she'd become way too focused on her career lately and had been ignoring his needs for intimacy. He needed someone who could satisfy his obsession with sex as well as his constant cravings. He couldn't look at a woman and not wonder what she was like in bed. Unbidden DaNikka ran across his mind.

"Damn it, Will. Get it together, man. You can't let thoughts of DaNikka consume you like this." Will shut his eyes tight, but his mind only flashed images of his young temptress dancing seductively for him and nibbling on his neck.

"Fuck it," Will said aloud and picked up his cell phone from the nightstand.

"Hello?" DaNikka answered the phone.

"Hey. Where are you at?" Will asked because he heard a lot of noise in the background.

"Hanging out with a friend. Are you back home yet?" she asked.

"No, I'm still in D.C. I'll be back soon though." Will paused. "Hanging out with a friend where?" Will became insecure. He didn't want DaNikka going anywhere without him knowing about it. She was his private delight and he didn't want to share her at all.

"I'm at home with my girlfriend Shantel. You remember my girlfriend Shantel, don't you?"

"Yeah, I do," Will said. His mind immediately thought about Shantel's succulent lips and long legs. "What are you guys doing?"

"We're just listening to the radio and talking."

"Are you talking about me?" Will asked. He wanted to know if DaNikka was thinking about him the way he was thinking about her.

"No. We're talking about stuff."

"Stuff like what?"

"Just stuff. I was thinking about trying to get my GED."

"You don't need a GED. You have me to take care of you."

"But—"

"But nothing, DaNikka. I'm everything you need. And right now, I say you don't need a GED."

"I hate it when you talk like that," DaNikka said.

"You just remember what I told you. You don't need to worry about an education because you have me."

"Are you still going to do what you promised?" DaNikka asked.

"I'll still come through for you as long as you remain loyal to me," Will assured her.

"You know I'll do anything for you. Why do I have to keep proving it to you?" DaNikka asked.

"Because I want you to," Will answered. There was a long moment of silence between them.

"What do I have to do, make another video of us making love?" Will could hear the nervousness in DaNikka's voice and it brought a smile to his face.

"Nothing right now. We'll talk about it when I get back. Have a good time with your friend."

"Okay," DaNikka answered. Once Will had finished talking to DaNikka, his wicked ego told him that he was a better player than his brother had ever been.

CHAPTER 10

ANGELA

Angela and Bobbi Franklin had just been seated for lunch at the Le Bistro French restaurant in Walnut Creek. Bobbi was a woman in her late fifties who was originally from Jackson, Mississippi. She had a mocha complexion, was tall and a little overweight, but not by much. Angela could tell that her hair had been recently braided by the way Bobbi kept playing with the cascading braids. Angela had met Bobbi several years ago at a fundraiser she'd attended with Will. Angela had always admired and respected Bobbi for her business savvy and intelligence.

"Order whatever you'd like. This one is on me," Bobbi said as she looked over the menu. Angela took her time to review the menu and decided to order the stuffed prawns. Bobbi settled on the pan-seared salmon.

"As I was saying to you earlier—" Bobbi rested her elbows on the table "—my entire team is very excited about producing your show, *Love, Lies and Scandal*. I truly believe that the show will draw a large numbers of viewers."

"I believe that women and men who watch television don't just want to watch some contestant try to win a prize. They want to be active participants. They also want to know about issues that others are afraid to talk about," Angela chimed in.

"I agree with you and so does the director of programming. We want to launch the show this fall, so that means we want to begin taping before the ink dries on the contract." Bobbi laughed. "I have the advertisers lined up and your time slot will be nine o'clock on a weeknight. I know this show is going to be a hit. You'll be a superstar."

"This is so exciting," Angela exclaimed. "I can see the show going on for no less than ten seasons."

"Well," Bobbi said, smiling, "we can hope for that. By the way, how does your husband feel about you hosting such a racy show? Is he okay with it?"

"Of course he is. Will has always supported me." Angela thought it was odd that Bobbi would ask such a question.

"Well, here's to a wonderful business relationship." Bobbi held up her glass of water. Angela did the same and they both toasted to their partnership.

Several weeks had passed during which Angela had handed in her resignation at the news station and focused on launching her television show. She, along with a team of programming directors, producers, writers, marketing experts and designers, hammered out everything from show topics to set design. The first episodes of her show covered the topics of men who watch too much pornography, dating while divorcing, why men and women cheat, turning Rambos into Romeos and sleeping with coworkers.

Before Angela's first taping, Will decided to treat her to a day of pampering. He'd made reservations for brunch and dinner and scheduled a couples' massage for them at the Claremont Resort and Spa in Berkeley. Angela was thrilled about spending time with Will because they'd been missing each other due to their work schedules. Angela had been on Will's back about making time for them to focus on each other, and now that they were about to have brunch together, she planned to remind him not to forget to make time for each other.

"Hey, stranger," Angela teased him as he sat down at the resort's dining table.

"Why are you calling me stranger?" Will asked as he unfolded his napkin.

"You're always gone and I'm always working. I feel like the only time we get to see each other is to have sex. Hopefully with the show's production schedule, my time will be a little more flexible, which means we'll get to spend quality time together." Angela reached across the table and placed her hand upon his. "Maybe we can even find enough time to schedule a vacation to the Virgin Islands."

"You know how busy I am. I'm constantly—"

"Too busy to spend time with each other?" Angela wanted Will to think carefully about what he was about to say. He seemed to have read her thoughts.

"A vacation would be nice. But right now is not a good time. I have too much going on."

"Well, then, find the time. I want to go the Virgin Islands. I've been talking to you about it for months and you keep putting it off."

"Don't start with me, okay?" Will warned.

"I haven't started anything with you. Why are you so defensive?" Angela leaned back in her seat and folded her arms.

"I hate it when you do that. Don't try to make me feel guilty. It won't work."

"I'm not trying to make you feel guilty, Will. All I'm saying is that I'd like to spend a little more quality time with you. What's wrong with that?"

"We do spend quality time together," Will corrected her. "We were spending quality time last night if I recall correctly." He gave her a lusty smile.

"Will, having lazy sex is not spending quality time, so don't get it twisted."

"What's that supposed to mean?"

Angela was silent for a long moment as she navigated through her feelings.

"Well?" Will wanted her to speak up.

"Will," Angela whispered. "We shouldn't talk about this here. It should wait until we get home." Angela searched for an exit out of the conversation.

"Oh, no. Tell me now. It's too late to back away."

"Are you sure you want to hear this?"

"Yes, I want to hear it. Lay it on me," Will said sarcastically. He leaned back in his seat and stroked the tip of his nose a few times.

"Will," Angela whispered. "I feel like I'm just some sex object to you. When we make love, you don't talk to me, you don't look at me and you don't pay attention to me."

"What the hell are you talking about?" Will said with irritation.

"I'm saying that it would help if I knew what you were thinking. It would help if you'd open your eyes and look at me. You keep your eyes closed so tightly…at times I think you're fantasizing about another woman. Do you fantasize about having sex with other women when you're making love to me?"

"That's ridiculous and you know it. I'm not even going to dignify your comment with a response." Will dismissed her statements. At that moment, his cell phone began to vibrate. Will removed his phone from its holster to check his message and grinned as if he'd just won an exquisite prize.

"What's that look for?" Angela asked.

"What look?" Will stopped grinning.

"Who just sent you a message? What did it say?"

"Why are you being so nosy?" Will asked curtly.

"Because as soon as you read that message, an expression washed over your face that I'd never seen before."

"I don't know what you're talking about, Angela. I think you're being paranoid or something. The message was just a joke someone forwarded to me," Will said as his phone vibrated once again. She could tell that her husband was trying hard not to let his excitement show.

"Either you put that damn phone away or I'm going to take it from you," Angela snapped at him. She didn't like the fact that Will wasn't paying attention to her. She was trying to have a meaningful conversation with him.

"See, that's your problem, Angela. You think that you can boss me around. I've told you a thousand times that I'm not the one. You don't threaten me on any level." Will raised his voice at her.

"I'm just trying to talk to you, Will," Angela defended herself.

"No, you're not. You're trying to break me down. Here I am, planning to take you out for a nice dinner and a little pampering and you want to attack me by saying I don't pay attention to you. Here is a news flash for you, honey. If I wasn't paying you any attention I would not have planned an afternoon like this for us." He waved his arms around.

"You're taking this all wrong, Will," Angela said in a loud whisper.

"No, I'm not, Angela. You're sitting here acting all sanctimonious, complaining about me not paying attention to your needs. Have you ever stopped to think about my needs and what I'd like? Maybe there is a *reason* I don't look at you when we make love. Maybe you're not *satisfying* me the way I need to be satisfied." Will glared at her. "I didn't think so." Will's cell phone vibrated once again.

"Let's just drop this conversation and enjoy the rest of our afternoon together," Angela suggested, trying to bury her hurt feelings.

"You know what?" Will removed his wallet from his back pocket and placed a one-hundred-dollar bill on the table. "I don't even want to spend the afternoon with you anymore. Enjoy yourself." Will got up.

"Will, don't you walk away from me," Angela warned him.

"Your threats mean nothing to me," Will said and continued on. Angela followed him. When they reached the parking lot, Will went to his car.

"Will, wait a minute." Angela stopped him by holding on to his arm.

"I don't want to talk, Angela. I'll see you later. It's a good thing we met up here and drove in separate cars because right now, I don't like you very much." Will walked away and got into the car. He pulled off before Angela could say another word.

CHAPTER 11

JoAnn

JoAnn rushed across the parking lot of Sandburg Junior High School to get out of the pouring rain. Once she stepped inside, she slid her umbrella closed and shook the excess water off of it.

"Oh, I can't believe how hard it's raining outside," she said to herself as goose bumps blanketed her skin. She headed toward the gymnasium and took a seat on the bleachers next to a handful of students and several parents. Once she got herself situated, she began searching for her daughter, Trina. She spotted her stooping down and lacing up her gym shoes.

Once Trina was done, she and her teammates formed a circle and yelled out in unison, "Let's go, Wildcats!" and then trotted out on the court for a game of volleyball against their cross-town rivals, the Winston Warriors. JoAnn watched with enthusiasm as the teams volleyed the ball back and forth, scoring points against each other. She watched as her daughter dropped to her knees several times to keep the ball in the air in order to keep it in play.

"Way to go, Trina!" JoAnn yelled out from the stands. Trina had her father's natural athletic ability. She was tall like Jesse and had a very competitive spirit.

Trina looked at JoAnn and smiled. JoAnn acknowledged her by waving. It was Trina's turn to serve the ball. Her team was down by five points and JoAnn was on the edge of her seat, hoping that all the time Jesse had spent with his daughter working on her serve would pay off. Trina hoisted the white ball in the air and struck it with just the right amount of force to send it rocketing across the court and over the net. The ball was moving so fast that the opposing team didn't have time to reach it. JoAnn clapped for Trina and shouted out her name once more. Trina went on a nine-point scoring streak before one of her teammates made an error and gave the opposing team one last opportunity to catch up.

"Work as a team, Wildcats!" Trina and her teammates howled out their battle cry.

Too bad they're not playing for money, JoAnn thought, *because I'd certainly put my money on my daughter and her teammates. With Trina and her killer serve I know they'd be unstoppable.* JoAnn tried to get thoughts of gambling out of her mind, but she couldn't. They were like concrete pillars securely cemented in the chambers of her mind.

"Damn it, JoAnn. Stop thinking about gambling," she mumbled to herself as she watched Trina and the Wildcats defend their lead over the Winston Warriors to win the game. After the game, JoAnn hugged her daughter and said, "Congratulations."

"Mom, don't hug me in public. I'll look like a baby." Trina unlatched herself from JoAnn and sat next to her.

"Well, you're *my* baby," JoAnn said defensively.

"I know, but we're in public and I don't want all of my friends to see."

"Oh Lord, girl. I'll hug them, too, if they come over here."

"Oh, please don't do that!" Trina looked horrified.

"You look just like your father," JoAnn said. "You certainly have his eyes and facial expressions."

"Where is Dad? I thought he was coming."

"I don't know. He's probably down at the store working," JoAnn said. She and Jesse hadn't been speaking much since they'd returned from Las Vegas several weeks ago.

"Are you guys getting a divorce?" Trina asked.

"No," JoAnn stammered. "Why would you ask that?"

"Well, he's been sleeping in the spare bedroom next to my room for, like, forever. And my friend Stephanie said that her parents slept in separate rooms before they got a divorce."

"Trina, stop worrying yourself about that. Your father and I are doing fine."

"Well, will you tell him to sleep in his own bed because his snoring is keeping me from getting a full night's rest." JoAnn chuckled and Trina asked, "What's so funny?"

"*I've* been sleeping beautifully since he's been in the spare bedroom. I don't have to hit him or make him roll over." JoAnn laughed out loud.

"That's TMI, Mom," Trina said as she waved goodbye to one of her teammates. "Too much information. Are you sure you guys aren't getting a divorce? I've never seen Dad this angry with you."

"No, Trina. We're not. Don't ask me that again, okay?" JoAnn got defensive. She hated the fact that her daughter was so perceptive at such a young age.

"I'm going to go change my clothes. Where did you park?" Trina asked.

"I'm right out front by the door. You'll see me when you come out."

"Okay. I'll see you in a few minutes." Trina turned and walked down the bleacher steps and ran across the gym toward the locker room.

JoAnn exhaled before rising to her feet. As she walked back to the car, her heart began to feel heavy. Jesse had emotionally severed himself from her. Over the last few weeks, she'd tried several times to make up with him. He'd rejected her at every turn—even sexually.

In her car, JoAnn turned on the radio. Anita Baker was singing her hit song "I Apologize." As JoAnn listened to the words of the song, she had to laugh a little in order to keep herself from crying.

JoAnn really wanted to move forward, and the only way she could do that would be to return the money she'd foolishly gambled away. The sound of Trina drumming her knuckles against the glass of the passenger window interrupted JoAnn's thoughts, and she unlocked the door so her daughter could get in.

"How come you had the door locked?" Trina asked as she rushed to get in out of the pouring rain.

"I'm sorry, honey, my mind was someplace else," JoAnn answered as she fired up the motor and began driving toward home.

"Have you called Daddy yet?" Trina asked.

"No. I haven't spoken to him," JoAnn admitted. "Go ahead and call him. Ask him what he wants for dinner." JoAnn knew that Jesse wouldn't refuse to talk to Trina. She listened as the child told her father about the game and how her team had won.

"You should've been there. I was serving up some monster serves. Coach said that if I keep playing in high school, I may end up with a college scholarship. If I get an athletic scholarship, can I have the money you've been saving up for me to go to school to buy myself a car?" Trina asked.

An idea on how to return the money she'd gambled away suddenly entered JoAnn's mind. While driving, she began calculating, plotting and mapping out how she could execute her brilliant idea. By the time she was pulling into the driveway, she had everything all figured out and was looking forward to the moment she'd be able to present Jesse with the money she'd lost.

"Dad said that he wouldn't be home for dinner," Trina said as she got out of the car and entered the house.

"Wait, what did you say?" JoAnn trailed behind her daughter. She needed to make sure she'd heard Trina correctly.

"He said that he wouldn't be home for dinner," Trina repeated.

"Did he say why? It's not like him to not come home for dinner." JoAnn was sharing a little too much worry with her daughter, but she couldn't help it.

"He didn't say why he wasn't coming, but I would appreciate it if you guys started speaking to each other again because I hate being in the middle of your argument."

"We're not in a dispute," JoAnn lied.

"Could've fooled me," Trina mumbled as she raced up the staircase.

"What did you just say?" JoAnn had become irritated and wasn't about to put up with any wisecracks from Trina.

"Nothing. Don't worry about cooking for me either. I'm not very hungry."

"Not now, but what about later?" JoAnn asked, although at that moment her main concern wasn't Trina.

"I'll eat some fruit or something," Trina said. "I just don't have an appetite."

JoAnn placed her car keys on the granite countertop and began pacing the kitchen floor nervously.

"It is so unlike Jesse to not come home. We've had plenty of arguments and disputes before, but never to the point that he stopped coming home," JoAnn said to herself. "Could he have begun an affair over this?" JoAnn began thinking about all of the Barbie bitches who she thought would leap at the chance to seduce Jesse during this shaky time in their marriage. The list was rather long. She knew for a fact that several of his young female employees at the sporting goods store would spread their legs for him in a heartbeat. Jesse was a handsome and successful man, and JoAnn had always felt if he were a man whose values weren't strong, he would be out sleeping around with scores of women.

"But Jesse is not like that." JoAnn tried to convince herself that her husband wouldn't betray her the way she'd betrayed him. Her thoughts began playing tricks on her. "The hell with it," she finally said and opened her purse. She removed her cell phone and called him. His phone just rang. Clearly he was refusing to take her call. She decided to call the store directly but then held the thought.

"No, I'm going down to the store to talk to him face-to-face," JoAnn said aloud. "Trina," she called.

"Yeah?" Trina answered.

"I'm about to run down to the sporting goods store to see your father. I'll be back in a little while. Come lock the door." JoAnn gathered up her belongings and walked back out to her car.

"I'm going to straighten this entire situation out," she said as she drove off.

CHAPTER 12

JESSE

Jesse sat in his office staring out of his window at a nearby building. The image of the neighboring building's rooftop generators offered very little in the way of visual stimulation, but Jesse didn't mind. Especially not now, since he was thinking so hard about his life, what he'd accomplished and how best to approach JoAnn about ending their marriage.

Jesse's parents were working-class people. His mother was a social worker who'd worked tirelessly to help poor people advance from their impoverished conditions, but he'd followed in his father's footsteps and attended the University of Illinois at Chicago on a cross-country running scholarship, and later earned his master's degree in business administration.

Upon graduating, Jesse began working for a marketing firm building brands for sports-equipment companies. He worked on marketing campaigns for shoe manufacturers, surfboard companies and even did some work building a presence in the marketplace for an organization that made skateboards. For several years he'd earned a handsome income, but he'd always wanted his own business. After putting the idea off for what he considered to be far too long, he'd decided at the age of twenty-eight it was time to go for it. Jesse used his home as collateral, got a small-business loan and pursued his dream. He'd been running a successful business for more than eleven years and he was looking to expand by opening up another store but he wouldn't achieve that goal married to a woman with a gambling problem, like JoAnn. Jesse was about to call his cousin Regina to vent with her about his circumstances and what he'd planned to do when he heard someone enter the store. It was after hours and he'd locked the door, or at least he thought he had. Jesse rushed to the front of the store.

"So, how long do you plan on being mad at me?" It was JoAnn. She'd let herself in.

"What are you doing here?" Jesse asked. She was the last person he wanted to see.

"I came here to clear the air between us," JoAnn said, as she locked the door behind her. She walked over and sat down on a small bench near the section of the store filled with running shoes. Jesse leaned against a glass display case filled with sunglasses and folded his arms.

"Are you in here alone?" JoAnn asked.

"What does that have to do with anything, JoAnn?" Jesse snapped at her. He didn't appreciate her intruding on his quiet time away from her.

"Come on, Jesse, we can't go on like this forever. I said I was sorry. What more do you want from me? Why can't we just move on?" JoAnn asked.

"You've got some damn nerve, JoAnn. Sometimes I'm utterly amazed by how bold you are."

"Okay, I'll admit, I'm foolish, I'm dumb, I'm an idiot. Is that what you want to hear?" JoAnn asked, locking her gaze on his.

"I've gone through the ups and downs of your gambling addiction once, JoAnn. I'll be damned if I'm going to go through it again." Jesse's words hurt her.

"I know." JoAnn placed her face in the palms of her hands. "I had a relapse. I'll admit to that."

"How long have you been sneaking around behind my back gambling?"

"I swear to you I haven't been gambling. Not like I was before."

"Bullshit! I don't believe you. I've had this business for almost twelve years now. You almost put us in the poorhouse once, and I'll be damned if I'll allow you to do it again." JoAnn remained silent.

"I went to counseling with you and stuck by you through all of your gambling addictions. When you were working nine to five, you couldn't even make it home on payday without going to the casino. Once we got over that, then you started betting on horses. After that relapse, I discovered you were gambling on the fucking Internet. I even stood by you through that shit. I've had enough, JoAnn. I can't take any more. I refuse to put up with it. I'll admit taking you to Las Vegas wasn't so smart on either of our parts, but I honestly believed that you'd gotten over your problem."

"So, what are you saying?"

"I'm saying that I can't give any more. You've pushed me to the point that I've tried to kill you. I believe that our relationship has gone as far as it can go."

"Jesse, baby." JoAnn stood up and approached him. "You don't really mean that. I know you don't. We can work through this. I swear I'll do whatever it takes to get better. And if from time to time you have to kick my ass to keep me in line, so be it. I know that sometimes I deserve to have my ass kicked."

Jesse swiveled his head disapprovingly. "What kind of example is that to set for Trina? I don't want her to think that I'm the type of man who beats up on women. Why would you even think that was okay?"

"Look, I agree with you on everything, but we can't throw in the towel. Not yet." JoAnn hadn't expected the conversation to take this twist. "Don't you still love me? When did you stop loving me?"

"I can't love a woman I don't trust. When we went to Las Vegas, I fully trusted you." Jesse paused. "It's not all your fault. I knew about your gambling problems, and, honestly, I

should have made sure the money made it to the bank myself."
Jesse paused again. "I trusted you, though. I never would have
thought you'd use sex to manipulate me in order to deceive me.
I will never let you do that to me again."

"I wasn't myself, Jesse." JoAnn's voice trembled. "I just—
It was a mistake."

"I'm going to file for divorce and for joint custody of Trina."

"Baby, give me another chance," JoAnn pleaded.

"You're out of chances, JoAnn. The moment I tried to choke
the life out of you, I knew it was over."

JoAnn began crying in earnest. "I'll do anything to make you
happy. I promise I won't ever do it again."

Jesse swallowed down his emotions. It wasn't easy for him
to let her know that he'd thrown in the towel on their marriage.
It wasn't easy to detach himself from all his emotions for her,
but he knew that he had to. He knew that JoAnn and her addiction would ruin him and his dreams. He wasn't about to
change his mind because she was shedding tears.

CHAPTER 13

WILL

After Will forced a public argument with Angela, which he knew was completely wrong, mean-spirited and inappropriate, he got into his car and drove away. Back on the highway, he called DaNikka.

"Baby girl, talk to me," Will said when DaNikka picked up the phone.

"Hey, baby." Will could hear the smile in DaNikka's voice. "Were you able to get away?" she asked.

"I can always get away. Now tell me what you've arranged," Will said. He wanted to make sure that what DaNikka had set up was worth pissing Angela off, because if it wasn't, he planned to make DaNikka pay dearly for it.

"I talked to my girlfriend Shantel," DaNikka teased.

"And?" Will wanted her to get to the point.

"She wants to get together with us. But—"

"But what?" Will asked.

"She wants some money," DaNikka answered. "Five hundred dollars. She said that she's not doing it for free."

"I don't pay for sex," Will snapped at DaNikka. "You know that." He was already thinking about turning around and rushing back to the restaurant to apologize to Angela.

"She said that she'd really make it worth your while," DaNikka continued. Will could hear her voice trembling a little.

"Really?" Will asked, feeling lust burning deep within him. He tried to fight the feeling but he couldn't. It was like having an itch and trying not to scratch it. No matter how hard he wanted to resist, he couldn't.

"Hello? Are you still there?"

"Yes. I'm here."

"Did I mess up? Did I do something wrong?" DaNikka asked.

"No," Will answered. "You've done well."

"Now, if I do this, will it prove to you how loyal I am to you?"

"Didn't I tell you that I was on the housing subcommittee?" Will barked at DaNikka.

"Yes, but—"

"But nothing. I have the power to get you, your momma and your siblings into a really nice place. All you have to do is what I ask."

"I know, baby. But I was just wondering when we'd be able to move? I'm tired of living in this crazy neighborhood."

"Just give me a little more time. Trust me. I'll make sure you get out, especially if you and Shantel satisfy the burning in my soul."

"We will," DaNikka said.

"Yes, you will. I'm going to make some hotel arrangements now. You and Shantel get ready. I'll pick both of you up in about an hour."

"Okay. Shantel just asked when can she get her money."

"Tell her she'll get it once the job is done."

"Okay," DaNikka said, and hung up the phone. Will started laughing. He felt an erection being born as he thought about how young, impressionable and gullible DaNikka truly was.

Will stopped at the drugstore and picked up a package of condoms. With Shantel being as young as DaNikka, he knew that her womb would be fertile ground for even the tiniest droplet of sperm. Then he stopped at a nearby liquor store and purchased some alcohol, knowing it would help the young ladies relax.

Back in his car, he began laughing to himself. "Oh, Angela," he said aloud. "You had the nerve to tell me that I wasn't satisfying you. But the truth of the matter is that you're not doing a damn thing for me. Well, at least not the way DaNikka is doing it."

Will pulled up in front of DaNikka's house and phoned to let her know that he was waiting for her. A few moments later, DaNikka and Shantel approached his black Mercedes dressed as though they were headed to a production shoot for a hiphop music video. Will smiled at the sight of them—DaNikka with her beautiful chocolate legs and Shantel with her voluptuous breasts and succulent lips. DaNikka got in the passenger seat and Shantel got in the back.

"Look at you," DaNikka said. "You look so happy. Doesn't he, Shantel?" DaNikka turned in her seat.

Will turned to focus on the swell of Shantel's breasts and licked his lips. Shantel was just as young as DaNikka and from the little information Will knew about her, she was in pretty much the same situation. She lived in the 'hood, didn't have a father and planned to use her body to get what she wanted.

"Don't worry. It's all good," Shantel said to him with a smile.

"It had better be," Will said, turning back and heading the car toward the hotel.

Once the three of them arrived, Will got the key to the suite he'd reserved and they headed on up. He placed the Do Not Disturb sign on the door. He didn't want to waste any time, so he immediately approached Shantel and began caressing her breasts.

"Wait a minute, slow down," Shantel insisted. "You're going to get it. Can I just unwind for a moment?"

"Start with me." DaNikka scolded Will for not paying attention to her first.

Will couldn't have cared less about DaNikka's feelings; he

just wanted the action to start. He had an erection and a large supply of condoms.

"Why don't we start by having Shantel mix up a few drinks?" DaNikka said, as Will got completely undressed in anticipation of what was to come.

"Cool. I'll do it," said Shantel.

"I have a special surprise for you," DaNikka said as she stepped closer to Will and glided her hand up and down his thick dick. She made sure he was good and hard and then moved him to the bed. Will sat down on the edge and DaNikka lowered herself to her knees so that his pride was directly before her.

"You're just full of surprises today, aren't you?" Will shuddered as he enjoyed the pleasure of DaNikka kissing his shaft.

"Yes, I am," DaNikka answered.

"Oh, you've been reading that book I got for you, haven't you?" Will could tell because DaNikka had finally learned how to perform oral sex correctly.

"I read it from cover to cover twice. I even let Shantel read some of it. I don't want you ever to forget this moment."

"Trust me, I'll never forget this," Will assured her. At that moment, Shantel joined them. She removed her top and, exposing her breasts, she poured a little alcohol on them. Will noticed how erect her nipples were and craned his neck toward her breasts so that he could place moist kisses on them.

"I have another surprise," DaNikka said. "I have a digital video camera. I want to make a porno for you. I'll make sure to give you the memory card so that you can view it whenever we're apart."

Will couldn't wait to show it to Smoky.

"That's good thinking, DaNikka." Will circled his tongue around Shantel's nipple. DaNikka went to set up the video camera.

"The three of us should take a shower together," Shantel suggested. "DaNikka, move the camera to the left a little so that you can record us there."

"That's what I'm talking about. Let's get this party rolling," Will said, standing and heading toward the shower.

In the tiled enclosure, Will lathered up Shantel's silky skin. The sight of her succulent apple-shaped ass standing before him with frothing soap cascading down her back and through the valley between her cheeks was almost too much for him to handle.

"Damn, this is so hot," Will said as he gave in to the pleasure of DaNikka scrubbing his back. "That feels so good, baby," Will uttered as he closed his eyes and became utterly lost in euphoria.

CHAPTER 14

ANGELA

Angela sat in her chair facing the makeup specialist. Butterflies were prancing around in her belly.

"You'll do fine," Candice assured her.

"Can you tell that I'm nervous?" Angela asked.

"Yes, because you're sweating," Candice said, laughing a little. "Don't. You'll spoil our makeup."

"Fifteen minutes before we go live, Mrs. Rivers," said Shaletha, one of her production assistants.

"You'd better go." Candice rushed her out of the chair.

"Thank you," Angela said and began to make her way toward the stage.

"There you are. I've been looking for you," Bobbi Franklin said as she approached Angela from behind. Angela turned to greet her with a bright smile.

"Are you ready?" Bobbi asked.

"As ready as I'll ever be," Angela said with confidence.

"Okay, this is your big moment. Now go out there and give birth to a hit show for my television station."

Angela smiled slightly at Bobbi. She knew that Bobbi was on her side, but she also knew that Bobbi wanted to see a return on her investment.

"Okay, Angela." Shaletha rushed up to her. Her headset was sliding to one side. "Ten seconds until showtime. The studio audience is hyped and the band is ready to play your theme music. I'll make sure that the guests come out on cue."

"Okay. Let's do this." Angela moistened her lips with her tongue and put on her game face. She heard the announcer call her name and stepped out from behind the curtain to a chorus of loud applause from the studio audience. All of the nervousness that she was feeling suddenly vanished.

"Thank you," Angela said to her audience who gave a thunderous applause. "Thank you," she said once again as the noise began to quiet down. "Welcome to *Love, Lies and Scandal*. On this show we get all of the juicy details of love gone wrong, lies that lovers tell and all of the celebrity scandals. But we also give no-nonsense advice to those who have lost their common sense." The audience laughed along with Angela. She immediately felt their energy and excitement, which helped her to relax even more. "Do you guys feel me on that one? Because sometimes people do some strange stuff. They get involved in bad relationships, mistake lust for love, or just flat-out lie." The audience laughed. "Don't you hate it when someone lies to you and then when you catch them in the lie they try to place another lie on top of the one they just told?" The audience shouted out their agreement. She could feel that they were all on the same page with her. She no longer felt as if she were talking to a crowd of total strangers; instead, she felt as though she was talking to very close friends.

"On today's show we're going to talk to men who watch too much pornography." All of the men in the audience howled. "We are going to discuss the reasons why men do it, and we even have a porn star as our guest today." All of the men howled again. At that moment, Angela got a brilliant idea. Ignoring the script that the writers had given her, she decided to go out into the audience and speak directly to men.

"You, sir." Angela picked a young white man, with sandy brown hair and freckles, who appeared to be in his early twenties. "Do you watch pornography?"

"Yes, I do," the young man answered with a smile.

"And what do you like about watching it?"

"It's fun," answered the guest, his face beginning to turn red.

"Do you ever invite your buddies over to watch with you?" Angela asked. The audience gasped at the question.

"No. Guys don't do that sort of thing," answered the guest.

"So you like flying solo?" The audience laughed and so did the guest.

"Is she your girlfriend?" asked Angela as she nodded her head toward the woman who was sitting next to him.

"Yeah, she's my girl."

"Let me ask you the same question." Angela turned to the woman. "Do you like watching pornography?"

"I don't believe you just asked me that question," shrieked the girl, clearly embarrassed.

"You can't play the shy role on my show." Angela forced the issue with a charming smile.

"I like watching it sometimes," the young woman confessed. "But I don't like watching the ones that are just all sex. I like them when they have some sort of story line."

"So you like porn stars to have some acting skills?" Angela asked.

"Yes," replied the woman.

"Thank you both for sharing with our audience. Well today we're going to speak with a man who says that he is addicted to pornography. So addicted that he lost a job paying him a six-figure salary because he was downloading pornography on his computer at work. We'll also hear from a guest who says that porn is what keeps him from cheating on his wife. Stick around. I know you'll want to hear this. We'll be right back after this commercial break." At that moment, the band began playing music and the audience began clapping.

Once the camera light went off, Angela knew that she was off the air. Shaletha came out onto the stage and gave her some water.

"How am I doing?" Angela asked her.

"You're doing it, girl. That was cool the way you went out into the audience to get them involved. You've got ten seconds before you're back on the air." Shaletha rushed offstage. Angela walked across the stage and sat down on the sofa.

"Welcome back," she said as she smiled into the camera. "My next guest says that he lost a job that paid him a six-figure income because he couldn't bring himself to stop watching pornography. Ladies and gentlemen, please welcome Mr. Walter Hyde."

The audience clapped, and Angela stood to greet Mr. Hyde as he came out. He was a very well-dressed man, well-groomed, with a pleasing smile. Angela shook his hand and they sat.

"Thank for being on the show," Angela said. "Now, Walter, you had a job paying you six figures, is that correct?"

Walter adjusted his position on the sofa before he began talking. "Yes. I held a position as the vice president of sales for an oil company."

"And you lost your job because adult material was located on your computer. Why did you download the material?"

"Well, Angela, like many people who suffer from addictions, it was something that I couldn't stop myself from doing. I found myself thinking about it all of the time. I just couldn't get enough of it. I wanted to see as much of it as it could. I wanted to see women from around the world getting it on."

"Wow. How long have you had the addiction?"

"Since I was a teenager. That's when my fascination with sex began. My curiosity was sparked when I purchased my first swimsuit magazine. After that I got into adult magazines and my fascination continued to grow from there."

"When did you realize that you had a serious problem?" Angela asked.

"Well, for a long time I didn't think I had a problem at all. I guess it was because watching pornography is such a private affair. I realized that I was having a problem on a flight from Dallas to Seattle. I was sitting in the middle seat with my laptop resting on the tray table. I had a significant amount of adult video loaded on it and the urge to watch a particular woman was eating away at me. Before I realized it, I began watching the film."

"On the plane?" Angela asked for clarification.

"Yes."

"With a person on either side of you?" Angela asked.

"Yes."

"Were they men or women?" Angela asked.

"Both women. They reported me, and I was asked to turn it off. It angered me because I wasn't harming anyone." Angela got a signal from Shaletha that someone in the audience had a question. Searching the stands, she saw a young woman standing at one of the microphones waiting to be recognized.

"The young lady at microphone one, do you have a question?"

"Yes, I do. My boyfriend loves to watch adult films. He likes watching them more than he likes making love to me, or at least that's the way I feel. Did you ever prefer to watch porn instead of making love to your woman?" the young lady asked the guest.

"Well, it depended," Walter answered cautiously. "Sometimes I didn't want to go through the hassle of turning a woman on. I just wanted to watch a flick, get an orgasm and go to sleep. Other times, I allowed women to watch with me, but they ruined the experience because they focused only on the imperfections of the performers' bodies. I tried to explain that I couldn't care about a scar or an odd birthmark. I only cared about how well they moved."

"So, did you view women as sexual objects without any emotions?" Angela asked.

"Well, yes. I viewed them as objects whose sole purpose was

to satisfy me sexually." The audience gasped at Mr. Hyde's comment. Angela noticed that another audience member had a question so she acknowledged her.

"The young woman at microphone number two, you have the floor."

"I'm a woman who enjoys watching adult films with my husband. I also watch so that I can learn how better to satisfy my husband. My question to you is, do you think you're a better lover because you've watched so much pornography?"

"I wasn't watching to learn how to do anything. Well—let me rephrase that. Watching adult films did teach me a certain amount of control as I learned exactly how to operate myself." Angela and the audience laughed.

"That's a good way of putting it. *Operate yourself*," Angela said. She took a few more lively questions and finished the show. When she made it back to her dressing room, Bobbi Franklin was there waiting to greet her.

"That was excellent! I can feel that this show is going to be bigger than I imagined it could be. You have such a natural way with the audience. They love you already."

Angela couldn't stop smiling. For the first time in recent memory, she was happy. Once Bobbi left, she found a moment to exhale and reflect. She thought about calling Will to share her excitement, but then she stopped herself because she was still pissed off with his immature behavior at the restaurant. She knew that when she got home, she'd have to address it head-on.

CHAPTER 15

JoAnn

JoAnn parked her car in front of the tavern where her sister Jackie worked. She sat in the car for a minute taking in her surroundings. *Chicago is such an old and historic city,* she thought.

"But this entire neighborhood needs a face-lift," she said in disgust as she studied two women smoking outside Lola's Beauty Salon. Next to the salon was an old church and then a tavern which had an Old Milwaukee beer sign hanging above the entrance. Outside the tavern, the ground was littered with beer bottles. The windows were gated and there was graffiti written on its door. There was no doubt that the tavern was a rough spot. When JoAnn stepped inside, she noticed that many of the bar stools needed to be reupholstered because the yellow foam was exposed. The tiles on the floor had come unglued in several spots, and the paint on the walls had chipped. A person wouldn't choose to come here to socialize; it was for those who wanted to check out from reality, drink to their problems and, on occasion, sleep with a stranger who happened to look good after several glasses of alcohol.

JoAnn was on her fifth glass of E & J, but the brandy still hadn't dulled the ache in her heart.

"So are you going to tell me what happened? Why are you in here drinking like this?" Jackie asked, pouring herself a shot of brandy.

"You're the bartender. Isn't it obvious what my problem is?" JoAnn's voice was filled with pain.

"No, it isn't. I'm not a mind reader," Jackie fired back as she gulped down some of the brandy she'd poured for herself.

"Jesse wants to leave me." JoAnn began sharing her misery with her sister. "He wants a divorce."

"Jesse has stood by your side for too long to call it quits now. He's helped you get over your gambling addiction—well, not completely over it, but he did try. He's cleaned up your credit so that you guys could buy a nice home for you and Trina. Plus he's been supporting your unemployed behind for close to three years now. He's invested too much time and energy into making your marriage work to call it quits now. He's probably just angry. He'll get over it," Jackie tried to reassure her sister.

"I'm not so sure about that." JoAnn tapped her glass, indicating she wanted a refill.

"Why not? You guys have had bad arguments before. What's so different about this time?"

"I fucked up," JoAnn said. "I fucked up big-time."

"What did you do?" Jackie tried to pry additional information out of her sister.

"Remember when we went to Las Vegas a few weeks ago?" JoAnn asked. "I gambled away all the money Jesse made at the fitness expo."

"How much money?" Jackie was now paying close attention to every word her sister was saying.

"About eight grand."

"You fucked up eight thousand dollars!" Jackie raised her voice in disbelief.

"I don't know what came over me. I caught the fever, Jackie. The palms of my hands were itching and you know that's a sign. You know that meant unexpected money was about to come my way."

"Here, have another shot," Jackie said.

"Jesse said that he just couldn't take it anymore. He doesn't trust me."

"Hell, I wouldn't either if you fucked up eight grand of my money."

"I just had a run of bad luck, that's all. I know I can make the money back," JoAnn said confidently.

"You sound just like Daddy," Jackie said.

"Don't start with me, Jackie." JoAnn didn't like it when her sister compared her to their irresponsible father.

"Well, you do. I remember Mama sending me down to that woman Rubylee's house on payday to beg him not to gamble his paycheck away because he had a houseful of babies to feed. But Daddy wouldn't listen. He'd lose his entire paycheck to that con woman. And no matter how many times he lost his money to her, he kept returning, because he was determined to win it back."

"My problem isn't as bad as Daddy's was," JoAnn shot back.

"Okay, if you say so, but I know better. Shit, I have the gambling bug, too, but I know when to stop." There was a long pause before Jackie continued. "Look. I'm your big sister and I've gone through my fair share of men. I've had men who were really good to me and I've had men who treated me like shit. One thing I know for sure is that Jesse is a good man and if I were you, I'd do whatever it takes to make this up to him."

"You're right," JoAnn agreed with her sister. "I know exactly what I'm going to do. If all goes well, everything will work itself out."

"What do you plan on doing?" Jackie asked.

JoAnn laughed a little. "I've already done it. I've taken some money out of Trina's college fund. I'm heading over to the casino in Hammond, Indiana, to win back the money I lost in Las Vegas."

"Gambling is what's gotten you in this fucked-up position to begin with," Jackie reminded her sister.

"I've got it all figured out this time though. I've won big in

Indiana before. If I can win big once, I can do it twice. I just have to play my cards right."

"How much money do you have on you?" Jackie whispered.

"A few thousand dollars."

"Shit, you owe me eighteen hundred dollars from the last time you went on a secret gambling spree and lost all of the money that was in the cash register. Can I get any part of my money from you?" Jackie asked.

"Jackie, how are you going to ask me for money in my time of crisis?"

"Because you owe it to me. I can't help it if your ass can't hold down a job and the moment money hits your hand it evaporates."

"I can hold down a job. I'm just helping Jesse with the store until something comes my way."

"He didn't need your help with the store before you became unemployed and I'm sure he doesn't need it now."

"Why are you tripping like this? You're supposed to be on my side," JoAnn whined.

"I would be if I could see some part of the money you owe me. In fact, if I don't get at least one thousand of it right now, I'm going to call Jesse myself and tell him what you're up to."

"You wouldn't dare do that shit to me. I'm your sister. We're flesh and blood. How are you going to go against me like that?"

"Because I'm tired of waiting on my damn money." Jackie raised her voice. "And I'm tired of your lame-ass excuses. Shit, you knew that I was going to ask about my money when you came up in here and that's exactly why I didn't care when my daughter beat you up the other week."

"That's a low blow, Jackie." JoAnn now realized that she should not have told her sister about the money she'd withdrawn. "Fine. I'll give you a thousand."

"It's about damn time. Now, when are you going to the casino?" Jackie asked.

"As soon as I leave here," JoAnn said.

"Let me ride with you. I might get lucky my damn self and win some money."

"And you got the nerve to say that I'm the one acting like Daddy."

"You are more like him than I am. Either way, we're both his children and we both picked up his bad habits. Now stop drinking and sit here for a minute so that you'll be sober enough to drive. I get off work in about a half hour."

During their journey, JoAnn called Jesse and asked that he pick up Trina. JoAnn and Jackie arrived at the Horseshoe Casino around 6:00 p.m. Jackie went directly to the blackjack table and JoAnn decided to start off small and try her luck at the video poker machine. This time she wasn't going to pour money into the machine and then get up so that someone could sit down and win big. JoAnn planned to stick around until the machine hit pay dirt.

It didn't take long for JoAnn to lose every dime she had. When she lost her last poker game, she began slapping the machine as if it was its fault.

"Fucking piece of shit! You could've let me win at least one damn time." JoAnn yelled out her frustrations as she continued to hit the machine as if it were going to automatically make her a winner.

"Damn it!" JoAnn hissed. She was ready to get the hell out of the casino, but she had to find Jackie first. She called her up on her cell phone to find out where she was.

"Hey, where are you at?" JoAnn asked.

"At the teller cashing out," Jackie said.

"Did you win?" JoAnn asked.

"Oh yeah." Jackie's voice was filled with jubilance.

"I quadrupled the amount you gave me." Jackie began laughing. "Woo, I'm going to have myself a good time."

"I'm walking toward the teller now. I'll see you in a moment." JoAnn quickly hung up the phone. She couldn't believe that Jackie had actually won four thousand dollars. When she arrived at the teller's booth, Jackie was placing her winnings deep down in her purse.

"Hey, girl," Jackie greeted her as she secured the zipper on her purse. "How much did you win?"

"Not a fucking dime," JoAnn growled.

"Well, how much money do you have left to put back into Trina's account?" Jackie asked.

"Nothing. I messed it all up. I don't have a damn dime. I'm broke. You get it?"

Jackie chuckled. "That's real fucked up, girl. I'm ready to go. What about you?"

"Yeah. Come on." The two women walked through the casino and headed toward JoAnn's car.

"Jackie, loan me that four thousand you just won so that I can put the money back into Trina's account."

Jackie laughed. "You must be smoking crack. You need to find a way to get me the other eight hundred dollars that you owe me."

"Jackie, I'm serious. When Jesse finds out that I've taken that money, he might kill me."

"Hell, I'd kill your ass, too, if you kept fucking up money the way you do." Jackie had no sympathy for her sister. "Daddy'd lose every dime, too, and then he would come around begging for some more money."

"I'm not begging, Jackie, I'm asking you for a loan," JoAnn snapped at her.

"I don't give loans to people who don't have a job," Jackie fired back.

"I know you didn't just go there with me."

"Yeah, I went there and left."

"Jackie, don't make me take that money from you." They both stopped walking.

"I know you don't want to go down that road," Jackie threatened.

"Jackie, if you don't give me that money, I'm not going to drive you back home!"

"Then don't. I can catch a damn cab!" Jackie began walking away from her.

"Jackie!" JoAnn called after her, but Jackie kept on walking. "I need that money," she shouted. Other casino patrons looked at JoAnn shouting at her sister's back.

"That's okay. You're going to need me for something. And when you come crawling to me, I'm not going to give you a motherfucking thing! Do you hear me, Jackie? Not a mother-fucking thing, girl!" JoAnn tried to catch up with her sister, but by the time she did, Jackie had already gotten into a cab.

CHAPTER 16

JESSE

Jesse and Trina were spending their Sunday visiting museums along Chicago's Lake Shore Drive. They visited the King Tut exhibit at the Museum of Natural History, they saw the dolphins at the Shed Aquarium, and now they were at the Museum of Science and Industry about to exit the U-505 Submarine Exhibit where they got to see what it felt like to be inside submarines from the First and Second World Wars. Jesse and Trina decided to head over to another exhibit called Yesterday's Main Street for ice cream. It was a section of the museum made to look like a city street from the year 1910. The cobblestoned thorough-fares were designed to take visitors back to an era when silent movies played and children waited in line for old-fashioned sodas and fountain drinks.

"Do you remember when I used to bring you here?" Jesse asked.

"Barely," Trina said. Her father draped his arm around her shoulder. "I'd bring you here because you got a kick out of me chasing you around the exhibits. And when we'd visit the caveman exhibit, I'd pretend that the cavemen were talking to you and you'd talk back." Jesse laughed.

Trina was perplexed and said, "I don't remember."

They finally arrived at their destination and looked over the ice cream menu mounted on the wall behind the countertop. Trina ordered a strawberry sundae and Jesse ordered a banana spilt. Jesse located a booth and claimed it before another customer had a chance to.

"Daddy, I remember you making my Mulan and Mushu dolls talk," Trina said.

"I almost forgot about how I used to do that." Jesse laughed.

"I got a kick out of that," Trina admitted.

"So did I. I loved coming into your room and sitting on the floor with you. I'd make Mulan ride her horse and make her dragon friend Mushu chase her. It was a joy watching you talk to your dolls as if they were real people. When we got bored playing with your dolls, I used to tickle you. You'd beg me not to and I'd act as if I wasn't going to, but then the moment you got close to me, I'd grab you and tickle you until you started farting."

"Dad!" Jesse had embarrassed his daughter.

"Well, it's true. You'd laugh so hard you'd fart."

"Okay, that was like, so long ago, and can we not talk about that?" Trina asked, then ate more of her sundae. There was a long pause as Jesse studied his daughter. She had beautiful eyes, high cheekbones and his smile.

"What?" Trina asked. Jesse didn't respond, just looked at her and smiled. "Okay, you're really acting weird, Dad," Trina said.

"You've grown into such a beautiful young lady." Jesse's heart had begun to swell with love and pride.

"Can I ask you a serious question?" Trina asked.

"Sure," Jesse said, as he corrected his slumping posture.

Trina paused for a moment. "Okay, it's like this. Ever since you and Mom returned from Las Vegas, I've been feeling as if something isn't exactly right. You guys are acting differently."

"In what way?" Jesse wanted to find out exactly how his daughter was feeling. He didn't think that she'd picked up on their marital problems—at least not yet.

"I don't know. It's hard to explain. It's more of a feeling

that I get. I feel like you guys are going to tell me you're getting a divorce."

There it was. The power of the word plunged a dagger deep into Jesse's heart. He took a few deep breaths and concealed his pain before speaking.

"Sweetie, your mom and I are having a difficult time right now," Jesse explained carefully.

"But you guys are going to try and work it out, right?" Trina asked. Jesse knew it was not the time to tell Trina the whole truth, so he sugarcoated his answer so that her heart would be at ease.

"I always try," Jesse whispered and smiled at her reassuringly.

"Good. I don't want to be in the middle of a divorce. I have two friends at school who are going through one and it's not pretty."

"Divorce never is," Jesse said as he scooped up more of his dessert. "So how is volleyball coming along?" Jesse needed to change the subject.

"We'd be doing much better if the other girls on the team would stop trying to look cute and hustle for the ball. It seems like they just stand around and wait for me to serve and score all of the points."

"Well, do they?" Jesse asked.

"Duh, yeah!" Trina said sarcastically. "We're still learning how to work as a unit but some of the girls are too stupid to understand the concept of teamwork. And Ms. Green, our coach, has to remind the girls constantly to stay focused because their minds will drift to the left in a minute."

Jesse laughed.

"I'm serious. They have trouble focusing on one thing. I can't wait to get into high school so that I can get around some kids who want to *play* the game instead of being in the game."

"Maybe I need to talk to the coach and give her some tips on team-building," Jesse said.

"Oh, no. Don't do that, please. Ms. Green hates it when parents try to tell her how to run her team. It drives her up a wall."

"Okay. I'll let that one go." Jesse finished off the last of his dessert. "Do you want to look around some more when you're finished?" Jesse asked.

"Not really," Trina said. "What I'd really like to do is go see that new dance movie about fraternities and black colleges."

"All right then, that's what we'll do," Jesse said, accepting the fact that his little girl was rapidly turning into a young woman.

JoAnn wasn't home when Jesse and Trina arrived late in the evening from their outing at the museum and movie theater. Jesse hung his jacket in the closet near the front door while Trina galloped up the stairs and into her room.

"Don't leave your clothes in the middle of the floor, Trina. Make sure they make it into the laundry basket," Jesse shouted.

"Okay," she answered back.

Jesse walked into the family room and sat down on the chocolate leather love seat and turned on the television. He flipped through the channels until he reached the Spike Television Network just in time to catch an episode of *The Ultimate Fighter*.

"Damn, I can't believe that guy is still standing after a hit like that," Jesse said as he turned up the volume. He sat and watched the fight, which, in his opinion, was better than boxing and wrestling combined. Once the program finished, he walked into his office and opened up a stack of mail that had been sitting on his desk for a few days. He decided to boot up his office computer and pay a few bills online. Just as he was typing in his password, Trina appeared in his doorway.

"Have you heard from Mom?" Trina asked.

"No," Jesse said. He hadn't thought about JoAnn much, especially since he'd told her he planned to divorce her. He honestly didn't care where she was or whether she came back. But for Trina's sake, he thought he should sound concerned.

"That's odd that she hasn't called." Jesse supported Trina's concern.

"I called her cell phone but she won't answer."

"She's probably with your aunt Jackie. You know they're like two peas in a pod. Are you hungry?" Jesse asked.

"Yeah. Let's order some Chinese food," Trina said, forgetting all about her concern for JoAnn.

"Well, go get the menu and place the order."

"Should I get the usual? Fried rice, egg foo young and egg rolls?"

"That sounds good to me," Jesse said, beginning to input his account information so that he could pay a bill.

"Should I get a large order so that Mom can eat when she gets home?" Trina asked.

"That's fine, honey. Tell them that I'll come pick it up," Jesse said as he focused on the account information before him. No sooner had he paid his bill than Trina walked back in with the mail.

"Here's the mail that was still in the mailbox." She placed the mail on Jesse's desk, gave him a quick hug and then went to order the food.

Jesse searched through the stack of mail and noticed that he'd received a letter from the university he'd graduated from. It was a request for him to make a donation. Jesse chuckled. "I just paid off my student loan." Inspired, he decided to pull up Trina's college fund account. He and JoAnn agreed to place a certain amount of their income into the account. As Jesse checked the online statement, he was baffled by the information.

"That amount doesn't seem right," he said aloud, clicking a link to check the account's activity history. "What the hell!"

Jesse grew angry as he discovered a withdrawal of four thousand dollars.

"Oh, no, she didn't!" Jesse's blood began to boil as he continued to punch the keyboard, demanding more information. "JoAnn, you didn't have to rob our baby!" He quickly checked his business account, their checking account and their savings account to make sure she hadn't attempted to drain them.

Jesse began to think. He knew that he needed to separate their accounts immediately so JoAnn didn't have direct access to them. But he'd have to wait until morning before he could do that, since the banks were now closed.

"I should've transferred all of my money and other assets before I told her that I wanted a divorce," Jesse mumbled.

"Why are you mumbling?" Trina had come back. "The food is probably ready for pickup now. They said that it would take twenty minutes."

Jesse inhaled deeply and released it slowly.

"Are you okay? You don't look so good."

"I'm fine, honey," Jesse said. "I'll run out to get the food in a moment." When Trina left, he continued to check their financial records before getting dinner.

At two in the morning, Jesse heard JoAnn pull her car into the garage. He'd been sitting in the dark, thinking about what she'd done and what he planned to do to her once she confirmed his suspicions. He planned to beat her again. This time with a leather belt which was already coiled around his fist. JoAnn quietly entered the house and tried to creep away to the bedroom, but Jesse startled her when he flipped the light switch.

"Hey!" JoAnn said. Jesse noticed that her eyes were wide with fear and guilt. "What are you still doing up?"

Jesse stood up and approached her. "Where have you been, JoAnn?" he asked.

"With Jackie." JoAnn offered little information. "Why do you have that belt coiled up in your hand?"

"I'm sick and tired of your bullshit, JoAnn!" Jesse yelled at her like a madman. He even whacked the belt against the nearby wall to let her know that he meant business.

"Okay." JoAnn held up the palms of her hands. "Let me explain. Let me tell you the truth." JoAnn cleared her throat. "I was thinking about what you said about divorcing me and I got very upset about it. When I got up first thing this morning I just went for a long drive. I was trying to clear my head and figure out what to do next. I drove all the way to Carbondale in Illinois before I realized how far I'd gone."

"And?" Jesse asked.

"That's it, baby. There is nothing else to tell." JoAnn stood straight before her husband.

"You want me to kick your motherfucking ass, don't you!" Jesse whacked the belt against the wall again. JoAnn flinched when the sound vibrated through the room. "You're a back-stabbing liar and a thief, JoAnn, and right now, at this very fucking moment, I want to kill you."

"What are you talking about!" JoAnn hollered back.

"You robbed our own daughter, JoAnn!" The expression that blanketed JoAnn's face was riddled with guilt and proved his words.

"Yeah, I checked the damn account today. How did you spend it this time, JoAnn? Huh? Did you give it away? Gambling again? Or did you pay off some gambling debt that I didn't know about?" Jesse moved closer to JoAnn, who was now walking slowly backward up the staircase.

"Answer me!" Jesse slapped the belt against the banister.

"I can explain!" JoAnn yelled as she lost her footing and fell backward on the steps. She began to crawl away from Jesse as he raised the belt high above his head. He was about to beat her until her skin was black and blue, but he stopped himself.

"I'm not a monster," Jesse said as he uncoiled the belt and dropped it on a step. "I don't hit women. I've never been that type of man. You're the first woman I've ever beaten up and I feel awful about it." Jesse turned to leave and added, "I need some air."

"Don't go, Jesse," JoAnn pleaded.

He glared at her for a long moment and then left without saying anything further.

Jesse drove himself across town to his cousin Regina's condo. He rang her bell several times before she buzzed him into her building. Regina was standing in the hallway waiting to greet him when he arrived on her floor.

"I need to crash at your place for the night," he said.

"You're lucky I don't have any company over here," Regina said jokingly.

Jesse didn't find her comment too humorous. He was so emotional that he couldn't even bring himself to speak. He could only look at Regina and speak through his tortured eyes.

"Oh, it's that serious, huh?" Regina asked. "Come on in. You know where the spare room is."

CHAPTER 17

WILL

Will, along with the mayor of Oakland, other city officials and several families, was standing at the entrance of the newly completed public-housing development. Will had helped to move it along through his hard work, dedication and commitment to the poor and disenfranchised. They were having the ribbon-cutting ceremony, and all of the local media had converged on the new development to listen to speeches given by public officials.

Will stood at the podium. "Thank you all for coming out to witness this joyous and wonderful occasion. Today, we are opening the doors to a better future for some of this city's most deserving citizens—citizens who will no longer have to deal with substandard living conditions or with gangs and drugs destroying their community. Today begins a new chapter in the lives of our citizens. Today, they will begin their journey toward achieving the American dream. Today, one hundred and thirty families will know what it is to walk with their children on streets that are safe. They will know what it is to have a sense of pride and purpose as they move toward a brighter future. Ladies and gentlemen, I want to thank all of you for your hard work and dedication to making this monumental project a reality."

There was a chorus of applause and whistles for Will's speech as he took a pair of scissors and cut a yellow ribbon symbolizing that the new housing project was now ready to receive its new tenants. After the ceremony, Will remained to speak with reporters about upcoming projects to help teenagers in underserved communities build a community center, as well as fight for funding for more computers and books in their schools. Will also spoke with several new tenants who had grievances about certain public-housing policies.

"How do you expect tenants who have small children to find a job as well as pay for day care?" one woman asked.

"Why do senior citizens get bigger apartments than other tenants?" asked another woman who had five small children.

"How come single mothers can't let their boyfriends spend the night?" asked yet another woman.

"Can you get tickets to your wife's television show for me?" asked yet another person from the rear of the crowd. Will laughed at that request. He graciously addressed as many concerns as he could and then left the rest up to the public-housing staff and other officials to answer, and set off to drive across town to pick up his new mistress.

He loosened his necktie and thumped the steering wheel with his thumb as he listened to Snoop Dogg. As he merged with highway traffic, he began to daydream about the threesome he'd had a few days ago and how mind-blowing it was for him. After he, DaNikka and Shantel had got out of the shower, they'd made their way over to the bed. He'd enjoyed lying flat on his back while Shantel straddled his face and suggested that he feast on her warm and moist pussy, and DaNikka had glistened his baldheaded champion with her succulent lips. The very image and memory of the experience caused Will to get an erection so hard that he had to unzip his pants and drive with his manhood exposed.

"Damn, that shit was good," he said, squeezing himself while changing lanes. Another image flashed across his mind— he was licking the folds of DaNikka's honeypot. He was flicking his tongue around her clit and driving her crazy. Shantel was kissing and nibbling on his back and shoulders. The sensations that Will felt then were like none he'd ever felt before.

Then, in a surprise move, Shantel had squeezed her cheek next to his and, in unison, they'd devoured DaNikka's pussy. The tips of their tongues ran the length of her pussy and together they took turns flicking her clit back and forth. DaNikka was twitching and screaming and cradling the backs of both of their heads. Then Shantel and Will had begun kissing each other passionately. The tips of their tongues danced with each other in passionate circles. He wanted to do Shantel first. She was the true freak in his mind. He commanded her to get into the doggy-style position. With her caramel ass perched in the air before him, Will gave DaNikka some instructions.

"Put it in for me." DaNikka took Will's manhood and inserted it into Shantel's paradise. The moment Will entered Shantel, her love box gripped and squeezed his penis so firmly he felt as if she had the strength to milk him completely dry. Shantel screamed out with pleasure as Will glided rhythmically in and out of her, while simultaneously spanking her caramel ass.

"Give it to me," he told her now that he'd taken control and gotten accustomed to her strong grip. Shantel obeyed and pushed back against him harder and faster. Will was working up a sweat. DaNikka rubbed his shoulders and watched as he enjoyed himself.

"Get it ready, DaNikka. You're next," Will said, feeling as if he'd been blessed. He felt masculine, powerful and unashamedly lustful all at the same time. When he commanded DaNikka to get into position, he took a moment to admire her chocolate ass.

"You like her ass?" Shantel was filled with lust, as well. Will could see it in her eyes and hear it in her voice.

"She does have a nice one, doesn't she?" Will answered.

"Yes, she does." Shantel began to kiss DaNikka's ass.

"Oh, damn. That's what I'm talking about. Get nasty with it!" Will told Shantel. Shantel ran her tongue up and down the valley of DaNikka's ass.

"You like watching me fondle your girl, don't you?"

"Yeah, you know I like that." Will was panting. His lust was matched by Shantel's ways. Will entered DaNikka, slightly disappointed that her pussy didn't have the same clutch that Shantel's did. However, DaNikka did have an orgasm immediately upon his entry. The moment DaNikka's orgasm came down, Shantel removed his manhood from her friend's wet cave and stroked and sucked on him until she got the prize she'd been seeking.

"Yeah!" Will cried out. "Damn, girl." Will was exhausted for the moment but he wasn't done. "This party is far from over," he'd announced. Will remained with DaNikka and Shantel the entire night.

Will's immoral desire for a threesome came at a price. After he'd taken DaNikka and Shantel back home, he had to deal with Angela, who was completely pissed off with him. As he drove home that morning, he checked his cell phone and noticed a number of phone calls from Angela as well as several nasty voice mails from her.

"Will, where in the hell are you?" Angela asked on the first voice mail.

"I can't believe you're being such an asshole. You're supposed to be supportive of me. You were supposed to be in the audience at my show. You're just a selfish, arrogant bastard, and you only care about yourself and your own needs," she said on another voice mail. Will decided to stop listening to her messages because her anger was messing up his sex high. Will wasn't too concerned with Angela's anger because he was supremely confident that she'd get over it and fall back in line with what he wanted.

"After all, she'd better remember how good a catch I am. I can have any woman and do anything that I want to and there isn't a damn thing she can do about it, so she'd better remember that fact like remembering her ABCs," Will had mumbled to himself as he drove home. As soon as he parked the car in the garage and entered the house, Angela started barking at him.

"Where the hell have you been?" she demanded to know.

"Out!" Will said.

"Do you know how much you embarrassed me? Do you know how humiliating it was to have you throw money at me and walk out? Who in the hell do you think you are?" Angela picked up a pillow from a nearby sofa and tossed it at him. Will caught the pillow and tossed it onto another sofa.

"Angela, look. I'm not in the mood to fight. I'm very tired and I just want to get some sleep. Can you let me do that?" Will said, as if he were the victim.

"Hell, no!" Angela screamed at him. "Where in the hell have you been?"

"Don't ask questions you don't want to know the answers to, woman!"

"Who in the hell are you talking to like that? I'm your wife and I want to know where you've been?"

"I told you, I was out!" Will snapped at her.

"Doing what?" Angela continued her demand for information.

"Look, if you want to take a vacation, fine. We can take one. Just make the arrangements and I'll pack my bags."

"Are you using drugs, Will?" Angela asked, her anger tamping down. "Because your behavior lately has been very odd."

"You know damn well I don't use drugs."

"Then what is it? You don't talk to me. You act as if I'm invisible half the time. You don't really listen to me and every time I try to have a decent conversation with you we end up arguing. I'm tired of walking around this house feeling like I'm on pins and needles. I want to know what's going on? Where is our marriage going? Do you still want to be married to me or do you want to get out?" Angela's voice trembled more out of anger than sadness.

"You know that I don't want to get a divorce. You know that I love you. Sometimes I just feel like you push too much," Will lied, hoping that Angela would take the bait and question what he meant by his statement. He was about to turn the tables on her.

"What are you talking about? I don't push you at all."

"You do. Maybe you don't realize it, but you were hounding me about taking a vacation when you know that I'm stressed out trying to navigate my way through this public-housing project."

"Will, just because you're stressed it doesn't give you the right to treat me like shit."

"I'm sorry about that. I truly am. I just felt boxed in and I lashed out at you. I'm sorry," Will said, moving closer to her to try to hug her. He was supremely confident that she believed every word he said.

"I don't believe a fucking word coming out of your mouth," she said firmly. "You're a bastard, Will. On the eve of the biggest night in my career, you couldn't think of anything better to do than fuck up my head."

"That's not true, baby."

"Yes it is, Will. You're becoming jealous of my success. Your ego can't take the fact that I might be in the spotlight more than you."

Will laughed on the inside. He couldn't believe that Angela had actually provided him with an excuse. He laughed even harder because she had no clue that he had other women.

"You're right, baby. I got jealous." Will confirmed Angela's false suspicions.

"I know you are, and your jealousy is ugly, Will. It's pulling us apart."

"I'm going to work on it, okay? Now can I please go to bed?" he asked.

Angela glared at him for a long moment. "You've lost the

right to sleep with me for a while. Sleep in the guest room," Angela said, marching off toward their bedroom.

Will smirked. "Don't worry," he whispered. "I've got more than enough backup pussy to tide me over."

Will was now exiting the highway. Thinking about his argument with Angela made his dick go soft. He tucked it inside his pants and pulled into a service station to fill up his gas tank. As he pumped his gas, he began to think about how much more sexually open Shantel was than DaNikka. After sampling Shantel's passion, Will yearned for more of it. After only one night, he found himself longing for the taste of her young, luscious pussy on his lips and tongue.

The morning following his threesome, he'd awakened to find that Angela had already left the house to go tape her show. He'd contacted Shantel and asked to see her again. She agreed. Will picked her up and took her to another hotel room.

"You can't get enough of this pussy, can you?" Shantel said, as she stepped inside the room and sat down on the bed. Will noticed how sexy she looked in her Apple Bottom jeans, tennis shoes and T-shirt.

"What's your story?" Will asked before he answered the question about how he desired her.

"You don't want to hear my tragic story," Shantel said.

"Where are you from?" Will asked.

"Nowhere special," Shantel answered.

"How old are you really?" Will asked.

"All you need to know is that I'm old enough to do it," Shantel said, approaching Will and dropping to her knees to unzip his pants. "Damn, your dick is as big as my head," Shantel said as she placed her lips on the mushroomed head of his manhood and began sucking.

"Wait a minute." Will stopped her. "Damn, girl. How in the hell did you get so experienced at such a young age?"

"Do you want to ask silly-ass questions or do you want to get fucked? Make up your mind." Shantel had become irritated. At that moment, Will adored her for her aggressiveness.

"You're just an untamed hellcat." Will smiled.

"With some damn good pussy. Now, the question is, what are you going to do with it?" Shantel stood up and sat back down on the bed. A sinister smile dawned on Will's face.

"Listen, I'll make you a deal. A girl like me has to survive. You know what I'm saying? Now, I'm not trying to be a street-walker with a pimp, but I do want a man who can take care of me. Shit, DaNikka doesn't know what she has in you. But I know what a man like you needs."

Will laughed at her boldness. "Oh really? Do tell." Will encouraged her to continue.

"I'm bisexual. I like pussy and dick equally. Make me yours and I'll supply us both with a variety of girls who like to get down like that."

Will loved every word coming from Shantel's mouth.

"But you've got to drop DaNikka. She's a boring fuck. I licked her pussy and ass and she refused to return the favor. I like a girl who knows how to get down the way that I do."

Will smiled. "I want you to be my mistress. But you have to do what I tell you to do. If you screw up, I will bury your ass. You keep your damn mouth shut, you don't see any other man and you keep yourself clean. I don't fuck crackheads, and I damn sure don't plan on being your baby's daddy."

"And I don't plan on having any baby for your old ass," Shantel fired back.

"I like your spunk. But make sure that your mouth doesn't write a check your ass can't cash. Understood?" Will placed Shantel's cheeks within the clutches of his fingers.

"Yeah." Shantel submitted to his demands.

"You will travel with me from time to time and I'll make sure you always have money in your pocket."

"I want my own apartment," Shantel said. Will chuckled. "I'm serious. If I don't get my own place then the deal is off."

"I'll see what I can do," Will said.

"And DaNikka?" Shantel asked.

"You let me handle her."

"No. Handle her now," Shantel demanded.

"What?"

"I'm serious. If we're going to do this I want you to drop her ass like a bad habit. Call her and tell her it's over."

"What's the rush?"

"I need to make sure you're not all emotionally attached to her. Here, call her on my phone and tell her." Shantel pressed the automatic dial button for DaNikka and tossed him her phone.

"Hey, Shantel." Will heard DaNikka answer the phone.

"It's me, Will," he answered.

"What are you doing calling me from Shantel's phone?" DaNikka demanded to know.

"I don't want to see you anymore, DaNikka. It's over between us. Don't call me anymore and don't expect any more money or favors from me."

"Will! What are you talking about? Where is Shantel? What the hell is going on?" DaNikka shouted. At that moment, Shantel took her phone back from Will.

"He belongs to me now, DaNikka," Shantel said to her friend. "I knew that he was going to like me better the moment he got a taste of my goodies. Thanks for letting me fuck your man and take him from you." Shantel shut the phone.

"You're insane!" Will said.

"And exciting, don't you think?"

Will knew that he was caught up in this young woman's web. His common sense told him what the right thing to do was, but at that moment Will didn't feel like doing what was right.

"When can you get us another girl?" Will asked.

"I'll see what I can do."

"Well, in the meantime, come make me happy." Will rested on his back and Shantel went about the business of removing his trousers. As she placed his manhood into her mouth, Will closed his eyes.

"I'm going to enjoy breaking your wild ass in," Will cooed as Shantel took control of his lust-filled soul.

Will stopped pumping gas and placed the nozzle back in its cage. He knew that having a relationship with a girl like Shantel was a big gamble, but it was a risk he'd wanted to take. It wasn't every day that he'd run across a girl as young, sexually free and exciting as Shantel. At that moment, his cell phone rang. He'd had to change his phone number after he'd broken up with DaNikka because she kept calling him. Now only Angela and Shantel had his new number. He removed the phone from its holster and saw that it was Shantel calling him.

"Hello," Will answered.

"I'm heading over to the Pittsburg Bay Point train station now with my luggage. It won't take me long to get to Oakland City Center train station."

"Good. I gave my speech this morning. We'll make it to the airport in plenty of time to make our flight to Philadelphia." Will couldn't wait to take Shantel to Secrets.

"I don't know why you have me taking the train when you could've just picked me up."

"I told you. I can't afford to have anyone in your neighborhood asking questions about me."

"That's why I need you to get me an apartment. We wouldn't have those problems if you'd take care of that."

"Don't worry. It's being taking care of. By the time we return, your apartment will be ready."

"Okay. I'll see you in a little while," Shantel said and hung up the phone.

Will had already set the wheels in motion to bump a pre-qualified tenant out of one of the new apartments so that Shantel could have it.

CHAPTER 18

ANGELA

It had been two days since Will had left for Philadelphia on another one of his secret business trips that he refused to explain to her. Her female intuition told Angela that Will was up to no good. She suspected that he might have a mistress. Angela decided to do a little snooping around the house to see if she could find any receipts that would back up her theory, perhaps for purchases he hadn't told her about or a copy of his cell phone bill with an itemized list of the phone numbers he'd been calling. She searched Will's desk drawers, the pockets of his suits and the shelves of his closet. When she didn't find anything, she went back into his office and began searching cabinets. Still nothing. She was about to give up when she decided to look in one of his file cabinets. She tried to pull one of the drawers open but it was locked.

"Shit," she hissed. She tried to pry the cabinet open but she couldn't. She then ran into the kitchen and retrieved a screwdriver from the toolbox beneath the kitchen sink. Angela then tried to force her way into the cabinet but was unsuccessful.

"What is so important in this cabinet that he has to keep it locked up?" Angela wondered. She glanced at the clock situated atop his desk and realized that if she didn't get going, she'd be late for her show.

As Angela drove to the television studio, she put Will out of her mind and thought about the quick success of her show. After the first episode had aired, the network had placed a few more marketing dollars behind *Love, Lies and Scandal*. The station had created a Web site and posted video clips from her show. Thousands of viewers logged on to view the clips. Television ads encouraged people to tune in.

Over the past few weeks, she'd taped a number of shows. Today, however, Bobbi Franklin wanted it live. Angela's topic today was "The Art of Romance: How to Turn Rambos into Romeos." She knew that the topic was going to stir up some wild conversation. The producers of the show had located a gigolo by the name of Franklin Crenshaw who'd been in the business of escorting and romancing women for a number of years. He'd came highly recommended by several elite women who could afford his services. Angela was looking forward to having a conversation with him.

When Angela arrived at the studio, Shaletha was there as always, making sure she was on track and that the show ran smoothly.

"Has my guest arrived yet?" Angela asked Shaletha.

"Oh, yes. And, baby, that man is fine. Do you hear me? I mean F-I-N-E."

"He can't be all of that," Angela joked.

"Okay. Wait until you see him," Shaletha gushed.

"Well, I'm sure the studio audience will have a great time listening to him."

"Don't forget. One lucky studio-audience member will get a chance to win two airline tickets and hotel accommodations for three nights at Royal Palms Resort and Spa in Phoenix, Arizona."

"Thanks for the reminder," Angela said as she headed off to get her makeup done.

"Are you ready?" Bobbi entered the room just as Angela was getting out of the makeup chair.

"I'm ready." Angela smiled at her boss.

"Good, now get out there and run a good show for me." Bobbi was fired up.

Angela stood in the shadows listening to her familiar theme music until she heard her name announced, then stepped out onto the stage and into the spotlight. The audience clapped loudly for her and rose to their feet.

"Thank you," Angela said as the roar of the clapping began to subside. "Thank you again. Ladies, today's show is all about turning a clumsy lover into a romantic god." The audience laughed. "Now none of us are born lovers, so everything that we've learned has been taught to us by practicing with a number of lovers." The audience began to murmur and giggle and Angela encouraged them to be silly with her for a moment.

"My guest today is a man who makes his living romancing women. But before I bring him out, I wanted to take a few comments or questions from you guys to see what your romantic lives are like." Angela scanned the audience to see if anyone was standing at a microphone. She spotted a young lady standing with her hands behind her back.

"Okay, you. Young lady at microphone one."

"My name is DaNikka, and I'm from Pittsburg."

"Welcome to the show, DaNikka from Pittsburg," Angela greeted her.

"I just want to know. How can you be up there giving people advice and telling them how to make their relationships work when you can't keep your own relationship in order?" The audience gasped at DaNikka's bold statement. Angela laughed and downplayed the insult.

"I've been happily married for a number of years, sweetie. My husband and I are madly in love with each other. And my job here is to share with fans the secrets to love, to expose lies and to shine the spotlight on scandals." Angela placed her best Miss America smile on her face and was about to move on to the next person, but DaNikka continued to speak.

"Your husband is Congressman Will Rivers. A while ago he told you that he was on a business trip in Philadelphia. But he wasn't on a business trip. He was with *me*. And I have a picture to prove it." DaNikka exposed the large envelope that she'd been hiding. She pulled out an eight-by-ten photo, held it up and showed it to the studio audience. The photo was of DaNikka and Will at Zanzibar Blue in Philadelphia. "You don't know too much about romance because your husband has been fucking me ever since I was seventeen years old." The audience gasped again. "I'm twenty-one now—"

"Cut off her microphone!" Angela commanded.

"That's okay!" DaNikka shouted. "Because I can speak loud enough for everyone to hear me. Your husband was suppose to leave you but—"

"Security!" Angela shouted out.

When DaNikka saw the three security officers approaching her, she ran away from them and onto the stage with Angela.

"I hate you, bitch!" DaNikka began attacking Angela. She pulled her hair and slapped her face several times before Angela was able to strike her back. She was able to knock DaNikka off balance. They both fell to the floor and wrestled around until security came out and broke up their scuffle. A chorus of screams billowed up from the audience as Angela's personal drama spilled over into thousands of households.

Angela was sitting in Bobbi Franklin's office holding an ice pack on her upper lip. A flat-screen television was mounted on the wall behind her. Bobbi kept the TV on the world-news station to be alerted to any story of significance.

"Don't you worry," Bobbi said. "I'm going to make sure that we press charges against that woman for attacking you."

"I don't believe this shit happened," Angela said.

"Are you okay?" Shaletha asked, entering the office.

"I'm fine," Angela said.

"Let me see your lip," Shaletha insisted. "Come on. Let me just take a look at it."

"See!" Angela removed the ice pack.

"It's not so bad," Shaletha assured her.

"My dignity is what is hurt," Angela said.

"Oh my God!" Bobbi picked up the remote and turned up the volume on the television.

"Oh, shit!" Shaletha said as she looked at the television that was behind Angela.

"What? What's going on?" Angela asked, turning to see what they were watching.

"Girl, isn't that your husband?" Shaletha asked.

"A warrant has been issued for the arrest of Congressman Will Rivers after this tape was forwarded to authorities anonymously. The tape shows Congressman Rivers engaging in a sexual act with two women, one of whom is a known prostitute. Our investigative team has also obtained documents, which show that Congressman Rivers has been using public funds to pay for expensive trips and purchase luxurious gifts for his lovers. In addition to that, our team has learned that Congressman Rivers used his power and influence to provide Shantel, the young prostitute, with a two-bedroom apartment at the new public-housing complex in Oakland, even though she didn't have an application on file. It has also been confirmed that Congressman Rivers planned to use public money to pay his prostitute's rent."

A video clip of Will lying on his back and two women lying next to him filled the screen. Angela reached for the trash can. Her stomach did several somersaults before she vomited violently.

CHAPTER 19

JOANN

"Jesse has filed for a divorce," JoAnn said as she took a gulp of her brandy. She was visiting her sister Jackie at work. They were the only two people in the bar.

"How much of your shit did you think he was going to take?" Jackie asked.

"I wasn't that bad." JoAnn still refused to admit that she had caused her marriage to fail. "Bring that bottle of E & J back and leave it here with me on the bar," JoAnn insisted. Jackie did as she asked.

"You know he almost kicked my ass the other night." JoAnn was searching for sympathy from her sister. "He was going to beat the shit out of me but he caught himself. Said that he wasn't that type of man and that I was turning him into something he wasn't."

"He *should* have beaten your ass. You took a lot of money, JoAnn. And you took it from your daughter's college fund. That was crazy."

"You know that I didn't plan to lose all of that money," JoAnn said as she poured herself some more brandy. She held her shot glass up to her lips but paused before she drank. "He wants to buy me out of our house. He said that he's not giving this divorce thing up. And he wants joint custody of Trina." JoAnn took another gulp.

"Well, it doesn't sound like a bad deal," Jackie said.

"What do you mean it doesn't sound like a bad deal! I'm losing my husband. Of course it's a bad damn deal."

"Here's a news flash for you, JoAnn. You lost Jesse and your marriage died a long time ago. It's just been waiting to be buried."

"You're supposed to be on my side, Jackie." JoAnn became irritated with her sister.

"I *am* on your side. No one knows you the way that I do. And I'm telling you that Jesse was too much of a good man for you. You need a man who will keep his foot in your ass. I know I should've said that before but I was being nice because you owed me money."

"What's that supposed to mean?" JoAnn was offended.

"Just what I said. You don't function right unless some man is stalking your every move."

"That's not true," JoAnn complained.

"Whatever," Jackie responded and walked away from her.

"You know, I'm not ready," JoAnn said after her.

"Ready for what?" Jackie asked, turning around.

"Ready for him to be done with me. I'm not ready for him to let me go. I want him to still want me. Do you understand what I'm saying?" JoAnn asked.

Jackie walked back and stood before her. "You can't make that man want you. He's decided to move on. He's gotten an attorney. He's made you an offer. That shit doesn't happen overnight. He's been thinking and planning this for a little while." Jackie took the bottle of E & J. "You drank an entire bottle of this. I think you've had enough."

"But I love him. Why can't you see that I love my man? Why can't you understand that I want him back? Why won't you help me get him back?"

"You're drunk, baby sister. You're a crying drunk."

"Fuck you, Jackie! Fuck you, fuck you and fuck you again. You've always wanted Jesse, haven't you? I know you have. You've always been jealous of me and my man. I know you are. I see the way you look at him. I know you want him." JoAnn stood up but she lost her balance and stumbled.

"He's mine, you hear me? And there isn't another bitch in this world who can have him or take him away from me. I'll cut a bitch fifty ways from Sunday if she tries to move in on *my* good thing. His dick only gets hard for this pussy right here." JoAnn grabbed her crotch and then tumbled backward into one of the booth seats. "Fuck it. I'm leaving," she said. She attempted to rise to her feet but suddenly felt like sitting down instead.

"You are drunk, JoAnn, and you're not going anywhere. I've already taken your keys from you. You might as well sit here and sleep it off."

"Why am I so stupid?" JoAnn asked and then began crying. "Why do I do stupid shit?"

"I don't know, JoAnn. But you're not the only one in the world who knows how to fuck things up for yourself. Plenty of people do it every day."

"You got any weed on you?" JoAnn asked and then drifted immediately off to sleep.

A few hours later, JoAnn woke up lying on a sofa with a blanket covering her. At first she had no idea where she was. It took her a minute to take in her surroundings and realize that she was at her sister Jackie's house, but she had no clue as to how she'd gotten there. She had a massive headache and her stomach was very sour. She sat upright and became dizzy.

"Jackie," JoAnn called. "Jackie," she called to her again.

"I'm in the bathroom," Jackie hollered out.

"Bring me some aspirin out of there when you're finished," JoAnn said as she ran her fingers through her hair. A few moments later, Jackie handed her a glass of water and a bottle of aspirin.

"Trina called here looking for you," Jackie said. "She's very upset about the divorce. You need to talk to her about it."

"Yeah, whatever. I'll get around to it," JoAnn said as she

took the glass of water and the aspirin. Jackie sat on the sofa next to her.

"You can't run away from your problems by trying to stay drunk. I see too many people come into the bar to do just that. You got so drunk that I had to have someone help me put you in your car so that I could drive you over here."

"Jackie, I really don't want to hear you preaching at me right now, okay?"

Jackie remained quiet for a moment. "Fine. I'll stay out of it. You're a grown woman who can do whatever you choose. We've been fighting about your mistakes all of our lives and, quite honestly, I'm tired of trying to change you." Jackie said her piece, then got up and walked away from her sister.

"I'm glad she took her preaching ass on," JoAnn uttered as she took her pills and rested a little longer.

CHAPTER 20

JESSE

Jesse dropped Trina off at school and told her that he'd be back to pick her up, then drove to his store. Once he opened the store, he gave his staff their assignments and then went into the office to do some administrative work. As he sat at his desk, he received a phone call.

"What's the deal, pickle?" It was his cousin Regina.

"Hey, Regina," Jesse greeted her dryly.

"Are you at work?" she asked.

"Yeah, I just got here," Jesse answered.

"Well then, take an early break. I'm around the corner from your store and I want to take you out to breakfast. And I will not take no for an answer," Regina said.

Twenty minutes later, Jesse and Regina were sitting having a cup of coffee at a nearby family-owned restaurant. Regina had ordered French toast and scrambled eggs and Jesse had ordered blueberry pancakes and an omelet.

"So how do you feel?" Regina asked.

"About what?" Jesse asked.

"Stop being a hard-ass. I know this isn't easy for you."

"There really isn't much to say, Regina. I'm divorcing JoAnn. I just want her out of my life so that I can start over."

"Well, what did she say when you told her about the divorce?"

"At first she just looked at me as if I wasn't serious. But she knew that I was when I explained my offer to her."

"And she was cool with that?" Regina asked. "She didn't go crazy or anything?"

"No."

"It hasn't hit her yet, then," Regina concluded. "She's not going to let you go so easily. Trust me on that one."

"Yes, she will," Jesse said confidently. "I told her she could stay at the house until she located a place to live. But she'd have to sleep in the spare bedroom and our intimate relationship was completely over. I'm looking forward to the attorney drawing up the paperwork and going before a judge to officially dissolve our marriage. I'm not putting up with JoAnn's silly shit any longer."

"What about access to your accounts?" Regina asked.

"I've already taken her off the business and checking account as well as Trina's college fund account. I was the one who set those up, so that was pretty easy. Her name is also off all my credit cards. As far as her taking large chunks of money, she will not be able to do it any longer."

"Don't you feel sad about getting a divorce? I know JoAnn wasn't the greatest person, but still, you have to feel a little unhappy."

"I'm unhappy about the time I wasted with her," Jesse answered. "JoAnn can't hurt me anymore. I'm too numb now. And her rotten soul is something that I will not have to deal with for the remainder of my life."

"Her rotten soul?" Regina echoed.

Jesse nodded. "My attorney told me that no matter how I feel about her at this point I have to be extra nice and be on my best behavior so that I don't get involved in any marital blowouts. And it's not easy, Regina, it is so hard. Every day I go through emotional turmoil pretending and Trina knows it. She sees it, and I'm trying to help her cope with everything, but she doesn't want her family split apart." Jesse sighed. "It's just not easy."

"I hope you realize that it's only going to get worse before it gets better. Especially with both of you still living under the same roof." Regina looked into Jesse's eyes and saw the pain he was in. She placed her hand over his. "It's okay. I'll be here for you."

"Yeah, I know. You've always been like the sister I've never had," Jesse said.

"What about her? Does she have to act nice, as well?" Regina asked.

"Yes, she does. She went and got some crackpot attorney to represent her. I think he's a washed-up lawyer with a drinking problem but I can't be certain."

"Once everything is finalized, what are you going to do?" Regina asked.

"Regroup. I'm going to take my time and get my life back in order especially since I'll have peace of mind."

"Well, for what it's worth, I hope that you have a seamless divorce free of mistakes, arguments and misunderstandings."

"Amen to that," Jesse said. However, in the back of his mind, a little voice told him that JoAnn was going to make his life a living hell.

CHAPTER 21

WILL

Will and Shantel's flight into Oakland was about to land. The two of them had spent most of their time at a swingers club in Philadelphia and were exhausted.

"You are goddamn amazing," Will whispered softly to her. "Never in my life have I been satisfied the way you have satisfied me."

"You were all right, too," Shantel said, glancing out the window.

"I was just 'all right'? I wasn't spectacular like you were?" Will asked, nervous about his performance.

"It was nice," was all Shantel said.

"Whatever." Will ignored her indifference. "My shit was good to you. You're just playing a role with me right now. I know my performance was off the charts." Will chuckled.

Their plane landed and taxied to the gate. Will and Shantel got off together and headed toward the baggage-claim area. As they came down the escalators, Will broke one of his rules and began kissing Shantel passionately. He couldn't help himself. She kissed him back with an equal amount of fervor. Will cupped her ass with his hands and pressed her hard against his body.

"There he is!" Will heard someone shout out from below followed by a roar of voices.

"Congressman Rivers!" A multitude of voices were calling his name.

"What the fuck is going on?" Will said, seeing media

cameras and law-enforcement officials waiting for them at the bottom of the escalator.

"You don't know me," Will said and moved forward in a feeble attempt to distance himself from Shantel. "What's going on here?" he asked as cameramen and reporters all jockeyed for position.

"Congressman, is it true that you've been having sexual relationships with underage girls?"

"What! That's preposterous? How dare you ask me such a question?"

"What about the videotape? Who are you having sex with on those tapes?"

"Tapes?" Will was confused.

"Congressmen, you have the right to remain silent." Several police officers surrounded Will and Shantel.

"I'm being arrested? On what charge!" Will was angry and utterly embarrassed by the media bloodhounds who were filming everything.

"Did you know that you were traveling with a twenty-one-year-old prostitute with a very long rap sheet? Is it also true you used public funds to pay her rent?"

"What! I don't know what you're talking about!" Will lied as the police clamped handcuffs on his wrists and escorted him to their squad car, the cameramen and reporters trailing behind.

Will posted his bail and exited the jailhouse through a rear door to avoid the barrage of media and citizens. He had to catch a cab back to the airport in order to pick up his car. Once he got it, instead of driving home, he drove over to see his brother. Will parked his car in front of Smoky's house and as soon as he got out, a team of media people were there to greet him.

"Congressman, may we have a moment with you?" said one male reporter whom Will had known for a number of years.

"I don't have any comment at this time," Will said as he quickly opened up the gate in the three-foot-high fence and stepped inside his brother's property line.

"Get the fuck away from my house!" Smoky wheeled himself down the handicap-accessible ramp. He rolled up to the fence, with his wheelchair making loud squeaking noises. A cigarette dangled from his lips and his pistol rested on his lap. When he reached the edge of the fence, he tossed his cigarette aside and aimed his revolver at the media crew.

"You got something to say? Huh? Say it now!" Smoky dared anyone to speak. "Come on. I don't have shit to lose. Say something about my brother!" No one said a word as they quickly scrambled to get away from Smoky.

"Come on back. What are you running for now? Don't be scared!" Smoky let out a menacing laugh. "I'm a wheelchair gangster!" Smoky hollered out as he turned and wheeled himself back up the ramp and into the house. "Oh yeah, the maid is on vacation. I don't think she's coming back," he said as he navigated his way through all of the clutter and trash.

"Smoky, it's filthy in here. You've got junk food on the cocktail table, clothes on the floor and—" Will paused to sniff the air. "Oh, you need to open up a window. It smells horrible in here."

"Hey, don't come in here with that shit or I'll give you a one-way ticket to the county morgue. What you need to do is clean off a spot on that chair over there and pick you up one of those joints sitting right there on the edge of the cocktail table," Smoky said as he positioned his wheelchair adjacent to the sofa. He sat his pistol atop the cocktail table and maneuvered himself out of his wheelchair onto the sofa. He grabbed the remotes for the television and DVD players and pressed Play. Will heard a stream of sexual moans come from the television. When he looked at the screen, he realized that Smoky had been sitting in the house watching pornography.

"This is the movie here, *Prison Bitches Four.* It's about this black prison guard who has to make sure all of the women in jail stay satisfied." Smoky let out a creepy laugh. "Look at this. Both of those girls are trying to suck on the brother at the same time and they're fighting over him." Smoky laughed some more as he rocked back and forth on the sofa completely amused by what he was viewing.

"I'm in trouble, man," Will said, shoveling a stack of *Hustler* magazines off a chair and placing them on the floor beside him.

"Yeah, yeah, hang on one second. I just want to see the money shot," Smoky said, and he took a few moments to get the thrill he was seeking. "Oh, it's all in her hair." Smoky laughed once again.

"Damn, man, can you turn that shit off for a minute?" Will was trying to concentrate so that he could determine what his next move would be. Smoky didn't turn off his television. Instead he just hit Pause.

"I'm in trouble, dog. And I don't know what to do," Will admitted.

"That's obvious." Smoky didn't cut his brother any slack as he tried to get a little more comfortable on his cluttered sofa.

"I don't need your sarcasm right now, Smoky." Will stood up and glanced out of Smoky's window. He noticed that the reporters were still outside swarming around waiting for him to come back out.

"They're some persistent bastards," Will complained.

"I've been watching the news," Smoky said. "They've got your ass all over it. They even got you when you had your tongue down the throat of that young girl in the airport. They zoomed in on the shit. You were all up in her mouth."

"They filmed that?" Will hadn't realized how much the media had captured.

"Oh yeah. They got all of that. You can always tell them that you were just giving her an oral exam." Smoky cracked up laughing. "Oh, I kills myself sometimes," he said. "Okay. I'm sorry. I'll be serious now."

"They're trying to ruin me, man, and you're cracking fucking jokes."

"How do you figure that they're trying to ruin your ass when you did all of this shit on your own?"

Will didn't answer because he knew that Smoky was right.

"I'm going to lose everything. The district attorney wants to press charges. I've got to find a lawyer who'd be willing to take this case. It's going to cost me a fortune to defend myself. Plus, I've got to find a way to explain this shit."

"You haven't said a thing about Angela. What about her?" Smoky asked.

"What do you mean what about her? I haven't talked to her. She's been calling my ass though and leaving me nasty voice-mail messages. I'm not ready to go home just yet, because Angela is inconsolable right now."

"How long were you out of town with that girl?" Smoky asked.

"A couple of days," Will answered as he eyed one of the joints sitting on the edge of Smoky's cocktail table.

"Oh, shit. Then you haven't heard everything yet, have you?"

"What do you mean *everything?*" Will looked at his brother.

"Hang on." Smoky picked up the remote and turned on the news. As expected, Will's scandal was the top story. "Look at this, Will."

"Talk show host Angela Rivers, wife of Congressman Will Rivers, was attacked by one of her husband's secret lovers while she was taping an episode of her show." Will was horrified when he saw DaNikka rush down from the stands and onto the stage to attack Angela. DaNikka was slapping and punching Angela as if she wanted to kill her.

"Oh, no! What the fuck is this shit, man?" Will was thunderstruck.

"They've been running this clip all day. I thought you said that you had all your women in check?"

Will sat back down on the chair and buried his face in his hands.

"Look, man, for what it's worth, you know you can stay here for as long as you need to," Smoky said as he turned off the television. "How many women were you holding down?" Smoky was curious and wanted to know.

"Three," Will answered. "Angela, DaNikka and Shantel."

"Goddamn, you were a busy man." Smoky tried to joke around in an effort to make his brother feel better, but his light-hearted humor wasn't working. "Look, man, on the serious tip. Angela has got to be all fucked up. You're going to have to talk to her."

"What am I going to tell her, Smoky? I don't have a lie that I could tell that would explain all of this," Will barked at his brother.

"Man up and tell her the truth! You liked fucking chicken-headed women and her, as well. It's an ego thing, nothing personal. You were man enough to go creeping around, now be man enough to admit it."

"I don't want to admit that, okay? It makes me look bad. It makes me look like an asshole with no values."

"Right now, that would be true. Shit, if that's who you are, then so be it. Stop trying to be someone you're not. It's better to be hated for who you are than it is to be loved for someone you're not."

"Smoky, I could go to jail for this shit, man! Don't you fucking get it? Or have you smoked so much weed that you can't comprehend how serious this is?"

"I know how serious it is. I'm not stupid! So stop talking to me as if I am."

"Look. Thanks for coming out there and getting those reporters off me. I appreciate that." That was Will's way of apologizing to his brother.

"Whatever, man. I'm your big brother. That's what I'm supposed to do." Smoky accepted the apology.

"I'm going to lose everything, Smoky," Will said.

"You'll still have me. I ain't going nowhere," Smoky said. Will glanced at his brother. They didn't break eye contact for a long moment. No words needed to be spoken.

"Get some rest. The bedroom is clean. I don't even go in that room. It's yours," Smoky said.

"Thanks," Will said, and took Smoky up on his offer. As he moved toward the bedroom, he heard Smoky turn his pornographic movie back on. Smoky was simple. Just give him a place to rest his head, some food, some weed and some adult movies and he was happy. He didn't pretend to be someone he wasn't. Will admired him for that.

Will woke up the following morning and thought first that it was all just a bad dream. When he realized that he was still at Smoky's house, he knew that he wasn't so lucky. He walked back into the front room and found Smoky asleep on his sofa. Will got himself a glass of water and went back into the bedroom. He decided to face the music and listen to his voice mail.

"You ignorant bastard! The least you can do is be man enough to call me back!" Angela raged. Will didn't want to hear the rest of her message so he deleted it.

"Mr. Rivers, this is Kim Campbell from ABC News. We'd like to give you a chance to tell your side of the story. I would like to get an exclusive interview and—" Will deleted the message.

"Will, this is Congressmen Walters. We need to talk. The majority of other congressional leaders are calling for you to step down in light of recent allegations. Many feel that it's the decent thing to do." Will deleted the message. There was no way he was about to step down. Will decided not to listen to any more calls for now. He walked back toward the front of the house and glanced out of the window. The reporters were gone and he was thankful for that.

"Smoky." Will shook his brother's shoulder so that he'd awake from his slumber.

"What?"

"I'm going to take off. I'm going to head on home. I need to apologize to Angela about all of this," Will said. "I'll call you later."

"All right. I'll be here if you need me. Make sure the door is locked when you leave," Smoky said as he turned over and went back to sleep.

CHAPTER 22

ANGELA

Angela was feeling vengeful. There was no way she was going to allow Will or his bitches to get away with humiliating her the way they had. She could not believe her life was now tabloid gossip. How could she have been so blind? The morning after DaNikka came onto her show and attacked her, Angela had gone down to the district courthouse and filed for two restraining orders—one against DaNikka and the other against Will. Angela claimed that he and his lover had threatened her, and she feared for her safety. The restraining orders were immediately granted, and that gave Angela the authority she needed to be merciless toward Will.

When Angela returned home from the courthouse, a swarm of media people wanted to speak with her. As she tried to pull into her gated community, they rushed up to the car with cameras and microphones pointed at her. She reached for her dark sunglasses so that they wouldn't take some hideous photo of her swollen, red eyes.

"Angela, just give me two minutes of your time," said one reporter from her old television station.

"Angela, come on, girl. Roll down the window so we can talk. You and I go way back," said another male reporter who was smashed up against her driver's-side window.

There were newspaper reporters and newspaper photographers snapping pictures of her. At one point, the swarm was so bad that she just had to stop driving because they wouldn't move. She put the transmission in Neutral and gunned the engine a few times, hoping the roar of the motor would frighten them off, but the reporters were fearless.

Many of the reporters she knew personally and had hoped they'd cut her a little slack during her time of crisis, but none of them did. They all wanted to use their relationship with her.

Angela had finally made it past the media storm and to her home. Once she got inside, she grabbed some tissues from the downstairs bathroom, sat on the sofa and let her tears go. When she had finally cried herself out and didn't have any more tears to shed, the scorn in her heart took over. She'd called Will time and time again, but he'd refused to answer his phone.

"The bastard is too fucking chickenshit to face the music!" Angela had hissed, and wished evil things upon him.

A full seventy-two hours after the scandal had hit the airwaves, Will came home. By that point, Angela was beyond pissed off, hell was in her heart and as sure as the sun was hot, she was going to have vengeance.

"So you finally found the fucking balls to come home!" Angela greeted Will at the door. Will stayed silent.

"Looking pathetic isn't going to change the way I feel about you."

Will still didn't say anything. He tried to move past her.

"Where are you going, Will?" Angela taunted him. "'I'm going on a business trip out of town, baby. I'll be back in a few days,'" Angela mocked him. "Isn't that what you told me?" Angela stood directly before him.

"I'm sorry, okay." Will finally spoke. "I am so sorry about all of this."

"Oh, you're sorry." Angela chuckled angrily. "I guess that makes the shit feel better."

"This wasn't supposed to happen, Angela. I never meant to hurt you. You weren't supposed to find out."

"How long have you been fucking around on me, Will?"

"You don't want to know the answer to that question, Angela," Will warned.

"Try me. You can't hurt me any more than you already have."

"Okay, you want the honest truth? We weren't married a good month before I had an affair. I've had several affairs over the years of our marriage. I get bored, Angela. I like having other women. It excites me."

"Well, why didn't you say something? Perhaps we could've had an open-door relationship. You could've fucked who you want to fuck and I could've fucked whoever I wanted to fuck."

"I didn't want you fucking anyone but me," Will answered honestly.

"That's called fucking marriage, you son of a bitch!"

"Angela, I'm willing to get help. But right now there is too much going on for us to be fighting like cats and dogs. Let's not get ugly with each other," Will said, and headed toward his office. Angela laughed as she trailed behind him.

"Oh, you haven't even begun to see ugly!" Angela shouted.

"I'm sorry that DaNikka showed up on the set of your show." Will turned and tried to touch her.

"Don't you put your fucking hands on me!" Angela barked at him. "That bitch of yours cost me everything! After I was attacked by your 'hood rat, advertisers started pulling their ads from the show. A newspaper article discredited me by asking, 'How can Angela Rivers give relationship advice when she doesn't know how to take her own advice to keep her marriage going?' Then I got a call from Bobbi Franklin, the station owner, telling me that she was pulling the plug on the show. My entire career has ended because of your bullshit, Will!"

"What about me, woman!" Will roared at Angela like a grizzly bear in the wild. "You're not the only victim here! I might go to jail over this shit. Other congressional leaders are asking me to step down. You're not the only one who is taking hits. So cut me some fucking slack and back off me!"

"Oh, you want *me* to back off *you?* You need your space right now, is that it?" asked Angela with sarcasm.

"Yes. We need to talk to an attorney and—"

"Hold on. There is no *we!* We ain't doing shit together, you stank-ass whore!"

"I'm not going to put up with that shit from you, Angela. I've already told you why I did what I did. What more do you want?"

"So you're telling me that our entire marriage has been a sham from day one?"

"It wasn't a sham. I just needed a little something on the side." Will broke eye contact, opened one of his desk drawers and began searching for something.

"So, in other words, you did what you had to, to remain happy?" Angela asked for clarification.

"Yes. That's exactly what I did." Will owned up to his behavior. "But I'm not going to admit that publicly. I've got to find a spin in all of this. I've got to find a good lie that can get me out of it."

"Do you know or even care about how you humiliated me?" she asked sadly. "Do you even care that you've ruined everything for me?"

"Angela. You need to check yourself and stand by my side during this crisis. We need to be united. Do you hear me?" Will pleaded.

After taking a deep breath, Angela spoke. "Okay, Will." She walked away.

"Angela? Where are you going?" Will called out to her, but she refused to answer him. She walked into the kitchen and called the police to let them know that Will was home in violation of the restraining order that she had against him. She also told the 911 dispatcher that he was acting violently and she feared for her life. Angela then called the guardhouse at the entrance of her gated community and told them to allow all of the media to come on in once the police arrived.

Moments later, the police and media had surrounded her property. In the bedroom, Angela pulled all of Will's expensive suits out of the closet and began tossing them over the balcony to the ground. The cameras were rolling as far as she knew. The world was watching. The doorbell rang several times, followed by loud knocks and calls from the police.

"What in the hell is going on?" Will shouted out to Angela. He took a page from his brother's book and retrieved his revolver, planning to scare the media people away. He made sure his gun was empty and rushed toward the door. He opened it and aimed the gun at what he thought would be a crowd of cameras.

"Drop your weapon!" police officers yelled at Will and drew their guns on him. Will was in shock.

"Drop the gun, Mr. Rivers!" an officer commanded him. Will slowly kneeled down and set the gun on the ground. The swarm of police officers immediately grabbed him and wrestled him to the ground outside his home.

"I'm in my home! Why are you doing this? I have my rights!" Will said as he was restrained in handcuffs and brought to his feet. At that moment, Angela appeared and handed the officers a copy of the restraining order.

"He was threatening me," Angela said.

"Wait a minute. I've never even seen that restraining order. Angela, tell them we were just arguing. I wasn't going to hurt you."

"You already have, you ignorant bastard!"

"Tell them to turn off the damn cameras!" Will shouted out demands as if he were still in charge. "You can't do this to me. This is my house! You can't put me out of my own house. Angela!" Will tussled with the police as they escorted him to their squad car. "This is wrong, Angela. Fuck you, you bitch! This isn't over! Do you hear me, Angela? This isn't over!"

CHAPTER 23

JoAnn

Several months had passed since Jesse had informed JoAnn that he planned to file for a divorce. He had allowed JoAnn to remain in the house until she was able to find a place of her own to stay. Yet the last thing JoAnn wanted to get was a divorce. She couldn't see herself being with any man other than Jesse, especially in the fall of her years. Since Jesse was allowing her to stay until the divorce was finalized, JoAnn decided that she was going to fight to keep her man. She cooked for him, she stopped gambling, she stopped drinking and she began to act more like a good mother as opposed to a careless one. Although Jesse didn't seem fazed by her efforts, JoAnn's plan was to wear him down until he agreed to stick it out with her.

At times, her need and desire for intimacy was strong and she yearned for Jesse to put out her flame. However, he was sleeping in the master bedroom and never gave in to her repeated attempts and huge hints. So, she decided to play dirty. She entered his room late one night, completely naked. She knew from his loud snores that he was in a deep sleep.

"God. I don't miss that part of our marriage," JoAnn whispered to herself, listening to Jesse's snores. She was hoping that Jesse's routine of sleeping naked hadn't changed, because if she had to wrestle him out of his pajamas, he'd wake up before she had a chance to do what she wanted to. JoAnn quietly moved toward Jesse who was flat on his back. She uncovered his body and was delighted to discover that he was indeed sleeping in the buff.

"Damn. I never thought I'd miss his body the way that I do," JoAnn whispered. She leaned over and began gently stroking his pride. In no time, she got him erect and circled her finger and thumb around his mushroomed head, smearing some of his nectar which he had exuded. JoAnn didn't waste any time. She mounted him, guided him inside her and allowed him to fully penetrate her. No sooner had she begun to ride him and take pleasure in the feel of his manhood deep inside her than he became fully aware and woke up.

"JoAnn?" Jesse was trying to get his eyes adjusted to the darkness.

"You need to stop holding out on me," JoAnn said, as she rode him more vigorously, hoping he'd just go with the flow of the moment.

"Get off me, JoAnn." Jesse quickly and easily tossed JoAnn off him.

"Come on, baby. I'm on fire. I know you want a divorce, but damn, can I still get a little dick on the side? I don't want to sleep with anyone else. You know that only you can satisfy me. Come, baby." JoAnn rubbed Jesse's chest. "We can even have some of that marathon sex you like so much. You can stay in it all night long if you want to."

Jesse immediately got out of bed. "I can't believe you came in here to fuck me in my sleep." Jesse walked over to the wall and flicked the light switch.

"Jesse, don't mess up the moment. Why do we have to fight?"

"Because that's the way it is now. I don't live or die for your pussy anymore. I don't ever want to feel you again. I don't feel anything for you anymore."

"Who is she, Jesse?" JoAnn wanted to know.

"What are you talking about?" Jesse asked, as he opened up one of his dresser drawers and removed a pair of pajama pants.

"You're too young not to have needs. If you're not giving it to me, then you're giving it to someone else. Now, who is the Barbie bitch that you're fucking?"

"Wouldn't you like to know?"

"What does she look like? Is it one of those skinny running Barbie bitches that are always up in your face?" JoAnn was now enraged.

"It doesn't really matter, JoAnn," Jesse said.

"Can't you see how hard I'm trying? I've stopped gambling. I've stopped drinking. I've apologized to you at least a thousand times. What is it going to take for you to see that I'm a different person?"

"JoAnn, I've been down this road with you so many times. You've put our relationship and marriage in several financial tailspins over the years. And every time you messed up, you've behaved yourself for a while, but when you think things are running smoothly, you revert to your old ways. I'm worn out from it. I am not into you anymore. My feelings for you are no longer there, and trying to screw my brains out isn't going to change my low opinion of you."

"Low opinion!" JoAnn got out of the bed and approached him. "Thanks for making me feel like I'm not worth a pile of hot shit sitting on a sidewalk."

"My feelings aren't going to change. We've discussed this already. I'm ready to move on with my life. I need peace of mind to survive and you prefer drama to get you through the day."

"The failure of this marriage isn't all my fault, Jesse. You're not perfect by any measure. You boldly flirt with women when I'm around, you don't like to listen to me and you don't give me the support that I need."

"I've given you all that I can give, JoAnn. I've supported you through your gambling problem, your drinking problem and your employment problems—"

"You never made me feel good, Jesse," JoAnn interrupted.

"I've always felt as if I couldn't measure up to you. You've always made me feel as if I wasn't good enough for you."

"JoAnn, I can't change your perception of me. If that's the way I made you feel—" Jesse held his words for a moment. "I want us to be as nice to each other as we can until you get your half of the money that I'm going to give you for the house." Jesse redirected the conversation.

"Well, I may not be as nice as you'd like me to be. I'm not going to make this divorce a cakewalk for you," JoAnn said as she exited the room.

"JoAnn, think about Trina. She's already going through a lot of emotional turmoil. Don't make it worse for her by fighting with me."

JoAnn went back into her bedroom and let go of her tears. She felt unattractive, undesired and, most of all, she felt bad about how she'd ruined her marriage. She was now more determined than ever to save it.

It took an additional two months before JoAnn and Jesse had their day before a judge to dissolve their marriage and sign the papers on their financial settlement. Jesse got what he wanted— joint custody of Trina—but the judge recommended that Trina reside with her mother. JoAnn wasn't allowed to move out of the state with their daughter and was required to consult with Jesse on anything that had to do with Trina's well-being. Jesse covered medical insurance for Trina as well as paying child support.

JoAnn signed the papers authorizing Jesse to deposit two hundred and thirty thousand dollars into her bank account, her share of their property and the business that Jesse had started.

"Damn," Jesse muttered as he signed the documents.

"I know you wish you hadn't done this now," JoAnn said boldly.

"Ms. Robins." The judge spoke directly to JoAnn. "Do not

go there." The judge issued a warning to her. Jesse didn't respond to JoAnn's comment. His attorney placed some more documents before him for his signature. Once Jesse had signed the papers, they were shuffled over to JoAnn for her to sign.

"Wait a minute," JoAnn said. "I'm not signing the papers because we've got a problem."

"What problem?" everyone in the room asked.

"Jesse knows what the problem is." JoAnn placed a vindictive smirk on her face and then glared at him.

"No, I don't. What are you talking about, JoAnn?" She knew that she'd rattled his cage. She could tell by the way his voice rose.

"I'm pregnant and need more money to take care of the baby," JoAnn said smoothly.

"It's not my damn baby!" Jesse hammered his fist against the table and exploded with anger. "You must have gotten impregnated by some idiot out in the street!"

"It *is* your baby. You know that we were still having sex. Don't deny it, Jesse, because you know it's true."

"You're a goddamn liar, JoAnn!" Jesse slammed his fist against the table once again.

"We *did* have sex. That night I came into your bedroom. Remember?"

"I tossed you the hell off me," Jesse yelled at her. "I didn't even ejaculate."

"It only takes a drop!" JoAnn fired back.

"Enough!" The judge stopped their squabbling. "Ms. Robins, are you truly pregnant?" he asked.

"Yes, I am!" JoAnn was hell-bent on making Jesse understand how bitterly angry she was about their divorce.

"Mr. Robins. Did you have sexual intercourse with your wife recently?" asked the judge.

"It wasn't even sex. She violated me while I was asleep. I should bring rape charges on her. I was asleep in my bedroom when she broke in, mounted me and tried to have her way. When I woke up, I had to toss her off me and kick her out of my room."

"Okay, we're going to have to adjust the divorce settlement to reflect an additional income for prenatal care."

"If her old ass has a baby, I want a paternity test to make sure it's my child!" Jesse blurted out.

"It *is* your damn baby! I'm not some tramp!" JoAnn roared back.

"I don't know that for sure! As far as I know, you could have gotten drunk and flopped open your legs to every Tom, Dick and Harry who was willing to have you."

"Enough!" The judge once again had to stop their bickering. "Let the amendment also reflect that upon the birth of the child, it be immediately tested to determine whether or not Mr. Robins is the father. Ms. Robins, I'm giving you exactly three weeks to get a written statement from your physician telling the court that you are indeed pregnant."

"And if she's not?" Jesse asked.

"Then I'll amend the divorce decree again. Ms. Robins, you had better be pregnant." The judge wrote down what the amendments were. "Now if those amendments are agreeable to both of you, we can move forward with this proceeding and officially dissolve this marriage."

"Fine with me," Jesse said.

"Whatever," JoAnn answered back. Once the divorce papers were signed and money had been transferred into JoAnn's bank account, the judge declared them officially divorced.

JoAnn and Jesse exited the judge's chambers and Jesse said, "Don't come to my house unless you bring the police with you to pick up your belongings."

"What are you talking about? I'm on my way back to the house right now." JoAnn fired her angry words at him.

"The locks were being changed while we were here in court.

You don't have a place to live anymore. You have enough money now to start completely over. So don't come to my house to pick up your belongings unless the police are with you. I'll pick up Trina from school since I know you're probably headed directly to the casino to gamble."

"Fuck you, Jesse!"

"You already have," he said and walked in the opposite direction.

CHAPTER 24

JESSE

"Oh, hell no! What do you mean she said she's pregnant?" Regina asked as she and Jesse drove up the departure ramp at Chicago's Midway Airport.

"She lied just to get more money and to try to delay the divorce proceedings. We were arguing so badly that the judge went ahead and made an amendment to compensate her for her unborn child."

"Did you have sex with her?"

"Hell, no. I told you the bitch told a bald-faced lie! But I got her back. As soon as we got in the hallway, I told her not to come back to my house unless the police were with her."

"Whew! I can't take all of this drama. Between you and Angela, ya'll have enough material to write a daytime soap opera."

"This ignorant shit that JoAnn is trying to pull is going to backfire on her. Which airline are you flying?" Jesse asked.

"Southwest," Regina said. Jesse drove down the departure lane and stopped in front of the Southwest terminal.

"Well, you have a safe flight and tell Angela I said to keep her head up."

"This is my third time flying out there to support her through this crisis she's going through. Be thankful that you don't have cameras in your face and some news reporter asking you about your feelings."

"Yeah, I don't envy her at all," Jesse said as he got out of the car to pull out Regina's luggage.

"I'll call you to remind you of when I return," Regina said. Jesse set her luggage on the ground and hugged her.

"Have a safe flight," he said.

"I will." Regina raised the handle of her suitcase and walked inside the airport.

Getting JoAnn and her belongings out of the house proved to be a bigger challenge than Jesse had initially anticipated. Instead of coming at a decent hour to retrieve her belongings, JoAnn, with the police, arrived at 2:00 a.m.

"I'm here to pick up some of my stuff." JoAnn stood at the door, two police officers behind her.

"Are you crazy? Do you know what time it is?" Jesse snapped.

"Sir, can she just get a few of her belongings so that we can go?" asked one of the officers.

"Come on in," Jesse said, and was about to follow JoAnn around the house to make sure that she didn't take anything that wasn't in the court order.

"You wait here with me, sir. My partner will go with her."

"Okay," Jesse said, not wanting to make the situation any worse than it was. Once JoAnn had gathered enough of her belongings, she left, but not before saying she'd be back for some of the furniture she was entitled to.

Just as promised, JoAnn came back at very inconvenient hours to pick up the remainder of her belongings. When the last of her things were finally out of the house, Jesse was able to breathe a little easier. But he missed his daughter being in the house with him and that pained him horribly.

At the end of the three-week waiting period, Jesse was back in the judge's chambers with his attorney. JoAnn had been ordered to bring documentation supporting her pregnancy claim.

"Ms. Walker—" the judge referred to JoAnn by her maiden

name "—do you have documentation from your physician stating that you are pregnant?"

"I miscarried," JoAnn answered bitterly.

"I knew your ass was lying!" Jesse pointed his index finger at her. "You're just doing this to make my life hell!"

"Get your damned finger out of my face!" JoAnn yelled back at him.

"That's enough!" The judge stopped them. "Okay. Let's cut straight to the chase here. Mr. Robins, the divorce decree will be amended so that you don't have to worry about paying additional money for child support."

"Wait a minute. He got more of the furniture than I did. I want the flat-screen TV, the stereo and the bedroom set," JoAnn said.

"Ms. Walker, I'm going to deny your request. The meeting is adjourned."

"I'm so glad you're out of my life!" Jesse said to JoAnn once they had exited the chambers.

"You haven't seen the last of me," JoAnn roared back. "If I have to live in misery, I'm damn sure going to make sure that you do, too."

Jesse ignored her and left her standing in the middle of the crowded hallway.

Time moved on and Jesse began to settle into his new life and his newfound peace of mind. However, JoAnn, as promised, didn't make it easy for him. She constantly interfered in his relationship with Trina. She denied him his visitation by making sure that at the times specified for him to pick up his daughter, she wasn't home. Then JoAnn filed a false police report saying that Jesse threatened her and she feared for her life. The police issued a restraining order, which pissed Jesse off because it interfered with his visitation with Trina.

"How am I supposed to pick up my daughter if I can't be

within one hundred yards of you, JoAnn?" Jesse called JoAnn up and blasted her when he was served with the restraining order.

"Well, I guess you can't see her now, can you?" JoAnn answered him.

"You know what? I'm declaring war on you, JoAnn," Jesse barked at her viciously.

"I declared war on you a long time ago," JoAnn said, and then laughed.

"That's okay. I will go back to court as many times as I need to," Jesse answered. "And if you keep fucking around, I'm going to apply for sole custody of Trina. I will not allow you to keep me from seeing her! Do you hear me! That's my daughter! Hello? Hello?" JoAnn had hung up the phone on him.

Jesse called his lawyer, who advised him to take his divorce decree and restraining order to the local police department and make arrangements for JoAnn to pick up and drop off their daughter there. No sooner had Jesse got off the phone than he did that. It made him happy that several police officers sympathized with him. An officer assisted Jesse by calling JoAnn and informing her that she had to honor the court order, and she had to bring Trina to the police station so that Jesse could have his visitation time.

As for the dating game, Jesse was confident. At thirty-nine, he felt that he was still fairly young. He was in great shape, he was handsome, college educated and a business owner. However, dating wasn't as easy for him as he'd hoped. He went on a date with a forty-seven-year-old lawyer named Bridget, whom he was interested in getting to know better. She was a full-figured woman with a nice personality. However, when she said she hated housework and had a maid, he got the impression that her house was nasty. Then there was Karen, a beautiful woman with honey-brown skin and freckles. Karen was in her early fifties but didn't look it.

"I need a man who will go to church. Every night I'm at church and on the weekends I'm there all day. The world is coming to end, you know. I can just feel it. All of this strange weather, global warming, earthquakes, hurricanes and tsunamis—you just wait. Those who aren't in the church praising God will burn in hell." Jesse had always considered himself to be a religious man, but Karen drove him crazy with doomsday conversation.

Jesse decided that dating someone his own age might be better. He met Darlene, a thirty-seven-year-old schoolteacher who'd been in and out of a series of bad relationships with a variety of bad men.

"But you are so different," Darlene said to him. "So much nicer and smarter. I know we've only known each other for a short amount of time, but if you're feeling the same vibe that I am, I know that we could settle down and start a family together." Jesse decided that she was certainly not the woman for him.

Jesse decided to dip a little deeper and try dating a young woman in her twenties. He met Denise. A twenty-six-year-old fashion buyer for a national retail chain.

Denise was like him. She loved to run and had been a cross-country runner during her college years. Although Jesse was thirteen years older, he didn't think their age gap mattered that much until he went out partying with her and her girlfriends. He'd gone to a club on the north side of Chicago, owned by rapper Kanye West. They walked into the club together and Denise introduced him as her date.

"Hi, nice to meet you," said all five of her girlfriends. Jesse kept looking at their faces and how young they were. Each one of her girlfriends reminded him of his daughter, Trina. As the loud hip-hop music played, Jesse tried to understand the words.

"Who is this?" he asked and all five of her girlfriends looked at him as if he was totally out of touch.

"That's rapper Lil' John," Denise said to him.

"Why doesn't he clear his throat?" Jesse joked, but no one laughed. Denise asked Jesse to dance with her. When Jesse hit the dance floor, he was confident that the moves he'd used for years would still work. As he danced around, he noticed Denise's five girlfriends laughing so hard at him that they had tears in their eyes. Jesse tried to ignore them, but when Denise realized how outdated his moves were, she took him by the hand and they left the dance floor. Jesse stopped dating Denise for several reasons but the biggest one was that every time he looked at her pretty young face, he felt like he was dating his daughter.

Over a twelve-month period, Jesse continued to date, but in each new person he found some flaw that he didn't care for. If anyone reminded him of JoAnn, even in the smallest way, Jesse immediately severed all communication. Eventually he gave up on the dating scene and took some time to do some soul searching. It was then that he realized that it wasn't the women he was dating who had the problems, it was him. Jesse realized that he was carrying baggage. He was carrying baggage from years of misery with JoAnn, and until he was able to get rid of it, he'd have a difficult time trusting anyone enough to build a new relationship.

CHAPTER 25

ANGELA

It was 6:00 p.m. on New Year's Eve and Angela was sitting on her sofa wearing nothing but a Mary J. Blige concert T-shirt and her panties while painting her toenails and watching television. The weatherman, one of her coworkers at the television station, was reporting that a snowstorm would be arriving on New Year's Day dumping a total of seven to eight inches of snow.

"Oh God," Angela said. "Why did I move back to Chicago?" She questioned her decision although she knew that her reason for coming to Chicago was to follow a job opportunity. Angela had purchased a two-bedroom high-rise condo just south of the city in the community of Hyde Park. She had a magnificent view of Lake Michigan as well as of the Museum of Science and Industry. There was a twenty-four-hour guard on duty and she even had valet parking.

She put the cap back on her nail polish and picked up the remote and changed the channel. She stopped when she came across an episode of a program called *Cheaters*. The producers of the show hired an undercover investigator to follow cheating boyfriends and husbands around and videotape their activity. Once enough evidence was gathered, the girlfriend or wife would be shown the video evidence and offered the opportunity to confront their cheating mate in the act.

I should have called up Cheaters *on Will's no-good ass,* Angela thought. She watched as a husband confronted his wife in the act of having sex with her husband's boss in the back of his car. A part of Angela wanted to watch the drama unfold but she decided that there was no joy in watching the suffering and humiliation of someone in the middle of an emotional crisis. Angela turned the television off and glared at the lifeless screen as she recalled all of the hardship she'd gone through with Will just over a year ago.

After she'd had Will removed from her home while several cameras were rolling, she'd slammed the door shut, closed all of the curtains and unplugged the phone from the wall. Angela had then gone into the guest bedroom, locked herself in and cried so hard that she'd given herself a headache. The following day, Angela had tried not to watch television but she couldn't help it. She sat on the sofa in the family room watching news reporters and fans of her show smear her name and pick her life apart.

"Respected journalist Angela Rivers, who created the talk show *Love, Lies and Scandal,* has found herself in the middle of her own scandal. Her husband, Congressmen Will Rivers, has apparently been involved in numerous sleazy affairs. Several other women have come forward claiming to have had an affair with him," said the news anchor. "Miss Rivers was brutally attacked on her show by one of her husband's lovers." Once again the network showed the clip of DaNikka swinging her fists at Angela.

"We've spoken to citizens to get their reaction."

"I don't think that Angela should be giving advice to her guests about love and relationships when she can't keep her own man happy," a woman on the street, wearing a weave that was platinum gold in color, said.

"I think that Will Rivers should step down. How can he possibly be a public servant dedicated to helping poor people and then turn around and exploit the very people he's trying to help? I feel sorry for the citizens of Oakland, sorry for his wife and sorry that I voted for him," said another man.

"I think it's just horrible to exploit young women who are obviously in crisis. There is just no excuse for that. And I feel sorry for Ms. Rivers. I can't imagine what she must be going through," said a woman with long, blond hair. Angela couldn't take any more so she turned the television off. At that moment, Will had walked in the front door.

"Angela," Will called out. Angela refused to answer him and contemplated calling the police once again to have him removed.

"If you're somewhere in this house calling the police, please don't do it," Will said, swiftly moving from room to room trying to locate her. "Oh, there you are." Will breathed a sigh of relief.

"So now you're going to ignore the restraining order, as well?" Angela quickly hid her tears; she wouldn't allow him to see her weakness.

"I have no place to go, Angela."

"Go back to one of the chickenheads you've been sleeping with."

"I know this is difficult for both of us. Angela, please." Will sat down in a chair on the opposite side of the room.

"Please what?" Angela barked.

"Look. I can understand you're angry. You have a right to be. I can understand the restraining order and calling the cops on me. You were looking to get revenge, but we need to set aside the rage and anger right now and pull together."

"Have you lost your ever-loving mind? In case you didn't pick up the huge hint, it's over."

"No, it's not over! We can work this out, Angela. Everything can be fixed," Will tried to assure her.

"This can't be fixed, Will," Angela screamed.

"I'll admit that I have a problem, but I'm not some monster." Will raised his voice. "I'll go to therapy. I'll do whatever it takes. I just need you to be with me right now." Will humbled himself. "I can't go through this alone."

"I don't have any sympathy for you at all. You've hurt me in a way that is indescribable. You come in here asking me to be strong for *you*. What about me, Will? What about what I'm suffering through? Who's going to be there for *me?*"

"I'll be there," Will quickly answered.

"I don't want you to be there. You've lost that privilege. I don't even want to be near you. Every time I think about what you've done, my stomach turns sour. I'm disgusted with you."

"Everything was consensual," Will argued. "I never took advantage of anybody."

"Did you know that girl was underage, Will? Tell me the truth."

Will paused for a long moment and then looked into her eyes. "Yes. I knew she was underage."

Angela hung her head in shame.

"Angela, baby. Listen to me. I'm going to fight this case, and once this is all over, I promise you, as God is my witness, I promise I will never do anything like this again."

"I spoke with a friend who is a lawyer, Will. She called me the moment the story broke. I asked her how much time you'd serve if you were convicted. And she told me you could serve up to four years in jail plus face civil lawsuits. You're not innocent in this crime, Will. I know it. You know it. And all of the media vultures know it. You've ruined everything we've worked so hard for. Our lives will never be the same. And even if you somehow walked away from all of this scot-free, I wouldn't want you back."

"Angela, think about what you're saying. What about the time we've invested in this marriage? What about our vows— for better or for worse—till death do us part?"

Angela had to laugh to keep from crying. "You should've thought about all that when you were out there getting your groove on."

"We wouldn't be in this position had you agreed to participate in my sexual fantasies," Will snapped. "It's because of you that I had to go outside our marriage to be satisfied! If you'd come to the sex clubs with me like I asked, and if you'd tried being bisexual like I asked you to, we wouldn't be dealing with this situation."

"Motherfucker, have you lost your damn mind!" Angela completely lost it. "I am not going to bring another woman into my bed and have sex with her. I am not going to some sex club filled with diseased souls humping everything that moves. You knew that I was a woman of integrity when you met me. You knew that I wasn't some trick-ass whore!"

"I had a right to be satisfied! If you weren't woman enough to do the job, it was my right to find a woman who could!"

"You went and molested a young girl, you dirty son of a bitch!" Angela stood up. "I don't want you in this house. You need to pack your bags and go live someplace else."

"Oh, no. You're not putting me out of my own damn house. I will burn the motherfucker down before I let you put me out of it." Will held his ground.

"Okay." Angela smeared away her tears. "Then I'll go." She went into their bedroom and removed several suitcases from the closet. She thought Will was trailing behind her, but he wasn't. She packed her suitcases and then placed them in her car. She went back into the house and found Will sitting in his office on a phone call.

"I'll be back for the rest of my things. And you can expect a phone call from my attorney."

"Hang on a second." Will placed the caller on hold. "Angela. You don't have to go. Stay. Please. I can fix this. I can make it go away."

"Goodbye, Will!" Angela said coldly as she turned her back on him and left. She drove herself to a hotel.

Will stepped down from his position as congressman and was eventually convicted of statutory rape and misuse of public funds and was sentenced to three years. Angela petitioned the court for a divorce from Will and it was granted. She sold their home and once she received her share of the money, she had left California behind and come to Chicago to start over.

The loud ringing of Angela's telephone startled her out of her memories. She leaned across the sofa and picked up her cordless phone.

"Hello?" Angela asked.

"What's the deal, pickle? Are you all set to party tonight?" It was Regina.

"I guess," Angela said.

"Come on now, Angela. Don't fake me out, girl. I got tickets to the hottest New Year's Eve party in town."

"The weatherman said that it was going to snow," Angela complained.

"Girl. You are in Chicago now. Snow doesn't mean a damn thing to us. Now, if I have to come over there and drag you out of the house, I will do it. You're coming out tonight."

"Okay," Angela conceded.

"Damn, trying to get you and Jesse out for some fun is proving to be a real damn challenge."

"Wait. Are you talking about your cousin Jesse? Is he coming with us?" Angela asked.

"Yeah. He had planned on going out of town, but he had to cancel his plans because the manager of his store had to have emergency surgery after she fell on a patch of ice and broke her ankle."

"Ouch." Angela cringed at the thought of breaking an ankle.

"I called him up to ask what he was doing tonight, and he said that he'd planned to spend the evening watching television. So I twisted his arm so he'd come hang out with us."

"So Jesse is doing well with his sporting goods store?"

"Yeah, you can ask him all about it when you see him."

"Okay." Angela perked up. "I haven't seen Jesse in ages. It will be nice to see him again."

"I'm sure he'll be happy to see you, as well. Now get dressed because I know your ass is probably sitting in your condo half-naked with the heat set on hell trying to keep warm."

Angela laughed, happy that her old college roommate knew her so well.

"I'm not going to keep you from getting dressed. Just make sure you meet me in the lobby of the Hyatt Regency hotel on time."

"Okay. I'll see you there," Angela said and hung up the phone.

CHAPTER 26

JESSE

Jesse had just exited the shower and toweled off. He placed a small foam mountain of shaving cream in his hand before applying it to his face. Once he was done shaving, he began applying moisturizer all over his naked body. The moment he touched his manhood, he achieved what he considered to be a magnificent erection.

"Woo, calm down, player. I know it's been a while but one of these days the right one is going to come along and we'll make up for lost time. This shit is for the birds," he said aloud as he exited the bathroom. He was about to put on his clothes when he heard his cell phone ring. It was JoAnn. Jesse thought that perhaps something had happened to Trina, so he answered.

"Hey, stranger," JoAnn greeted him. They'd been cordial to each other over the past few months.

"What can I do for you, JoAnn?" Jesse asked.

"I just called to see what you were doing. I can still do that, right?" she asked.

"It's a free country," Jesse answered.

"If you don't have any special plans perhaps—you know, maybe we could talk." Jesse knew what JoAnn was after, but no matter how many times he told her that he refused to have hit-and-run sex with her, she kept on trying.

"I actually do have plans for this evening," Jesse informed her. "I'm going to a New Year's Eve party."

"So you're not sitting around the house thinking about me at all, are you?" JoAnn got a little snippy with him.

"JoAnn, you're not going to ruin my evening."

"Well, I certainly wouldn't want to do that. It doesn't matter. I'm going out myself. I'm going to have me a great time. I'll bring in the New Year with a bang," JoAnn said.

"Good for you. Is Trina okay?" Jesse asked.

"She's fine. She and Jackie ran out to the store," JoAnn said.

"I'll call her tomorrow to wish her happy New Year. I'll talk to you later," Jesse said and hung up.

Jesse parked at the Hyatt Regency hotel garage. He got out of his car and followed the crowds of partygoers into the hotel.

"Happy New Year, bro!" yelled out some young partygoer who'd obviously begun celebrating long before he'd arrived at the hotel. He was traveling with several friends.

"Happy New Year to you, man." Jesse returned the greeting with a smile.

Once inside the hotel, Jesse was stopped in his tracks by a sea of people wearing party favors, cheering, drinking and dancing in place to pass the time. In the background, he could hear the thud of loud music bouncing against the air. Jesse began to feel the energy of the crowd and began popping his fingers to the music. The hotel was festooned with Christmas trees and other holiday decorations.

"Excuse me," Jesse asked a hotel worker passing by. "Which way is the ballroom?"

"Straight ahead, sir," the man shouted above the music. Jesse maneuvered his way through the crowd. He paid his entrance fee and got the back of his hand stamped. Once inside the ballroom, Jesse could see people dancing, drinking and having an all-around great time. He felt his cell phone vibrating. He looked at the caller ID and saw that it was Regina.

"Hello." Jesse held the phone up to his ear.

"Where are you?" Regina asked.

"I just walked in. Where are you sitting?" Jesse asked.

"Toward the back of the ballroom near the exit doors on the right side." Jesse glanced in the general direction that Regina said she was at.

"Okay. Give me a minute and I'll make my way over there." A short time later, Jesse found Regina and Angela sitting at a table drinking cocktails and rocking to the music as they sat. Regina was wearing a hot, red strapless dress and a top hat that said Happy New Year. Angela was wearing a black dress with straps that tied together at the back of her neck and a New Year's tiara.

"What's up!" Regina stood up and rushed over to Jesse and hugged him the moment she saw him. They embraced each other and Regina kissed him on the cheek. "I'm so glad you could make it." Regina released her embrace so that Jesse could give Angela a hug, as well.

"How are you doing, girl?" Jesse asked, genuinely happy to see her. They embraced for a long moment. "You look fantastic," Jesse said.

"No, you're the one who looks great," Angela said, squeezing on his arms. "You and Regina have been keeping yourselves in shape running marathons. I can stand to lose a pound or two."

"Jesse, I've been trying to convince her to come out and train with us," Regina said. "Shit, if I can do it, anyone can."

"Girl, you know I can't even *imagine* running a marathon. I might—and I say might—hang in there for five or six miles, but after that, I wouldn't make it."

"You're just afraid to try it," Regina said.

"I'm afraid I've turned Regina into a marathon junkie," Jesse said laughing, then he smiled at Angela and said, "You look fine." All three of them finally sat down at the table.

"I can't wait for that damn waitress to come back with our

drinks," Regina said as she continued to groove to the music. "Hell, I need a dance partner!" Regina began looking around for a man who appeared to be single.

"Girl, you are so crazy," Angela said.

At that moment, the waitress returned with the drinks Regina and Angela had ordered. Jesse then put in an order for two beers. Regina continued to dance in her seat and look at the crowd of people on the dance floor.

"So, how have you been?" Angela asked Jesse.

"I've been pretty good. My business is doing well and I can't complain too much right now," Jesse said, happy to brag a little to Angela.

"You're still as handsome as ever," Angela complimented him.

"You're not looking too bad yourself. What about you? How have you been?"

"Well, I'm doing okay. I'm sure you've heard about my divorce." Angela grimaced.

"And I'm sure you've heard about mine." Jesse chuckled. "I've seen you on television a few times. I saw you were doing some story about a high-school girl and some ecstasy drug ring."

"Oh yeah, the Keysha Kendall story. Come to find out the poor girl was set up by her best friend. Anyway, so why haven't you called me?"

"Same reason you haven't called me," Jesse responded.

"I didn't have your phone number."

"And I didn't have yours." Jesse removed his cell phone from its holster. "Give me your phone number so that I can put it into my phone."

"Do you want to dance?" A young, handsome, white guy came up to Regina.

"Do you know how to dance?" Regina asked with skepticism.

"I got you covered, baby," the young man said and Regina laughed.

"Angela, watch my purse for me?" Regina asked and allowed the young man to escort her to the dance floor.

"That girl will never change," Angela said. "She has always been a party girl."

"That's Regina. She can walk into any room and instantly make friends. She was like that when we were kids," Jesse said as he watched Regina get swallowed up into the crowd. "So, what is your phone number, Angela?"

"I'm not going to give it to you if you don't plan to call me," Angela flirted.

"I'm going to call you. I promise." Angela gave Jesse her phone number, then took his, as well. "So, how do you like being back in Chicago?" Jesse asked.

"Oh my God. I forgot how cold it gets here. I've become a warm-climate girl and this cold weather takes some getting used to."

"How did you end up back here anyway?" Jesse asked. "I mean, I know about the divorce, but why did you come back to Chicago? The last time I spoke with you, remaining in Chicago wasn't an option."

"I had to get the hell out of California. Even after Will was convicted, the local media just wouldn't leave me alone. Lucky for me, Bobbi Franklin, my boss at one point, had a friend here in Chicago who was a station manager. She put in a good word for me and the rest, as they say, is history."

"Do you like being a reporter?"

"It's kind of a demotion for me, but it pays the bills. I'd rather be at the anchor desk but I have to pay my dues, I suppose. I heard that you're a dad now."

"Yes. I have daughter who is in eighth grade. She's growing up very fast. It seems like yesterday she was born. What about you? Do you have any kids?" Jesse asked.

"No, not yet. I was too busy with my career to settle down to be a mom," Angela said, taking a sip of her drink.

"Are you dating anyone?" Jesse asked. Angela choked on her drink and began coughing.

"Are you okay?" Jesse patted her on the back a few times.

"Yeah, I'm fine," Angela said as she caught her breath.

"I must have asked you the wrong question," Jesse excused.

"No, that wasn't it," Angela assured him. "I just never thought I'd be in my thirties trying to date and start all over. But to answer your question—no, I'm not seeing anyone. I'm not interested in dating anyone right now."

"Okay. I can understand that," Jesse said.

"What about you? Are you seeing anyone?"

"Who me? No, I'm not."

"Yeah, right. You've probably got women falling all over you. You're probably one of those playas," Angela teased him.

"Now, that's funny." Jesse laughed. "I went on a few dates, but I was traumatized by the type of women I kept meeting."

"Traumatized?" Angela encouraged.

"I just haven't found someone I'm compatible with yet," Jesse said. "Plus, after I divorced, I needed some time to myself. You know what I mean?"

"Oh, yes." Angela nodded. At that moment, Regina returned.

"Hey, y'all," she said as she sat down. Regina reached into her purse and found a handkerchief to wipe the sweat off her face. "That guy could dance. He was moving like he was a member of the Backstreet Boys or something." Regina laughed as she picked up her drink.

"Speaking of dancing, would you like to dance?" Angela asked.

"I don't know. Last time I went out on the dance floor, my moves were a little rusty."

"Come on, Jesse. Everyone here is drunk. Trust me. No one is going to notice you."

"Okay." Jesse took her hand and headed out to the dance floor.

At the stroke of midnight, Jesse, Angela and Regina gathered at their table for a champagne toast.

"To friends and family," Regina said as she held up her glass.

"And to new beginnings," Angela added.

"Cheers," they all said as they clicked their glasses together.

CHAPTER 27

ANGELA

Angela was sitting at her desk working on an online article which had to be done before she left the office. She worked hard for the television station. Not only was she often outside braving the bitterly cold weather, she also had to keep pace with her writing assignments for the station's Web site. The Chicago market was very competitive, and she didn't have the luxury of writing one story and going home. The widespread use of the Internet meant that the public was hungry for more news, more information. The public had also shifted from becoming a passive audience to an audience who wanted to get involved. Citizens were creating their own Web sites and blogs filled with news that interested them and their community. In the past, television stations had decided what was newsworthy but that was rapidly changing.

After she e-mailed her story, Angela shut down her computer and headed home. Once inside, she changed, sat on her sofa and picked up the television remote. She flipped through the channels, but nothing interested her.

"There is absolutely nothing on television," she whined. Angela went into her bedroom and picked up a book by Beverly Jenkins, one of her favorite authors. Just as she began to read, her cell phone rang.

"Jesse," she said aloud as she read the caller ID. "What's up, Jesse?"

"Hey. Did I catch you at a bad time?" he asked.

"No. I'm just sitting on my sofa at home reading a book. And you?"

"I'm still at my store working. I was just thinking about you and decided to give you a call."

"Well, it took you long enough. You had a sister wondering if you were ever going to call. It's been about three weeks since I saw you at the New Year's Eve party."

"I know. I'm sorry about that. I've just been doing a lot of work here at the store, as well as spending time with my daughter. Plus, I have a running club that I have to manage."

"It sounds as if you're trying to do too much." Angela adjusted her head on the sofa pillow, preparing for a long conversation.

"That would be true. I need to hire more staff, but it's hard to find good help who will be as dedicated and as passionate as I am. Say, do you like Chinese food?" Jesse asked.

"Yeah, I love it but I haven't found a good place here in Chicago yet," Angela admitted.

"Are you kidding me? There's a great place right in your neighborhood. Tell you what. Why don't you let me take you out one day this week. We could go there."

"Are you asking me out on a date?" Angela wanted clarification.

"No. Let's just call it two friends getting together to have conversation," Jesse explained.

"Sounds like a date to me and you know that I'm not ready for that," Angela joked.

"Okay, then I'll just drop it," Jesse said and she could tell he would hang up.

"You gave up too easily."

"Look. Let's not play games. Would you like to go out for dinner or not?"

"Yes, Jesse. I think I'd love to have dinner with you."

* * *

Friday evening of that week, Jesse and Angela were enjoying each other's company over dinner. The Asian-themed restaurant was crowded with couples, families and university students. They discussed their failed marriages in detail and how they had been changed by them.

"One thing is for sure. I'm not going to get into another relationship and be made a fool of," Angela said.

"It's hard being with someone, especially after trust has been lost. I thought that going through therapy with JoAnn would really help and it did for a while. I started to trust her again, until she made a fool of me. Again," Jesse said.

"Trust, communication and love. Without those elements, no relationship will survive," Angela agreed. "At least not for the long haul."

"So, how do you know when you've found the right person?" Jesse asked.

"I don't know exactly. I think it just kind of happens. You know, you find yourself living your life and then the next thing you know you find yourself singing a Jill Scott love song first thing in the morning." Both Angela and Jesse laughed.

"Look." Jesse scanned the restaurant quickly and noticed they were the only ones still sitting. "We'd better get out of here before they put us out." He removed his wallet and paid for dinner.

Over the next several months, Angela enjoyed getting to know Jesse again. She'd even gotten to the point that she'd get upset if he forgot to call her at least to see how she was doing.

During the spring, Angela was given a special assignment to do a series of inspirational stories about Chicago and its citizens. She interviewed a woman who'd lost one of her legs serving as a soldier in Iraq yet had been inspired to run a marathon. The soldier was about to start training for her third consecutive marathon.

"I started crying when the woman said she ran to show her

family that she was still strong," Regina said of the inspirational story. She and Angela were spending Sunday afternoon volunteering at church. They were speaking to young people about their careers as part of the church's mentoring program. They were sitting by themselves at the moment.

"I was touched by her strength, too. Living through what she had and still finding the will, strength and determination to carry on is incredible," Angela agreed.

"Her husband was great. I could tell that he loved and supported her," said Regina. "One of these days, I'm going to find me a husband who loves me that much."

"Take your time, girl, and make sure you find the right man—" Angela stopped in midsentence.

"What's wrong with you?" Regina asked.

"A strange idea just popped into my head."

"What idea?" Regina asked.

"When does marathon training begin?" Angela asked.

"Next Saturday is the first day of orientation for Jesse's training program."

"Are you going, Regina?"

"Of course I am. I help Jesse with registration every year," Regina said.

"I'm thinking about running it this year," Angela said.

"Girl, stop playing." Regina dismissed Angela's comment.

"Regina, I'm serious. I'm inspired. I want to do something challenging and different. I want to do something I've never done before."

"That's a reason that many people join. They want to push and challenge themselves."

"Do you think I can do it?" Angela asked.

"Of course you can. You can do anything you want to." Regina was encouraging.

The following week, Angela got up early on Saturday morning, put on her new running gear and headed down to the 63rd

Street YMCA to register for marathon training. When she arrived, there was a large gathering of people of all ages and from various walks of life. Many of them appeared to be old friends who had not seen each other all winter and were looking forward to spending the next several months training together. Angela saw a large truck with the name of Jesse's sporting goods store on the side of it.

When Angela finally reached the registration table, she was happy to see that Jesse was ready to take her information.

"Do I really have to give you information that you already have?" Angela flirted.

"Yes, you do," he said seriously, focused on the paperwork.

"Oh, it's like that, huh?" Angela asked as she filled out the form that Jesse handed to her.

"Hey, I have to have every participant fill out a medical release form. It keeps a brother out of court, if you know what I mean." Jesse laughed.

"I understand," Angela answered. When she finished filling out the form and gave Jesse a check to cover her registration fee, he handed her another form.

"Now, what's this for?" Angela asked.

"This year after the marathon, we've put together a seven-day cruise package for anyone who wants to reward themselves with a vacation. The ship sets sail five days after the marathon and cruises to San Juan, Puerto Rico, Barbados, St. Lucia, St. John's, St. Thomas and then back to Puerto Rico."

"Now that sounds like fun," Angela said. "Are you going on the cruise?"

"Who are you?" Trina, Jesse's daughter, who was also helping out with registration, interrupted the flow of their conversation.

"Trina, this is my friend Angela." Jesse introduced her. "Angela, my daughter, Trina."

"Hey." Trina looked at Angela suspiciously as she protectively hugged her father.

"Hello. I've heard so much about you, Trina," Angela said.

"Well, I haven't heard about you, so stay away from my daddy. He's not interested."

"Trina, that's not nice." Jesse got on her about her bad manners. "Go help Regina over at the other tent." Jesse unlatched Trina from her embrace. Trina whined about having to leave, but she did.

"I'm sorry about that. She's a little overprotective of me."

"Yeah, just a little. I can understand why."

"Well, I'm glad you're here. Now you need to head over to the table across the field. You're going to run three miles today and be timed so that we can determine which group you'll be in."

"What if I want to be in your group?" Angela toyed with Jesse.

"You'd better get on out of here before you get yourself in trouble," Jesse teased her.

"Okay," Angela said before turning and heading across the field.

Angela listened as one of the running coaches instructed her on how to stretch properly to prepare her body to run three miles. Once this was done, she, along with several other runners, were shown the three-mile course they had to run. Angela went to the starting line with a group, and when the whistle blew, she began. She tried to keep pace with the fast runners but quickly learned that she couldn't compete with individuals who had more training and experience than her. She slowed down and shuffled along at a pace that was comfortable for her. Her pride was bruised a little because everyone seemed to be passing her by. At the one-mile mark, her thighs began to tighten up.

"Damn, girl, you are completely out of shape," she said to herself as she stopped to stretch. She began running once again and before long her left calf muscle began to tighten up. After that, her back began to ache. Angela slowed down and began to walk.

"Come on, girl, don't stop." A silver-haired woman offered words of encouragement as she zoomed by. "Keep it moving."

"Hell, if she can do it, I know that I can," Angela told herself and began running again. She ran faster than was comfortable and her breathing became labored, and once again she had to stop running and start walking. Angela was now at mile two and was practically exhausted.

"I know that I am not this far out of shape," she told herself. "I'm not overweight but I certainly feel like I am." Once Angela caught her breath, she began to run once again. As she approached the finish line, a gathering of runners stood there to cheer her on. Angela crossed the finish line and was given her time and the group she'd be running with. She leaned forward and rested her hands on her knees. She looked down the lane at the other runners coming and said, "At least I wasn't last."

After the three-mile run, Angela went and soaked in her whirlpool. While there, she received a phone call from Jesse.

"How are you doing?" he asked.

"Everything hurts and nothing works," Angela complained.

"Give yourself time. It was the first day," Jesse said.

"I don't know if I can do this. Some old lady passed me by," Angela said, adjusting her position in the water so that the pressure from the water jets concentrated on a particular area.

"That's one of the things that you shouldn't do. Never compare yourself to another runner."

"Well, you're going to have to teach me all of this stuff because I don't know it. All I know is that my body is aching right now and I'm having second thoughts."

"I *am* going to help you. I'll be the running coach for your group this year," Jesse informed her. "So that means we'll be spending a lot of time together."

"Okay. I'll hang with you for a little while but you'd better not make me hurt myself."

"Oh, if I make you hurt yourself, you're going to enjoy the sweet pain that I put on you." Jesse decided to give Angela something to think about.

By the time mid-June had arrived, Angela had been training with Jesse's running club for eight weeks. She'd learned so much during that time period and could feel herself getting stronger with each run. She learned about the proper clothing to wear, she learned how to pace herself and she'd met several other women who were sharing their journey with her. It was just the thing that Angela needed to keep herself going and to keep herself from getting depressed. And an extra bonus was that she'd lost several pounds.

"Today we're going to run ten miles," Jesse said to his group of runners. "We're going to keep the pace nice and smooth and we're going to take our time. It's going to be hot, so make sure that you have plenty of water with you."

Angela was nervous about running so far because she'd never done it before. Jesse gave out a few more instructions before the group began its journey. Angela put on her headphones and listened to the music she'd downloaded to her iPod. At the halfway point, the group took a water break.

"How are you feeling?" Jesse came up to Angela. She studied him for a long moment. He was so sexy to her. His succulent lips, strong arms and sexy legs were making her hot. Running behind him, looking at his magnificent legs, was driving her crazy. She wanted to do Jesse, but wasn't ready to let him know that.

"Why are you looking at me?" Jesse whispered so that no one would hear but her.

"Wouldn't you like to know?" Angela teased.

"Don't write a check your ass can't cash." It was obvious to Angela that Jesse was just as attracted to her as she was to him.

"And you'd better be sure you can handle this when the time comes," Angela said and put her headphones back on.

Angela had already made up her mind that she wanted to be intimate with him. Over the past eight weeks, they'd gone out on several dates and thoroughly enjoyed each other's company. Angela felt good about dating Jesse. He was supportive of her, he listened to her and he didn't place any pressure on her. She liked Jesse's intelligence as well as his drive to succeed. The other quality about Jesse that stood out was his integrity. He was surrounded by women who would have dropped their panties and spread their legs for him in a heartbeat, but he wasn't driven by wild lust the way Will was.

By the time the ten-mile run was over, Angela felt a sense of pride because she'd made it across a new milestone. As she made her way over to the refreshment stand, she stopped to ask Jesse a question.

"I've been trying to stretch out this muscle in my hip, but no matter what I do, I just can't get it to loosen up."

"Have you ever done yoga before?" Jesse asked. Angela gave him a sarcastic glare. "Okay, I guess not. Yoga really helps to loosen up your stiff muscles," Jesse said.

"Now I have to pay a yoga instructor?" Angela pouted.

"No. I can teach you." Jesse held her gaze.

"What else will you teach me?" Angela played along with him. Jesse swept his tongue over his lips.

"You'll just have to come by for a few lessons," Jesse said.

"When?"

"Tomorrow morning at eleven," Jesse said.

"Where?"

"My place." Jesse removed his cell phone and sent her a text that contained his address. "I'll see you then."

The following morning, Angela arrived at Jesse's house. She was wearing her black running shorts but didn't have on any panties. She was also wearing a matching top that could be easily removed in the heat of the moment. Jesse welcomed her into his home. He showed her around and then took her into the enclosed patio area where he had two mats on the floor. He also had some very relaxing music playing and a waterfall ornament sitting in the corner emitted a soothing, tinkling sound. The enclosed patio had a wonderful view of the backyard, which was in full bloom.

"Wow, this is nice," Angela said.

"Yeah, it is. I fell in love with the house the moment I saw it." Jesse shared his love of his home. "So, shall we begin?"

"Okay," Angela said.

"Now, which side is hurting?" Jesse asked. Angela pointed to her hip. Jesse stepped closer to her and massaged her hip. Angela felt butterflies prancing around in the bottom of her tummy the moment he touched her.

"Okay, I need you to take off your shoes and stand on the mat and face me," Jesse said.

"Do I need to take off anything else?" Angela was ready to make love to him. As far as she was concerned, hot sex would loosen her hips up just fine.

Jesse laughed and then scratched the back of his neck. "If I didn't know any better, I'd swear that you were trying to seduce me," he said.

"And if I am?" Angela stepped closer to him.

"Then I'd have to say that I like being sedu—" Jesse's and Angela's lips finally met. Jesse caressed her cheeks with his hands and cradled the back of her head. She felt his erection pressing against her tummy. She allowed one hand to slide down to touch it, curious to know what he was working with. At that moment, she exhaled and broke away from his kiss.

"Damn," Angela said, catching her breath.

Jesse was about to taste her sweet lips once again, but the doorbell rang.

"Are you expecting company, baby?" Angela asked.

"No," Jesse said and continued to kiss her.

The doorbell rang again and again.

"You sure you don't want to get that?" Angela asked, slightly irritated.

"Yeah, I'm sure," Jesse said, trying to kiss Angela again, but the noise of the doorbell was too distracting.

"I'll run them away," Jesse said.

"Which way is your bathroom?" asked Angela.

"Follow me. There's one near the front door." As they walked toward the front of the house, the doorbell continued to ring.

"I'm coming. Damn!" Jesse yelled out.

"The bathroom is right here." Jesse opened the bathroom door and hit the light switch. After that, he kissed Angela once more and then went to see who was at the door.

"JoAnn!" Jesse snapped. "What are you doing here?"

"I tried calling you but you wouldn't answer your damn phone," JoAnn shrieked at him.

"Is something wrong with Trina?" Jesse asked, concerned.

"She told me that you have a girlfriend." JoAnn tried to peer past his shoulder.

"That's none of your business, JoAnn." Jesse tried to be patient.

"It is my business if she mistreats or harms my daughter!"

"What the fuck are you talking about?" Jesse lost it. He couldn't believe that JoAnn was actually violating the restraining order that she'd put against him to come talk about some trivial bullshit.

"It's that Barbie bitch in the black shorts, isn't it? I saw her when she bounced her ass up to the door. It looked like she didn't have on any panties."

"Have you been spying on me?" At that moment, Jesse smelled alcohol on JoAnn's breath, and he was about to explode.

"I wasn't really spying. I just happened to be in the neighborhood and saw a strange car sitting in the driveway."

"Damn! How long have you been sneaking around like this?" Jesse now realized that JoAnn had gone completely crazy.

"Jesse. Is everything okay?" Angela asked as she exited the bathroom.

"Hell, no, everything isn't okay, bitch! You need to get the fuck out of my house," JoAnn exploded, and tried to force her way past Jesse. He grabbed her and held her still.

"This is my damn man, and this is the house that we bought together!"

"Jesse? Are you still married?" Angela was confused.

"No! I'm not still married. She's just crazy!" Jesse pushed JoAnn back out.

"I'm not crazy, bitch! Get out of my house!" JoAnn continued to assault Angela with angry words. "That's my bed that he's fucking you in!" Jesse slammed the door in her face.

"Open this damn door, Jesse!" JoAnn began pushing against the door like a madwoman. "Open the damn door. Let me in, Jesse!" JoAnn began ringing the doorbell repeatedly.

"I think I'm going to go now. I don't fight over a man," Angela said and hurried back to the enclosed patio to get her shoes.

"Angela, wait. It's not what you think," Jesse tried to explain.

"She's obviously still in love with you, Jesse," Angela said as she quickly put on her shoes.

"But I don't love her. Our marriage ended over a year ago."

"Well, if she's crazy enough to show up unannounced like this, she's probably crazy enough to pull a gun on me." Angela now had her shoes back on. "I can't deal with this type of drama, Jesse. I just won't."

"Angela. Please." Jesse captured her gaze. "I think we're on to something special. I want to continue."

"There your black ass is!" JoAnn had walked around the house and entered the backyard.

"Goodbye, Jesse," Angela said and rushed toward the front door and her car.

"That's right. You'd better run!" JoAnn tried to race around to the front of the house but tripped and fell over the garden hose.

Jesse picked up a nearby telephone and dialed 911.

When Jesse spoke to Angela again, he explained that JoAnn had been spying on him and that he had absolutely no feelings for her. He reassured Angela that he was indeed divorced.

"I'll even show you a copy of my divorce decree," Jesse said to her over the phone.

"Jesse, I like you. I really do. But I can't deal with drama in my life right now. I've been through too much already."

"Angela, I know. And believe me, I don't want to put you through any more. And Lord knows that I don't want any drama. JoAnn was drunk when she came over. By the time the police arrived, she'd passed out on the back lawn. I had to call my daughter, Trina—" Jesse stopped talking for a moment. "It was just a mess." Jesse was afraid that all of his baggage would scare Angela off.

"I think I need a little more time," Angela said. "Just give me a little space right now, okay?"

"What does that mean?" Jesse asked.

"I just need to take my time before I jump into another relationship. I need to make sure that I'm ready to trust someone again."

"So, are you saying that you don't trust me?" Jesse asked.

"No, it's not that. I think we're both still kind of vulnerable right now. I was married for eight years and you were married for longer than that. It takes time to get a person out of your system. I think we just both need a little more time."

"I'm not going anywhere, Angela."

"I know, Jesse," Angela said.

Thirty thousand people had registered for the running of the annual Chicago Marathon. It was going to be unseasonably warm for October and runners were being told to hydrate in advance of the run. Jesse had rented tent space so that everyone from his running club would have a place to gather prior to the race. Everyone was buzzing with excitement, anticipation and nervous energy. When the time was right, herds of people began making their way from the tent area over toward the starting line.

"Are you ready to do this?" Both Jesse and Regina asked Angela as they moved toward the starting line.

"Yes," Angela said.

"Now, here is what's going to happen." Jesse was speaking directly into Angela's ear so that she could hear his voice above the noise of the crowd. "The first ten miles or so will be very crowded and we'll be moving slowly. Once the crowd begins to thin out, you'll be able to find your stride and knock down the rest of the miles."

"Jesse and I will be running with you, so you'll have plenty of support," added Regina. The buzzer sounded and the three of them began their journey toward completing the 26.2-mile run. Just as Jesse had explained, the crowds were bad for the first ten miles. After they passed the ten-mile mark, there was much more room. Angela moved along and was feeling very strong. By the time they reached mile fourteen, Regina said that she was feeling stronger and needed to pick up her pace.

"Go ahead," Jesse said. "Get your run on. We'll see you back at the tent."

"Is that okay with you, girl?" Regina asked Angela.

"Yes. Go ahead. Run your race," Angela said. Regina picked up her pace and left them.

"Are you doing good?" Jesse asked.

"I'm good, but it's very hot," Angela said.

"I know. It's hotter than it normally is this time of year. Make sure you drink plenty of water. And pour some on your head to help cool you off." The two of them pressed on. By the time they reached mile twenty, Angela was in trouble.

"I can't make it, Jesse." Angela stopped running. "I need to sit down and get some rest."

"No, you can't stop now," Jesse said and forced Angela to keep on moving. At mile twenty-five, Angela was completely exhausted.

"Jesse…I can't make it. I feel like I'm going to fall flat on my face. It's too hot and I feel so weak. My feet are killing me. I feel like I'm running on my bones."

"Just a little farther, baby. Dig a little deeper," Jesse encouraged Angela. It was quiet then, and every runner around them seemed to be moving at a zombie's pace, with barely enough energy to remain upright.

"My foot is bleeding, Jesse." Angela glanced down at her right foot. "My shoes have rubbed the side of my big toe raw."

"Damn." Jesse looked down at Angela's foot. Some blood had soaked through the fabric of the shoe.

"I know this is going to sound horrible, but you don't have time to bleed. You're one mile away from accomplishing something you never thought possible. So suck up the pain and let's keep it moving."

"Jesse, I don't want to," Angela complained.

"Angela. You're only running twenty-six miles. Slaves who were running to freedom had to run across entire states through the wilderness with no shoes. Now you mean to tell me that you can't find the will to carry on?"

Angela thought about what Jesse had said for a moment and willed herself to move. Four hundred meters from the finish line, Angela's legs gave out completely and she collapsed. Jesse caught her before she hit the ground.

"I can't…" Angela began to cry. "I tried, but I can't make it. I'm sorry. My feet, my legs, my back, everything just hurts."

"I know, baby, but we're right at the finish line. Look right there. Do you see the banner? That's the finish line. Don't come this far and stop."

"Is that your wife?" A female police officer who was sitting in a nearby squad car asked the question. "Is she okay? Does she need help?"

"Angela. Don't give up now," Jesse pleaded and then answered the officer. "Yes, she is my wife and no, she doesn't need help. She's going to make it."

"What's her name?" shouted the officer.

"Angela," Jesse answered.

The officer then turned on the squad car's loudspeaker and began cheering for Angela. "Come on, girl," the officer encouraged. "A couple that runs together, stays together. You can finish this race. Get up, Angela, and fight!"

"See there, babe." Jesse beamed. "Complete strangers are pulling for you."

Angela released a big sigh and allowed Jesse to help her to her feet. She began walking slowly and painfully toward the finish line. She was crying, she was in pain, but she continued to move with what little energy she had. About a hundred meters from the finish line, Angela realized that she was about to complete the race. A swell of energy rushed through her body and she found the strength to begin running again. She ran hard.

"There you go, Angela!" Jesse shouted out as he ran alongside her. "Go get your medal!"

Angela crossed the finish line and collapsed into Jesse's arms.

CHAPTER 28

JESSE

Jesse was in his room listening to Fantasia while packing his luggage for his flight to Miami the next morning. He looked forward to the post-marathon cruise and enjoying a long-overdue vacation. He turned up the radio and began singing along with Fantasia. Jesse was feeling so good that he began dancing until Fantasia stopped singing, then he continued to pack. Once his bags were completely packed, he set his suitcase by the front door. Just as he was about to walk away, he noticed a man approaching his home.

"Good morning," Jesse said, opening the door.

"Good morning to you, as well," said the man. Jesse quickly noticed the police badge dangling from a chain around the man's neck and deduced that he was an off-duty police officer.

"What can I do for you?" Jesse asked.

"Are you Jesse Robins?" the man asked.

"Yes," Jesse answered. The officer handed Jesse an envelope and asked him to sign a document which stated that he'd received it.

"You've just been served," said the officer and then left.

"Served!" Jesse looked at the envelope. He stepped back inside the house and opened it. Once he'd read it, he flung it across the room.

"Damn you, JoAnn. Why won't you just let shit go!" Jesse yelled out. He was being summoned back to court so that JoAnn could make an adjustment to their joint custody arrangement. At that moment, Jesse's doorbell rang once again. As he approached the door, he could see Regina's silhouette. Jesse opened the door.

"What's the deal, pickle? Are you all set to get out of here?" Regina was her usual perky self.

"Hey, Regina," Jesse greeted her dryly and then turned to head toward the family room.

Regina came inside and closed the door behind her. "What's wrong with you?"

Jesse picked up the envelope he'd thrown across the room. "Come and listen to this shit," he said. They both sat down in the family room and Regina listened as Jesse read his summons to appear in court.

"She's just doing this shit to be vindictive, Jesse."

"Why won't she just let it go? I don't want her. Our marriage is over. Why can't she get that through her thick skull?"

"I know some people who could walk up on her and beat her ass for you," Regina offered.

"Regina. She's the mother of my child. I can't do that."

"I'm just saying. If you need somebody to get in that ass, I have a few girlfriends who roll like that. Well, what *are* you going to do?" Regina asked.

"Nothing right now. I'll deal with this madness when I come back from vacation."

"Damn, I wish I was going with you. I should've signed up back when you did. Next year I'm doing it for sure," Regina said.

"You and Angela could have gotten a cabin together," Jesse said.

"I don't want a cabin with Angela. Shit, if I was going I'd have a man in my room with me. I don't know why you and Angela are wasting money on separate rooms. Ya'll know that you're going to end up together on that ship."

"Hey. I tried to get sister girl to go there, but after that move JoAnn pulled a few months ago, she got cold feet."

"She was just nervous, that's all," Regina said. "Well, give me your spare set of door keys so I can come by and check on your house while you're away. I have to run a ton of errands today," she said as she stood up. "Call me after you've boarded the ship."

"Okay," Jesse said as he exited the room to retrieve the spare set of house keys.

"All right then. Have a good trip. Remember what I said now. If you need me to make a phone call to take care of JoAnn—"

"Regina. I can handle my own affairs." Jesse laughed. Regina gave him a hug and left.

The following day, Jesse met up with Angela and several people from his running club. Many of the group sat near the Jetway, talking about the race, their completion times and how much fun they planned to have on the cruise. When it was time to board their flight, Jesse and Angela sat next to each other and watched a movie on Jesse's portable DVD player. When they arrived in Fort Lauderdale, a shuttle service from the cruise line picked them up and drove them to the dock in Miami where they'd boarded the ship.

On the ship, Angela and Jesse found their cabins. Jesse had splurged and reserved a suite with a private balcony while Angela's cabin was located on the interior of the ship. Jesse was very pleased with his suite; it opened into a narrow foyer which led to a seating area with a small dining table and four chairs. There were several cupboards and a small television. On the other side of the dining area were a sofa and two chairs. Just to the right of that was the sleeping area that featured a queen-size bed, a walk-in closet and a bathroom with two vanities. There was a whirlpool in the suite as well as a separate shower area.

"Very nice," Jesse said aloud as he turned on the water in

one of the sinks to see how strong the pressure was. He walked back toward the dining area and moved toward the two large windows that opened out to the private balcony. The balcony held a small table and two recliners.

An hour later, the ship was setting sail and scores of passengers were out on their balconies and on the upper decks waving goodbye to friends and family members. Once the shore was receding from view, the ship's crew herded the passengers to the upper deck to hear the safety instructions in case of an emergency. While the drill was going on, Jesse saw Angela.

"How is your cabin?" he asked her.

"Cozy." Angela laughed. "Just enough space to take off your clothes and rest. And yours?"

"You should come by to take a look at it. It's very nice. I have a suite," Jesse boasted.

"Oh, so you're playing the role of a baller." Angela attempted to make Jesse's ego swell with the idea that he was making as much money as a professional athlete.

"You only live once." Jesse smiled at her for a long moment, and as they got lost in each other's gazes, Jesse could feel the intensity of their desire for each other.

"You're going to get me into trouble, aren't you?" Angela murmured.

"I'm planning on getting you into a whole lot of trouble," Jesse said, as he took her hand into his. Angela didn't resist his advances as she had done over the past few months since the incident with JoAnn.

"After dinner with the running group tonight, why don't we go to the dance hall and have some fun?" Angela suggested.

"Are you sure you're up for it?" Jesse asked. "After all, you did just finish a marathon. How is your toe?"

"Yeah, I did, didn't I?" Angela said with pride. "My foot is fine, but I'm still having problems with tight muscles in my hip."

"I can stretch those out for you." Jesse played along.

"Are you sure you can loosen me up?"

"I have all of the skills needed to relax your entire body," Jesse answered.

"Umm, I like the way you said that," Angela cooed, and Jesse stepped in to embrace her. He took her face into his hands and kissed her. Angela's body responded to him immediately, and she broke away from the kiss.

"It has been so long, Jesse. I need you," Angela admitted breathlessly.

"I need you more," he said as he hugged her. "You have no idea."

Later that evening, Angela and Jesse joined the rest of their marathon colleagues and enjoyed cocktails, dinner and conversation. Afterward, at the ship's dance club, Jesse located a table for them and they sat for a moment watching as people gyrated and howled with joy as Buster Poindexter sang "Hot, Hot, Hot," a song which had become very popular among vacationers in the Caribbean.

"I'm going to go over to the bar and get us something to drink. What would you like?" Jesse asked Angela.

"Have the bartender mix me up a pineapple martini," Angela said excitedly.

Jesse returned with their drinks and snuggled up to Angela. Angela took a few sips of her drink as she grooved along with the music. She placed her hand on Jesse's thigh and began rubbing it under the table. She guided her fingers under the fabric of his shorts until they reached the prize she'd been searching for.

"I hope you know I'm not going to tell you to stop," Jesse said with a smile.

"You know that I'm so hot that I'll suck on your dick right here at this table." Angela spoke into his ear and nibbled on his earlobe as she freed his manhood from its confines. Another couple sat at a table next to them but it seemed that Angela didn't give a damn about being watched and neither did Jesse. Angela glanced down at Jesse's dick.

"Oooh, shit," she said as she began to stroke him. His manhood was standing at full attention. "Damn, Jesse." Angela licked her lips.

"Do you like what you see?" Jesse asked.

"I can't help it. I've got to know what you taste like," Angela said as she bowed her head down and placed Jesse inside her warm, wet mouth. Jesse hissed, cooed and sighed as Angela stroked and sucked hard on him. After a few moments, Angela resurfaced, took another drink of her pineapple martini, left the liquid in her mouth and went back down to suck on Jesse some more.

"Oh, damn. Shit, Angela," Jesse called out as he cradled the back of her head and ran his fingers through her hair. When Angela stopped, she drank the last of her alcohol and kissed Jesse passionately.

"Okay, whew," Angela said as she pulled away from the kiss to take a deep breath.

"We need to take this party back to my suite." Jesse tried to calm his manhood down in order to leave the table.

"I agree," Angela said, rubbing the back of his head. She kissed his cheek, then his ear, followed by his neck. "You've got my pussy pulsating and in need of something to squeeze," Angela confessed as she clamped her thighs together.

"Let's get out of here," Jesse said. He and Angela left the club and headed back to his suite. Angela was impressed by the size and decor of the room. She immediately walked over to the bed and kicked off her shoes, then got undressed, turned on the shower and stepped inside. A few moments later, Jesse joined her. Angela scrubbed his back and marveled as soapy water cascaded down his back and through the valley of his muscled ass.

"You have a nice, spankable ass," Angela said as she caressed his behind. Jesse's back arched and he exhaled as a wave of passion washed over him.

"Squeeze my nipples," Angela directed Jesse. He did as she asked.

"Harder, baby. Don't be shy."

Jesse complied and applied a little more pressure. Angela released several loud moans. Her body was alive and excited.

"Spread your legs," he commanded, then squatted down. Angela did as he requested. With water streaming down the valley of Angela's breasts and flowing down her tummy, Jesse positioned his lips before her pussy.

"You have a landing strip," he said, noticing how she'd trimmed her pubic hair. Jesse swept his tongue over the lips of her paradise. He positioned his right hand on her ass and allowed his middle finger to make small circles around her anus. With his left hand, he parted her pussy lips and brushed his tongue slowly and rhythmically up and down.

Jesse felt Angela's clit swell up and become hard. He focused on it, sweeping his tongue clockwise around it. He could feel Angela opening up. The first knuckle of his index finger was now in her ass. He made sure that his footing was solid and skillfully placed the middle finger of his left hand inside her honeypot, then maneuvered it up toward the back of her clit and applied gentle pressure.

Angela began thrusting her hips hard as she felt her first orgasm swelling up. Jesse paid attention to every detail of Angela's body language, her undulations and echoes of pleasure.

"Jesse! I'm about to come, baby," Angela cried out as her orgasm exploded deep within her body. She lost her breath for several moments as the sweetness of the orgasm bathed her soul. Angela felt weak and had lost her breath for a moment.

"Okay, baby. You've made me cry," Angela confessed. Jesse stood up. He had a bright smile on his face because he'd gotten his reward. Not only had he given her an exquisite orgasm, but he knew that they had connected with each other emotionally. Now that she'd had her first release, she wanted more.

"Are you ready for round two?" he whispered in her ear.

"You know I am," Angela responded.

"Follow me." They stepped out of the shower, and Jesse turned off all the lights in the cabin. He moved toward the balcony and opened the door.

"You are a big freak!" Angela whispered.

"You're a bigger freak. Place your hands on the railing, lean forward and put your ass in the air. I want to take you from behind."

Without hesitation, Angela did exactly as Jesse had requested. Jesse stood behind her and, with his right hand, guided himself inside her. The moment he penetrated, her pussy squeezed him.

"Damn, girl, you've got a death grip," Jesse said.

"That's Coco grabbing you like that. She likes you." Angela was referring to the name she'd given her goddess.

Jesse slowly pushed himself deeper inside her. As he did, Angela cried out, her voice filled with both pain and pleasure.

"Oooh, you are hitting every wall inside of me," Angela said, trying to adjust her position by leaning forward a little bit more. Jesse was now deep inside her, slowly stroking her. Angela cried out more as Coco squeezed Jesse's dick with all of her might.

"Harder, Jesse," Angela begged him. Jesse was completely in tune with Angela's desire. He grabbed her long hair and pulled on it, causing her chin to crane upward. He began pounding her. He looked down at his pride, which was glistening with her juices. He glided in and out of her with the erotic rhythm that made Angela quiver uncontrollably.

"Fight back," Jesse began. "Come on. Take this dick. Show me that you like what I'm doing to you."

Jesse spanked her ass and Angela responded, "Oooh, yes. Slap my ass, baby."

"Come, give it to me. Give it all to me. Don't cheat me," Jesse said.

"I'm not cheating you, baby. You're all up in my shit. You have Coco wide open." Angela cried out with sweet pleasure as she bounced her ass against him.

"Do you like the way I'm fucking you?" Jesse asked as he kept thrusting in unison with the rhythm of her movements.

"Yes, baby." Angela's breathing became labored as another orgasm rose up. Angela spread her legs a bit wider, raised herself upward until she was standing on the balls of her feet, and then began shaking as her orgasm exploded.

"Jesse!" Angela pushed her ass back harder against him. "Oh, keep going," she insisted. A series of consecutive orgasms detonated inside her.

"Damn. Wooo, you are hard," Angela said as she slowed down. Jesse stepped back and wiped the sweat that had formed on his forehead.

"Come on. I want to ride you." Angela led Jesse back inside and moved toward the bed.

"Oh, your bed feels so comfortable." Angela stretched out on the smooth sheets.

"Turn around," Jesse ordered. "I want to get you from the back again." Angela positioned her ass in the air once again. She was anticipating more long and deep strokes from him before she got her opportunity to ride him, but to her surprise, Jesse didn't penetrate her. Instead, he placed both of his hands on her ass, gently opened her up and exposed her valley. He then began sweeping his tongue up and down her ass, stopping every now and again to circle his tongue around her anus.

"Oooh!" Angela cooed. "I've never had this done before."

"Do you like it?" Jesse asked.

"I'm not telling you to stop," she answered as she perched her derriere higher in the air for him. Jesse once again toyed with her by placing his fingers inside Coco.

"Let's get in the sixty-nine position. I want to bury my face between your thighs, pussy and ass. I want us both to lose our minds."

Angela didn't argue with Jesse, but honored his request. She steadied herself, parted her lips and placed his strong cock inside her wet and warm mouth. Angela swirled her tongue up and down the length of his manhood, then held him in her hand, enjoying the silky feeling of his skin as she stroked him.

"Oh, that's it right there, Angela. Stroke it just like that," Jesse moaned.

Minutes later, Angela spoke. "Lie on your back. I want to ride you." Jesse did as Angela requested. She mounted him, placed his long, glistening shaft inside herself and swallowed him up. "My turn," she said.

"Show me how good you can ride," Jesse said with untamed anticipation as he placed his hands on her ass. Angela circled her hips so that his dick kissed every wall of her honeypot.

"Is this my dick?" Angela asked as she listened to Jesse's orgasm stirring inside of him.

"Yes. This is your dick," Jesse grunted.

"Then give me my juice," Angela demanded. She reached behind her and toyed with his balls while riding him.

"Oh, fuck!" Jesse began shooting his essence inside her.

"Yes, baby!" Angela screamed out as she felt his release. She was exhausted. She leaned forward and nuzzled her face next to his. Jesse held on to her.

"You are so beautiful," he whispered.

"You make me feel beautiful," she said as she drifted off to sleep.

* * *

The following morning, Angela walked back to her cabin and picked up a few necessary items. While she was gone, Jesse ordered room service. When she returned, she got comfortable again and disrobed down to her white bra and panties.

"Will you rub my feet for me?" she asked as she positioned herself on the bed. She wanted to watch television while he rubbed them.

"After last night, I'll do anything for you." Jesse slipped into his black silk pajamas and positioned himself so he could rub her feet and watch TV.

"There is so much for us to enjoy on this vacation and I want to spend as much time as I can with you— Oooh, that feels so good. Right there. Rub that spot," Angela instructed Jesse. She wiggled her toes and tickled his tummy. "I could get used to you rubbing my feet every night."

"You know that I want a serious committed relationship with you, right?" Jesse asked.

Angela turned and captured his gaze. "No. But now I do."

"I'm serious. I don't want to lose you again."

"What are you saying?" Angela asked.

"I'm saying that I'd marry you in a heartbeat."

"Damn, Coco. Girl, you must have really put it on him." Angela glanced down between her thighs and spoke directly to her goddess. Jesse laughed.

"I want you to be my woman. I don't want to see anyone but you. Do you have a problem seeing only me?" he asked.

"No." Angela focused her attention on him once again.

"Good, because I want to build something special with you," Jesse said. Angela repositioned herself on the bed so that she could hug him.

"Don't hurt me, Jesse. I don't want to be hurt again."

"I won't hurt you. I promise."

"And I won't hurt you. I promise," Angela vowed as she squeezed him tighter.

CHAPTER 29

Will was glad to be getting out of jail a few weeks early for good behavior. He'd been locked up for three years and never wanted to see the inside of a prison again for as long as he lived. Once all of his release paperwork had been completed, he was free to go. He exited the prison, which was located in a rural area, and walked along the side of the highway until he reached the spot where he was to wait for an hour for a bus that would take him back toward his home.

As he rode the bus, he thought about his former life, which was completely gone. He had no career, no house and no wife. When Angela had sold their home, he *did* get his share. However, most of that money was gone due to levies placed against him by creditors. Will was now in the position of having to micromanage his limited financial resources until he was able to get on his feet.

The bus dropped Will at the Bay Area Rapid Transit station in Oakland. From there he caught the train back to Pittsburg where his brother, Smoky, lived.

When he arrived at Smoky's home, he stood in front of it and took a deep breath. The grass in the front yard was completely overgrown with weeds and needed to be mowed. The outside of the house needed cosmetic work, as well. Two windows were boarded up, the screen door was dangling from its hinges and the old Ford, which should've been towed away to an auto graveyard long ago, was in the driveway.

"I'm going to have to put money into this dump if I'm going

to sell it," Will said to himself. He stepped inside the chain-link fence and headed up the sidewalk to Smoky's front door. He rang the doorbell, and a few moments later he heard the cantankerous voice of his brother.

"Who the hell is there?" Smoky barked.

"It's me. Your brother, Will."

"My brother is in jail." Smoky didn't believe the voice on the other side of the door.

"Smoky, stop playing and open up the damn door," Will shouted.

"If you're my brother, then tell me, who was the first girl you had sex with?" Smoky asked.

"Smoky, I really don't have time for this, man. Open the damn door."

"Answer the damn question," Smoky fired back.

"Marcia Moore. She'd come over to the house one day after school and we had sex on the sofa."

"That's my brother!" Smoky began laughing. Will heard a series of dead bolts being unlocked. Smoky opened the door and wheeled himself out of the way.

"What's up, boy!" Smoky was delighted. Will dropped the one duffel bag he was carrying and leaned over to embrace his brother.

"I forgot you were coming back home today. Come on in. The maid is on vacation."

"The maid is always on vacation, Smoky. How do you live in this pigpen?" Will asked, looking around. Unwashed clothing, trash and boxes were piled up everywhere. A musty odor was wafting through the house, and Will couldn't tell if it was due to a plumbing problem or if it was from old trash and spoiled food.

"Don't start with me, man. You know damn well I'm in a wheelchair. It's not like I can get up and mop the damn floor. I have to depend on other people to help me, but they don't like to come around because they think I've gone crazy. But I've got more sense than any of those fools running around out there. I've got a college degree." Smoky tapped his index finger against his temple indicating that he was very intelligent.

After clearing off a spot to sit down, Will focused his attention on Smoky, and assessed his appearance. "Why are you missing two teeth and what are you doing with that black ankle bracelet on?" Will asked.

"I'm under house arrest," Smoky confessed as he put the brake on his wheelchair.

"What did you get in trouble for this time?" Will asked.

"Prostitution. I was having myself a party. You should've seen it, man. I had three girls, man, and I was handling all of them. Everything was going fine. We were getting our heads bad. Next thing I knew, the police busted out my damn windows and came charging in, this motherfucker ready to shoot anything that moved. They arrested the girls, but I wasn't going down without a fight. When one of those cops tried to handcuff me, I grabbed him. I told them not to fuck with me because my brother was a congressman and would put all of their asses on the unemployment line. While I was on the police officer, I fell out of my chair. Then one of those bastards kicked me in the face and knocked out my teeth. I told them I would be filing a police brutality report, but they all said that my teeth fell out when I tumbled out of my wheelchair."

Will exhaled loudly.

"They tried to say that I was running a cathouse." Smoky laughed. "When I got in front of the judge, I told him that I wasn't running a cathouse, I was trying to get some pussy. To make a long story short, the motherfucking judge put me under house arrest. I told him it was fine because it wasn't like I was going any place special."

"Look, man. When I get on my feet, I'll hire a maid to come through once a week," Will said.

"Make sure she's pretty and young. I don't want to look at some old, bloated lady bending over."

"You're never going to change, are you, man?" Will asked.

"Change? What the fuck for? I like being me. Hey, check this out." Smoky picked up the television remote sitting on his lap and pointed it at the television.

"I am watching *College Girls in Heat*. It's a damn good porno." Smoky laughed as he wheeled himself back in front of the television. "Remember how we used to sneak around and steal pornos from Uncle Fred? He had boxes of them. He had seen so many that he could just look at a woman and tell what kind of pussy she had." Smoky began rattling on. "Look over there." Smokey pointed to a stack of VHS tapes scattered all over the floor. "I got a collection just like him. I even taped myself a few times. I could be a big porn star if I wanted to." Smoky laughed. "I'm flexible like a motherfucker."

"You've gone crazy, haven't you?" Will asked him. "You've been sitting in here alone for too long."

"I'm not crazy, so stop calling me that," Smoky snapped at Will. "Why does every motherfucker in this world think I'm crazy? I like watching porno all the damn time. So fucking what! I'm a grown-ass man, living in my own damn house doing what the fuck I want to do."

"I did a lot of thinking while I was in jail about why I was so lustful and careless," Will said slowly. "As I thought about my life I realized that my problem started when we began watching Uncle Fred's pornographic movies. We were both too young to be watching those movies, Smoky."

"You don't know what the hell you're talking about. It's a rite of passage. Young men are supposed to watch pornos and be interested in them. Look at the damn Internet. That's the porno superhighway. If you type in the word *sex,* about two million Web sites come up. Somebody's watching a lot of it and it's not just my black ass."

"I just think that in the back of my mind it taught me to believe that women were only objects to be used for my sexual pleasure."

"They *are* there for your damn sexual pleasure. What are you trying to say, man?" Smoky paused in thought for a moment. "Oh, no. They didn't take your manhood away from you while you were locked up, did they? Who was it, man? When he comes out, we'll roll up on that fool and blow his damn brains out!"

"No. That didn't happen, Smoky," Will explained. "I'm just saying I did a lot of thinking. That's all."

"Well, that's your problem, man. You think too damn much."

Will realized that a mature conversation with Smoky about their views on women wasn't going to happen.

"Smoky, I don't want to fight with you," Will said. "Look, man, I'm going to attempt to put my life back in order. I'm going to try to run for office again. I'm going to talk to Angela and pick up where we left off."

"Angela?" Smoky chuckled. "Man, that woman is gone," Smoky said as he repositioned himself in his wheelchair.

"What are talking about? She's not dead, is she?" Will asked.

"I don't think she's dead but when you got locked up, she sold all the furniture in your house. Those boxes stacked up right there." Smoky pointed to the boxes Will noticed earlier. "That's some of your shit. She packed up all your stuff and dropped it off over here. Your clothes, your shoes and your books are packed up in boxes. Most of your stuff is down in the basement."

Will moved over and opened one of the boxes. It contained his cell phone, music CDs and newspaper articles that had been written about him. Will sighed. "Do you know where Angela is?" he asked.

"She said that she was moving back to the Midwest," Smoky said.

"Midwest?" Will asked, a little bit perplexed.

"Yeah. Chicago, I think. She said she was moving back to Chicago."

"Regina," Will said. "Her girlfriend Regina lives in Chicago."

"Yeah, that's who she was with when she dropped off all your stuff. Boy, that Regina was a fine-looking woman. I told her that she needed to get with me so—"

"Smoky." Will cut him off. "I don't want to hear it."

"Suit yourself. But Angela has moved on," Smoky said.

"I can get her back," Will said confidently. "We were good together. We had a good life. She'll always love me."

"Did she come to see you or write to you while you were locked up?" Smoky asked.

"No," Will admitted.

"And you're calling me crazy? Huh, that's a laugh." Smoky chuckled.

"I'm going to find her. But first I'm going to reach out to some old friends, schedule some interviews and start making my way back."

"How are you going to do all of this when you've been in jail? I'm dying to know," Smoky said.

"I don't know, but if the mayor of Washington, D.C., can get caught smoking crack and get reelected, so can I."

Will didn't waste any time. Within a month, he'd scheduled a press conference and was able to generate local media interest. The conference took place at a local community center.

"Mr. Rivers, what will you do now that you've been released?" asked one of the reporters.

"I'm going to run for office again," Will answered. He was glad to be back in the spotlight and he was beginning to feel the confidence he'd once lost return.

"Mr. Rivers, do you feel any remorse or regret about the crime you committed?" asked another reporter.

"I've had plenty of time to think about what I've done. Of course, I feel remorse. I realize that I was wrong, and I've paid my debt to society for my actions. That chapter of my life is now behind me. I feel that my best work and service to this community is still ahead of me."

"Since your release, have you had any contact with the young women you were involved with?" asked another reporter.

"As I stated, that chapter of my life is behind me. I'm moving forward and with the help of the citizens of this community, we'll build a place where there is opportunity, economic growth and prosperity," Will countered. He began finding his voice and the combination of words that had served him well in the past.

"What about your ex-wife, Angela? She's a reporter in Chicago now. Have you had any contact with her since your release?" asked one of the female reporters.

"Angela is an amazing woman." Will couldn't speak for a moment because he'd lost the words he wanted to say. "She is strong and I can still learn a lot from her. She and I have a lot to catch up on," Will said.

He answered several more questions, and then cornered the woman who'd mentioned that Angela was working as a reporter in Chicago. Will milked as much information from her as he could, but he didn't get much to go on.

When Will returned to Smoky's house, he told him that he was headed to Chicago for a few days.

"You're leaving already? You just got here, man. Why do you have to rush off?" Smoky asked.

"I've got to find Angela. I promised her that I'd make things right, and that's what I'm going to do," Will answered as he carried his suitcase from the basement back up the stairs.

"Will. You need to slow down and think, man. It's been what—two years now? That woman has moved on. You have to let her go. There is plenty of pussy out here that you can have."

"Smoky, she was more than pussy to me!" Will snapped.

"Okay, so she was more than pussy to you, but you fucked that shit up, man. She's probably remarried by now."

"No, she's not," Will said as he began packing his things.

"How do you know?" Smoky was trying to talk some sense into Will.

"Because I do. Angela isn't like that. She just isn't going to go out and get a new man. No one understands her the way that I do."

"You've flipped out, man." Smoky didn't hold back his words. "You've barely got money. You don't know where the woman is in Chicago. You haven't talked to her and you don't know if she even wants to deal with you. Let it go, Will."

"No! I sat in that rotten prison for two years thinking about her. She's just hurt, that's all. And *I'm* the only one who can fix her broken heart. Do you understand what I'm saying?" Will asked.

"You still love her," Smoky answered.

"Yes," Will returned.

"Well, remember this, brother. Love will make you do some crazy shit. Don't let love drive you crazy," Smoky said.

"Whatever, man," Will said.

"When does your flight leave?" Smoky asked.

"I'm taking a red-eye flight to Chicago. I'll be there by morning."

"All right, man. Be careful," Smoky said, and left Will alone to continue packing for his trip.

CHAPTER 30

JESSE

Jesse sat far away from JoAnn in the courtroom. He was angry about her summoning him to court once again to try to get their custody arrangement amended. Jesse knew that her request was just another attempt to make his life miserable. The judge finally called their case, and both Jesse and JoAnn approached the bench. JoAnn stood at the plaintiff's podium and Jesse stood at the defendant's podium.

"Ms. Walker, you want to make an amendment to the custody arrangement you have with your ex-husband, Jesse Robins," the judge began.

"Yes. I want it to be written down that Jesse can't have other women around when my daughter visits him at his house."

"And why is this?" asked the judge.

"Because that's what I want," JoAnn stated. "He shouldn't be dating around anyway. I just don't feel comfortable with other women being around my daughter."

"Ms. Walker, do you know of any direct threat or danger posed to your daughter by anyone who has been visiting Mr. Robins?"

"No."

"Your Honor, may I speak, please?" Jesse asked.

"Yes, you may," the judge said.

"Your Honor, this is an attempt by JoAnn to make my life more difficult, which she's been trying to do for the past three years. She's placed a restraining order against me, but then violated it by coming unannounced to my home. A friend came by my house for a visit and JoAnn showed up at my home drunk and belligerent. I have a police report of the incident right here." Jesse handed a copy of the report to the bailiff who handed it to the judge. "Your Honor, for the record, I want to say that I value the time I have with my daughter, and I've never had other visitors at my home when she's there."

"Ms. Walker, why were you at his house when *you'd* placed a restraining order against him?" asked the judge.

"I wanted to see who he was dating and to make sure that whoever it was wouldn't harm our daughter."

"Do you have any record or written reports that show any harm has come to your daughter while she has been in the care of Mr. Robins?"

"No," JoAnn said.

"Case dismissed." The judge slammed down her gavel and called the next case. Jesse exhaled a sigh of relief and began walking out of the courtroom.

"Jesse," JoAnn called after him, but he wouldn't stop walking. "Jesse, wait." JoAnn finally got him to stop outside the courtroom. He was angry and breathing hard.

"What do you want, woman?" Jesse snarled at her.

"Calm down, okay?" JoAnn tried to ease his tension. "You look good." JoAnn made small talk.

"I'm not in the mood for cheap talk, JoAnn. Don't you call me again unless it has something to do with Trina. You understand me?" Jesse pointed his index finger at her.

"Okay. I'm sorry."

Jesse turned to leave her where she stood when she asked, "Jesse, um, is there still a chance for us?"

Jesse began to laugh. "Are you delusional? No."

"Are you married to your friend?" she asked.

"That's none of your business," Jesse said.

"I'll take that answer to mean no, you're not married to her. That being the case, there *is* still a chance for us to work things out and get back together. We can do it for Trina's benefit, don't you think?" Jesse was stunned that after JoAnn had hauled him back to court, she had the nerve to ask him for a reconciliation.

"Trina is sixteen now and soon she'll be eighteen years old and on her way to college. I am doing everything that I can to make sure she has every opportunity to succeed. One thing that I know for sure is we are no good together. I almost lost who I was because of your intolerable behavior. I'm going to be the best father that I can be to my daughter but I'll never ever be your husband or lover ever again."

"Jesse, wait!" JoAnn pleaded.

"Bye, JoAnn. I'm going to pick up Trina from school," Jesse said and turned his back on her.

"Jesse! Don't do this. I need you!" JoAnn's voice trembled with emotion. "I need you, Jesse. Do you hear me?" Jesse didn't look back as he rushed out the door.

Trina was scheduled to stay with Jesse for the weekend. He'd made prior arrangements with JoAnn to pick their daughter up from school instead of the police station. He pulled up in front of Trina's high school and waited for her to exit from the side door. When the bell rang, a flood of teenagers rushed out of the building. Jesse spotted Trina and waved to her. Trina acknowledged him and headed in his direction.

"Hey, how are you?" Jesse asked Trina as he held the car door open for her.

"Fine," she answered as she got in. As they drove home, Jesse began asking a series of questions.

"How was your day?" he asked.

"Fine," Trina answered.

"Anything exciting happen?"

"No."

"What were your friends talking about today?"

"Nothing."

"Come on, Trina. Cut me some slack here. Talk to me," Jesse pleaded with her.

"You're driving the wrong way," Trina informed him.

"What are you talking about? We're driving to your mom's house so that we can get your bags for your stay with me this weekend," Jesse said.

"We don't live on that side of town anymore. We live in Westside now."

"Westside!" Jesse's voice was filled with surprise.

"We live in an apartment on the corner of Laramie and Augusta."

"Wait a minute…" Jesse was trying to process this new information as he made a U-turn and began heading in the opposite direction. "When did this happen?" Jesse asked.

"Recently. Didn't you talk to Mom today?" Trina asked.

"Not exactly, Trina."

"Well, she told me that you guys were going to get back together. Is it true?"

"Oh God." Jesse's heart began to ache. "Honey, it's complicated. Your mom and I haven't been together for three years and—"

"Well, my life is complicated, too, Daddy." Trina's chest began heaving and her breath came in spurts. She started crying, and in a trembling voice began to explain what was going on. "We live in a horrible place. It's not safe. We've only been there a week, and the first night someone broke into Mom's car and snatched out the radio. On the second night, the neighbors below us got into a massive fight in the hallway. I was walking down the street headed to the corner store to get something to eat on the third day and a group of boys started following me. They were talking about my butt, my breasts and my vagina. They said that if I didn't date one of them they'd all break into the apartment and catch me and all of them would have sex with me. One of them even said that he had a gun." Trina swallowed heavily and then continued to speak. "And our apartment isn't safe and I don't feel safe in it. It's old, musty and infected with rodents. It's a real shit hole, Dad." Trina's chest continued to heave uncontrollably, making it all the more difficult for her to speak.

"I had no idea. What happened to all the money?" Jesse asked.

"It's gone, Daddy. She's broke. She gambled it all away, I guess. She's been trying to find a job but hasn't had any luck. I don't want to go to school in that horrible neighborhood, Daddy. If those boys find out that I go to school over there they're going to catch me. I don't want to live over there. You have to take me and Mommy back. We're not going to make it in that neighborhood. We're two girls who live by ourselves and those people are crazy."

Jesse felt as if someone had poured a pail of ice water down his back. For a moment he felt as if his heart had stopped beating. He was in shock and he was numb. He managed to pull the car over and put it in Park. He unlatched his seat belt, reached over and embraced Trina who finally let out all her emotions. Jesse stroked the back of her head.

"It's okay, baby. Daddy is going to make sure that you're safe." He comforted her as he held back his own tears of fear and anxiety.

CHAPTER 31

ANGELA

Angela and Regina were at the gym sitting side by side on exercise bikes pedaling slowly before their cardio spin class began.

"Girl, I am in love," Angela said to Regina.

"You're in love with Jesse?" Regina asked.

"No. The man on the moon." Angela was being sarcastic. "Of course, Jesse."

Regina laughed. "Well, I'm happy for you. I know he feels the same way. He's always cared about you."

"He is such a good man. He's smart, he's caring, he's ambitious."

"He must've been thrown down on that cruise you guys took," Regina whispered so only Angela would hear her.

"Forget you, Regina. This isn't about lust." Angela wanted to be perfectly clear about her feelings.

"I know, girl. I'm just teasing you. So what does all of this mean? What are you going to do?" Regina asked.

"Well, I wouldn't say no to him if he asked me to take our relationship to the next level."

"And what's the next level?" Regina wanted to be clear.

"Marriage," Angela said. "I'd marry Jesse. Settle down again. Plan a pregnancy, become a mother." Angela smiled. "We'd have a pretty baby."

"Does Jesse know how you feel?" Regina asked, as she took a gulp of her water.

"Yes. He knows exactly how I feel. And I know exactly how

he feels about me. I'm not one to make bold predictions but I know Jesse is going to ask me to marry him."

"Okay, now you know that I'm going to charge you a finder's fee if y'all get married," Regina joked.

"Whatever." Angela dismissed her comment. "What about you? I haven't heard you talking about anyone special in a while."

"Girl, please, these brothers out here can't handle this on a 24/7 basis."

"Oh Lord." Angela laughed. "You'd better settle your hot-ass down soon."

"Well, I'm working on it. I'm dating this new guy, Nick, who teaches English over at DePaul University. He's thirty-five, single, no kids and has never been married. He's a handsome brother and loves to travel. Every year he takes a group of students to visit a different country. He's been to Egypt, Italy and Kenya."

"Wow. How come you haven't mentioned Nick before?" Angela asked.

"It's still a new relationship. But so far, so good," Regina answered truthfully.

"Well, I'm so glad that Jesse and I have reconnected," Angela said, just as the instructor began the class. After working out, Regina and Angela went to get a quick bite at a nearby café, and Regina started talking about a few local news stories to get Angela's viewpoint.

"So, what do you think about the police discovering the body of that judge who has been missing for all of those years?" Regina asked.

"What do you mean, what do I think about it?"

"I mean, how do you think they found the remains after so long?" Regina asked.

"I think someone tipped off the police as to where the body was buried. I've heard rumors around the television station that the new state prosecutor is making deals with felons to solve the backlog of unsolved cases. Criminals can get their sentences reduced depending on how helpful the information they give is."

"Isn't that going to upset people?" Regina asked.

"Probably, but that's politics for you. Will taught me that with the right amount of money, clout or damaging information, a lot of things can get done or undone, which seems to be the case with the state prosecutor." At that moment, Angela's cell phone rang. She looked at the caller ID but didn't recognize the number.

"Who is that?" Regina asked.

"I don't know. I don't recognize the phone number." Angela was perplexed by the odd phone number.

"Well, are you going to answer it or just look at it?" Regina asked.

"Hang on," Angela said and answered the phone.

"This is Angela," she greeted the caller.

"Hey, baby," the voice said.

"Who is this?" Angela asked.

"Come on now. It hasn't been that long, has it? Surely you still recognize my voice."

Angela stopped breathing for a moment.

"Angela, what's wrong? Did something happen?" Regina was filled with concern when she saw the look on Angela's face. Angela held her hand up for her friend to be quiet and to listen.

"Will?" Angela asked to confirm.

"Yes. How have you been?" he asked.

"How did you get my phone number?" Angela asked.

"Come on, Angela. You know that I have connections and I still have a few friends that I can call in favors to."

"Okay, so you called in a favor. Why are you calling me?" Angela said, feeling irritation rise.

"I want to see you," Will said.

"I'm not in California anymore, Will, and if I were I certainly would not be coming to visit you in prison."

"I know you're not in California. You're in Chicago. And so am I," Will said.

"What! You're in Chicago?" Angela's heart began beating hard.

"Yeah, baby. I'm out of jail now, and I want to see you."

"That's not a good idea, Will," Angela said.

"Why? Are you married now?"

"No," Angela answered him.

"Good." Angela could hear Will exhale.

"Will…" Angela paused in thought. "I am not going to see you. Our relationship is over. We have nothing to say to each other."

"Wait a minute now. I've traveled a long way to see you. I think you could at least see me once. Just for old time's sake. I just want to explain things to you and set the record straight."

Angela could hear the anger in his voice. "Goodbye, Will. And don't call me anymore."

"Angela. You don't want to hang up on me. You do not want to piss me off," Will barked at her. Angela felt a bolt of anxiety flow through her.

"Whatever, Will," Angela said and then hung up.

"Please tell me that wasn't the same Will you were married to." Regina was sitting on the edge of her seat waiting for Angela's response.

"Yes, it was," Angela whispered softly, her mind still in a daze.

"What the hell is he calling you for?" Regina demanded.

"He said that he wanted to talk and set the record straight." Angela captured Regina's gaze.

"Well, that fool should know that there isn't shit to talk about. It's over. Finished. Done."

"I know," Angela said. "I'm not going to tread old waters

or even entertain a conversation with him," Angela said. "I've suddenly lost my appetite." Angela excused herself and headed toward the bathroom.

Later that evening, Angela was resting comfortably in her bed watching a Will Smith movie. As the movie was drawing to its conclusion, she decided to give Jesse a call.

"Hey, babe," Jesse greeted. "Sorry I didn't call you earlier, but it's been one hell of a day."

"You can say that again," Angela agreed. "What are you doing?" she asked.

"Lying in bed and watching television," Jesse said.

"You sound really sad. What's wrong?" she asked.

"As much as I hate to say this, I've got baby-momma drama."

"Well, come on. Talk to me about it. What's going on?" Angela pried for more information. There was a long moment of silence. "I'm petitioning the court for full custody of my daughter. Her mother has run into some catastrophic financial difficulties. She's not able to provide a safe environment for her," Jesse said, and then went on to explain everything that had happened and how Trina had broken down in tears.

"You should become the custodial parent. It's a damn shame that JoAnn has fucked up that much money in such a short amount of time."

"That's only part of my problem. Trina doesn't want to leave her mother behind. I've tried to explain to her the best way that I know how that her mom can't come live with us. It's been a very long and difficult night," Jesse admitted.

"Well, do you want to get back with her?" Angela asked, fearing that Jesse was trying to find a way to end their relationship so that he could go back to his ex-wife.

"I am done with JoAnn. No. I don't want to get back with her," Jesse answered.

"Well, I mean, you have a child to consider in all of this." Angela was being honest as well as supportive.

"I know, and I want to be a good father to Trina, but I can't raise grown people. I can't raise JoAnn. She has deep issues and more baggage than I'm willing to carry."

"Well, since we're both talking about our exes, Will called me today." There was a long moment of silence once again. "Hello? Jesse, are you still there?" Angela thought she'd lost the call.

"Oh my God!" Jesse exclaimed.

"Jesse, what's wrong?" Angela was confused by his exclamation. "Are you mad that he called me? I didn't give him my phone number—he called in some favors to get it."

"Angela, turn to channel seven." Angela picked up the remote and changed the channel. There, on the evening news, was Will, sitting in his hotel room giving an interview to a reporter.

"So, Mr. Rivers, what you're saying is you admit that you were wrong to have an inappropriate relationship with a minor, but you're saying that your ex-wife was also involved?"

Angela was speechless. She watched as Will repositioned himself in his chair and began talking.

"Yes. My ex-wife, the journalist Angela Rivers, was also involved in the sexual acts. So I'm not the only one who should've served time for that particular crime."

"What!" Angela shouted out. "You low-down, dirty, lying son of a bitch!"

"Angela, what is he talking about?" Jesse wanted to know.

"He's lying, Jesse. The bastard has crawled out from under his rock and is trying to ruin me." At that moment, Angela was notified of an incoming call. She looked at her phone and saw that Regina was trying to reach her. Angela figured that Regina was watching the news and wanted her to know that Will was on there slandering her. Angela decided to call Regina back later.

"Why would he do something like this?" Jesse asked.

"Because I refused to listen to his bullshit. He called me today and wanted to talk to me, but I said that there was nothing to talk about."

"But what's he doing here in Chicago?" Jesse asked.

"I guess he thought he still had a chance with me."

"Shit," Jesse hissed. "Now let me ask you the same question you asked me. Do you still want him?"

"No," Angela said with absolute certainty.

"Then why is he doing this?" Jesse asked again.

"Because he doesn't have shit else to do. But two can play this little game of his." Angela felt vengeance rise in her chest. "I'm going to squash this shit, once and for all. I am not about to allow him to get out of jail and fly across the country just to ruin my life and my new beginning," Angela proclaimed.

"So, what are you going to do?" Jesse asked.

"Something that he isn't expecting me to do," Angela answered. "Babe, let me call you back." Angela was about to end the call.

"Angela," Jesse called out to her before she hung up. "Love you."

"Love you," Angela said and hung up.

The following morning, Angela called Will first thing.

"Hello," Will answered. She could tell that he'd still been asleep.

"How long will you be in town for?"

"I have interviews scheduled for the rest of the week," he answered. "Everybody in this town wants to hear my side of the story."

"Your side of the story is twisted and filled with lies," Angela snapped at him.

Will laughed. "You've made a good name for yourself here in Chicago. If I keep on talking, you're going to lose everything—especially when I go on that new daytime talk show *Exposure*."

"I know the show. When are you scheduled to go on it?" Angela asked.

"End of the week. But I'll pull out of my interview and stop my smear campaign if you'll come back to me so that we can rebuild our life together."

"Go to hell, Will," Angela said and hung up the phone. She called her office and took a few days off. She was thankful that the station's management thought highly of her and allowed her to take the time on short notice. Angela then logged on to her computer and booked a noon flight back to Oakland. She didn't care how expensive it was because getting back to Oakland was paramount. She landed in Oakland at 2:30 p.m., grabbed her luggage and then took the shuttle service over to rent a car. Once she got her car, Angela drove toward Oakland. She made one special stop before she continued on to Smoky's house.

When she arrived, she parked the car, grabbed the bag of goodies she'd picked up for Smoky and walked up to the house.

"Who is it?" Smoky called out, when she knocked on the door.

"It's me, Angela. Open the door," she said.

"Angela who?" Smoky asked.

"Your sister-in-law. Open the door, Smoky." For a long moment nothing happened, then the door finally opened up.

"What are you doing here?" Smoky asked. Angela could tell she'd surprised the hell out him.

"I need a favor from you, Smoky," Angela said as she stepped inside and shut the door behind her.

"A favor?" Smoky laughed as he wheeled himself to an open spot on the floor. He was thankful Will had picked up a little before he'd rushed off.

"You came to see old Smoky because you need some good loving, don't you?" Angela could see Smoky undressing her with his eyes.

"You might be a little too much man for me to handle, Smoky." Angela smiled. She knew exactly how to get what she needed from him.

"Yeah, that's true. Because I can get down all night long," Smoky boasted.

"So I've heard," Angela said.

"You know Will is in Chicago looking for you. I thought that's where you went. I didn't know you were still here in California," Smoky said.

"Smoky, I need to find out something from you," Angela said, completely ignoring his comment.

"Well, I know a lot of things about a lot of shit," Smoky said confidently.

"I need to find DaNikka, Smoky," Angela said.

"DaNikka. As in Will's woman on the side?" Smoky asked.

"Yes. Where can I find her?" Angela asked.

Smoky began laughing. "Girl, you're trying to set old Smoky up. It goes against the player code of honor to give up information like that." Smoky paused, and then looked at Angela lustfully. He moistened his lips with his tongue. "What's in it for me? Do I finally get to get a little taste of you?"

"I taste rather bitter right now, Smoky. And I know that a smart pussy connoisseur like yourself doesn't want bitter pussy. But I do have a little something for you." Angela reached into the bag and held out a bag of marijuana.

"Girl, where did you get that from?" Smoky was blown away by the fact that Angela had marijuana on her.

"It's the good Jamaican shit. It's got something special in it. Do you want it?" she asked.

"You know damn well I want it. Stop playing with me. But that's not enough to get you that type of information."

"How about these, as well?" Angela emptied out the bag and an assortment of pornographic films and male sex toys designed to heighten the masturbation experience fell out.

Smokey exhaled. "Oh, that's not nice. You're not playing fair, Angela. You got me some Jamaican weed, a shitload of porno and some sex toys. You're a straight-up freak, girl."

"Do we have a deal, Smoky?" Angela asked.

"She lives in the projects about a mile away. Building 363, door number 3."

"Thank you, love. Enjoy yourself," Angela said.

As she turned to leave, Smoky asked, "Hey. You want join me? You don't have to do anything, you can just watch me."

"Maybe next time," Angela lied and then left Smoky to entertain himself until he fell into an orgasmic coma.

Angela pulled up in front of DaNikka's home and sat in the car for a long moment. It was the first time since she'd left Chicago that she'd stopped to think about what exactly she hoped to get from DaNikka. The one thing she didn't want was to get into a confrontation with her. She just wanted her to publicly verify that Will was lying and that at no point had Angela, Will and DaNikka ever had a sexual relationship. Angela hoped that DaNikka had matured at least a little over the past two years. Angela grabbed her purse and then popped the trunk to remove the digital video recorder she'd brought with her. She walked up to the door and knocked. Angela heard the sound of slow-moving house shoes sweeping against the floor. A moment later, the door was opened.

"Yes?" An old woman who could barely stand erect opened the door. Angela looked into the woman's face. Her mouth and neck were twisted and fixed into one position. The woman had to turn her body completely in order to look at Angela. "Sumpin' I can do for you?" the old woman asked.

"Is DaNikka here?" Angela asked.

"Yup. She stays here. Come on in. Have a seat." The old woman, who was clearly a kind and trusting soul, didn't ask Angela for any additional information, she only welcomed her into her home. Angela sat down on a worn-out sofa. The room was brightly lit and filled with eclectic furniture which seemed to have been collected during various decades.

"Nikka!" the old woman hollered out.

"Yeah, Momma?" DaNikka answered from another room toward the back.

"Somebody here to see you," the old woman said, as she methodically moved toward the kitchen. Angela felt bad. She got up from her seat and helped the woman to sit down.

"Thank you, sweetie. Go on in there and talk to Nikka. I won't bother y'all none."

"Okay," Angela said. As she turned, she came face-to-face with DaNikka. DaNikka exhaled.

"Momma, I keep telling you to stop opening the door and letting strange people in here."

"Isn't that your sister?" her mother answered back. It became clear at that moment that the woman was also suffering from memory problems.

"Look, I didn't come here to cause any trouble," Angela explained. Just as she was about to give the reason for her visit, a naked, wet child about two years old came running into the room, leaving a trail of wet footprints behind him, and attached himself to DaNikka's leg. There was a long moment of silence between DaNikka and Angela.

"Let me go put him in some clothes. Have a seat. I'll be right back."

Angela sat down, completely thunderstruck as she attempted to puzzle out DaNikka's situation. DaNikka and the young boy rejoined her a few minutes later.

"So, what's this about?" DaNikka asked as she sat down in a chair on the opposite side of the room.

"He's beautiful," Angela said.

"I know you didn't come all the way over here to look at my son," DaNikka said defensively.

"I didn't know that you had a son," Angela said. DaNikka didn't respond. She just nervously shook her leg.

"Is Will the father?" Angela asked.

"Yeah," DaNikka answered.

"Jesus. Does he know?" Angela asked.

"I told him that I was pregnant, but he said that it wasn't his."

"Will can't deny this child. He looks just like him." Angela hoped that her words could offer DaNikka some comfort.

"Well, he ain't helping me none with this baby, and it's not easy trying to take care of my momma, my baby and keep my grown-ass brothers and sisters from coming in here and stealing what little my mother has."

"How long have you been taking care of your mother?" Angela asked.

"A long time. Since I was about sixteen," DaNikka answered.

"I know what I'm about to say is going to sound really weird, but can you explain to me why you dated Will?" Angela asked. DaNikka's son tried to crawl onto her lap but DaNikka made him sit next to her.

"That *is* a strange question," DaNikka said and was silent for a moment. "Fuck it. If you want to know, I'll tell you.

"Will and his brother, Smoky, used to come around the neighborhood flashing money and talking to young girls. They were just looking for girls to have sex with. But I wasn't going out like that. They both tried to convince me to do it with them. But I said no. I guess the fact that I said no pissed Will off because he wasn't used to being turned down.

"So, he comes around here one day and catches me as I'm coming home from school. Actually, the day he saw me I'd just dropped out of school because of my mother's condition. There was no one to take care of her and there was no one willing to help, so I had to do what I had to do. So, Will starts asking me questions about my family. And I told him that I was the baby of the family and about how my other brothers and sisters drove my mother crazy to the point she had a stroke, which left her like that. Once my mother got sick they stopped coming around and left me to take care of her.

"I didn't have money for her medicine and the public aid people kept giving me the runaround. I didn't know what to do. So Will tells me that if I agree to be his mistress, he'll arrange for an apartment in the new public houses the city was building. He said he'd make sure our name was pulled from the waiting list, and we'd be assigned a unit. He even said he'd provide me with money for clothes, medicine and stuff.

"I wanted to get out of this area so bad. I wanted my momma to be safe and I didn't want her kids coming around messing everything up for her because they fight, they do drugs, they steal, you name it. So I said okay.

"I told myself that I could do it. I told myself that I was doing it for my momma. I did it because I needed to survive. He told me that he wanted to train me on how to fuck him. He said that he wasn't getting fucked right at home." DaNikka paused.

"You cry, Mommy. Why you cry?" asked her son, as he wiped away her tears.

"I'm okay, Eric," she said to the little boy. "So, anyway, I did my best to give him whatever he wanted. I did my best to keep him happy, but it wasn't enough. Then he wanted to have a threesome with my girlfriend Shantel. I didn't want to do it so he threatened me. He said that if I didn't do it, I wouldn't get the new public housing apartment and I believed him. This was around the time that the city had just finished construction on the new houses. I was so close to getting my mother out of here that I said okay.

"Shantel would fuck anything and anyone for money, so she was down for it. We made a videotape of it. Partly because I knew that he'd want to brag about the experience to his brother, but something told me to take the memory chip out of the digital video recorder. So I did. Then I found out I was pregnant. And I told Shantel, but she turned on me and stole Will away from me. Said that I didn't know how to please a man like him.

"I was so mad and angry. I had been used. I couldn't reach Will or Shantel so I sent the video recording to the media and the police. Then I came to your show and attacked you because I was hurt so bad and I wanted to show Will that he couldn't treat me like that. I was upset when he went to jail. I didn't want that to happen. I just wanted him to treat me right."

DaNikka wiped away more of her tears. "I'm sorry for all of the trouble I caused you. I really am. And I'm sorry for messing up your career and getting your show cancelled because I really liked it. I even admired you because I wanted to be a journalist. But every time I talked about going back to school, Will didn't want me to. I'm back in now but it is so hard. Especially with trying to take care of my baby and my mother." Angela looked at DaNikka's mother who was laughing to herself, and her heart sank.

"What happened to Shantel?" Angela asked. DaNikka released a painful laugh. She drew back the curtain behind her chair and pointed out the window.

"There she is right there. She's a crackhead now." Angela glanced out of the window and saw a thin, frail-looking woman standing on the corner, begging from people as they walked by. "I feel sorry for her. All the media attention she got drove her crazy. I give her food sometimes because she'll tell me that she hasn't eaten in days."

"I had no idea that Will was that twisted," Angela confessed. "I'm so sorry that he put you through all of that."

"So, is that the real reason why you came here? To find out why he did this?"

"Partly," Angela admitted. "I also came for my own selfish

reasons. I came to get even with Will for trying to fuck up my new life back in Chicago. He's going around saying that the three of us were involved in a love triangle and that I should also go to jail for having sex with you."

"That's a lie," DaNikka said. "You can't let him get away with that shit!" DaNikka was angry once again.

"Tell you what. If you'll help me shut this bastard's mouth once and for all, I'll make some phone calls and cash in on a few favors to help you get out of here. I'll also help you make sure that Will financially supports his son."

"How do I know you're not just bullshitting me? I'm so tired of lame motherfuckers coming around me with bullshit," DaNikka said.

"Because I didn't travel all the way from Chicago just to come and bullshit you," Angela answered.

CHAPTER 32

JESSE

Jesse parked his car in front of a brown-brick apartment building on the corner of Laramie and Augusta. The neighborhood was everything that Trina had described to him. Bands of young men and women were wandering streets filled with condemned and boarded-up buildings. Drug dealers were loitering on the streets, hovering around their expensive cars trying to appear legitimate. Jesse exhaled as he prepared to go inside and deal with JoAnn and her dismal situation. He rang the doorbell but got no answer. He rang it again and waited. A moment later, he heard the sound of a window being lifted open above his head. He stepped back from the door and looked up.

"Hey, Jesse," JoAnn said, her head stuck out of the window above him.

"Hey," he said.

"I'll be right down." JoAnn closed the window and then came downstairs to open the door. When Jesse stepped inside the vestibule of the building, the distinctive odor of urine assaulted him.

"I know it stinks a little bit in this hallway, so let's hurry up and get upstairs," JoAnn said. "I've called the landlord about that but he doesn't seem to care."

Once Jesse entered the apartment, he headed toward the kitchen where there was a small table with two chairs.

"I'm so glad you came by." JoAnn tried to sound upbeat. Jesse took a seat at the table and JoAnn joined him.

"I'm taking Trina." Jesse didn't waste any time. He got

right to the reason he'd come. "She told me that you were broke and that she didn't feel safe living here."

JoAnn's smile quickly disappeared. "You mean you didn't come here to ask me to come home?" she asked.

"No," Jesse answered honestly. "I came to pick up Trina's belongings."

"You really don't want me anymore? Not even a little bit?" JoAnn began crying.

"No. I was just a lifeline to you, JoAnn. I've lost hope of you ever changing your ways." Jesse gave her a direct answer.

"I fucked up, okay? I know this—"

"JoAnn, please don't make this harder than it already is," Jesse pleaded with her.

"No, Jesse, hear me out. Please." JoAnn wiped away her tears. "I had a good man in you. And I fucked that up with my drinking and gambling and carelessness. I'm just like my father, I suppose. When things are going well I just have a way of fucking shit up. I don't know why I'm like that, I just am. You should take Trina. I won't fight you."

"I'm not saying that you can't see her, JoAnn. You're always welcome to come by and see her. And when you get yourself settled in a decent place, she can come stay with you if she wants to," Jesse said.

"I don't know what I'm going to do. I have very little money. I don't have a job. I live in this shit hole. My daughter is afraid to live with me and all of my attempts to get my husband back have failed. But I still love you, Jesse." JoAnn looked directly into his eyes. "I never stopped loving you. And I am so sorry that I bruised your heart and killed the trust in our marriage. I'm responsible for that, and I'm getting what I deserve."

"JoAnn, you don't deserve this. You're like a teenager who wants to do anything and everything without any consequences. You're paying the consequences for your actions. If you change what you're doing, you'll get a different result."

"Yeah, I know that." JoAnn paused for a moment, and in the background they heard the sound of a couple arguing in the next apartment unit.

"Look, I should get Trina's things to take with me now. I'll bring her by later on to pick up the rest of her belongings."

"Just so you know, this is my last week in this apartment. My mother is going to take me in for a little while. That's where I'll be. She doesn't have much of a place but at least I won't be alone."

"Okay," Jesse said, pleased that they'd arrived at a point where they could be civil with each other. "It's going to be hard on Trina. I'm still going to need your help with her."

"I know," JoAnn said. Jesse gathered up some of Trina's belongings and headed out the door and down the stairs.

"Jesse?" JoAnn called out his name. Jesse turned and looked up at her.

"I—um—if things don't work out with you and your friend, look me up, okay?" JoAnn asked nervously.

"Yeah," Jesse whispered and continued on his way.

CHAPTER 33

ANGELA

Angela was at Jesse's house. It was midday and they were sitting on his sofa watching the daytime talk show *Exposure*. The local reality show was similar to Angela's in that it sought to bring out the truth about scandalous affairs, forbidden pleasures and other topics with shock value.

"You know he's been on a lot of radio shows this week really bad-mouthing you," Jesse said. "I know he was your ex-husband and all, but he's a real jackass."

"Don't worry." Angela laughed. "This show is taped live and he's about to publicly put a noose around his neck and hang himself."

"I still can't believe that you got DaNikka to let you video-tape her side of the story. And then you sent it to the producer of the show."

"Well, it wasn't right what Will did to her. He took advantage of a young girl who was in a very desperate state. Then he gets her pregnant and says that it's not his. He's about to get everything he deserves," Angela stated.

At that moment, the show came on. Will walked out and greeted the studio audience and the show host. They sat down and Will began talking about his career as a congressman. He talked about the public housing project he helped to get finished and other highlights of his political career. After a commercial break, the show resumed and Will spoke about his sex scandal.

"I know that I was wrong, but I served my time and paid

my debt to society. I'm not some monster who preys on the less fortunate or teens at risk," Will said with conviction. The host of the show lured Will into deep waters by encouraging him to continue to talk about the affair.

"My wife at the time was aware of what was going on and even participated," Will lied.

"Oh, what an ignorant bastard," Angela said aloud.

"Well, you know this show is all about exposing the truth," said the show host. "Will has come onto our show and exposed what he says is the truth about Chicago journalist Angela Rivers and her past. But there are two sides to every story. Angela Rivers has provided the producers of our show with an exclusive interview that she conducted with Will's former lover."

"What are you talking about?" Will asked.

Angela smiled as she watched him squirm in his seat. "Payback is a bitch," she said.

The videotape of her interview with DaNikka was played for the audience and viewers to see. When the audience got the full story of what Will had done, he was booed. He refused to talk, unhooked his microphone and left the stage.

Twenty minutes later, Angela received a phone call from Will.

"Yes?" she answered.

"That was low-down, Angela," Will snapped at her.

"You got everything you deserved, Will. Now go back to Oakland and take care of your child," Angela snarled.

"How did you find her, anyway? Just tell me that."

"Give my regards to Smoky. It didn't take much to get him to talk." Angela heard Will sigh. "It doesn't feel so good now, does it? Don't you ever call me again."

"I just wanted you back, Angela. I just wanted to start over," Will confessed.

"I *have* started over," Angela said and hung up the phone.

ABOUT EARL SEWELL

National bestselling author and award-winning author Earl Sewell has written eight novels which include *The Good Got to Suffer with the Bad*, *Through Thick and Thin*, *The Flip Side of Money*, *When Push Comes to Shove*, *Keysha's Drama*, *If I Were Your Boyfriend*, *Love Lies and Scandal* and his debut title, *Taken For Granted*, which was originally self-published through his own publishing company, Katie Books. His work has also appeared in four separate anthologies which include *On the Line*, *Whispers Between the Sheets*, *Sistergirls.com* and *After Hours: A Collection of Erotic Writing by Black Men*. He has written numerous romantic short stories for *Black Romance* magazine and has been featured in *Black Issues Book Review* magazine. He is also the founder of Earl Sewell's Travel Network, www.earlsewellstravelnetwork.com, which is a travel agency. In addition, Earl is a lifelong athlete who has completed several marathons and triathlons. Earl lives in Chicago with his family. To learn more about Earl Sewell, visit his Web sites at www.earlsewell.com and www.myspace.com/earlsewell.

*Their marriages were shams,
but their payback will be real....*

Counterfeit
Wives

Fan-favorite author
PHILLIP THOMAS DUCK

Todd Darling was the perfect husband...to three
women. Seduced and betrayed, Nikki, Jacqueline
and Dawn learned too late their dream marriage
was an illusion. Struggling to rebuild their lives,
they're each invited by a mysterious woman to
learn more about the husband they thought they
knew. But on a journey filled with surprises, the
greatest revelations will be the truths they learn
about themselves....

*Coming the first week of December
wherever books are sold.*

sepia™